PAINT YOUR WIFE

Lloyd Jones was born in New Zealand in 1955. His best-known works include *Mister Pip*, winner of the Commonwealth Writers' Prize and shortlisted for the Man Booker Prize, *The Book of Fame*, winner of numerous literary awards, *Hand Me Down World* and his acclaimed memoir, *A History of Silence*.

PAINT YOUR WIFE
LLOYD JONES

TEXT PUBLISHING
MELBOURNE AUSTRALIA

The Text Publishing Company
Swann House
22 William Street
Melbourne Victoria 3000
Australia
textpublishing.com.au

First published by Penguin Books (NZ) Ltd, 2004

This edition published by The Text Publishing Company, 2014

Book design & illustrations by W. H. Chong
Typeset by Midland Typesetting
Printed and bound in Australia by Griffin Press

National Library of Australia Cataloguing-in-Publication entry

Creator: Jones, Lloyd, 1955– author.

Title: Paint your wife / by Lloyd Jones.

ISBN: 9781925095371 (paperback)

ISBN: 9781922182395 (ebook)

Subjects: Painters—Fiction.

Dewey Number: NZ823.2

PAINT YOUR WIFE

1

I've been visiting our son Adrian in London. He is a year or two older than I was the first time I flew there, dropping out of the clouds, glancing down at the storybook burst of Westminster and the serpentine crawl of the Thames. This time around it's been ten days of lounging about, filling in time reading the newspapers, musing on the crazy things that happen out there in the world. Hungry car thieves in Sao Paulo mistake AIDS-infected blood for raspberry jelly. That sort of thing. I was enjoying myself and London was big and scrambling. I showed up in the shop windows as a smiling amiable fellow, someone I hardly ever am at home. There were the same row houses in their grainy white that captured my interest more than twenty years ago as a newly graduated paint technician. London seemed to be painted in the colours of mist. The contrast with home was striking. Our houses were like bright coloured marbles let loose over the plain, shining down from hillsides, beaming up at the broad sky. More importantly, our paint was guaranteed not to blister or peel, to withstand extreme conditions. Our white was a cat's-eye white.

Opaque, unpleasant to touch. London's white was creamy; its grime charmed.

This time London had never looked so green. The weather was brilliant. Blue skies, the pavements hard and cheerful. I spent much of my time walking and looking for a park bench on which to sit and open my paper. St James's Park. Holland Park. Hyde Park. Squirrels running up trunks. Foreign nannies with prams. Boys and girls tongue-kissing over the rolling park grass.

Around six I'd totter off to some pub or bar rendezvous suggested by Adrian. He'd ask me what I got up to that day and I might begin to tell him about 'Thieves in Sao Paulo...' But he was only interested to know if I'd visited any of the second-hand shops.

'If you were over near Portobello Road you could have looked up Mr Musty at least. I was in there the other day and said you might drop by.'

I had to shake my head and look away guiltily. 'Afraid not. Ran out of time.'

Adrian seemed put out. I knew he'd gone to some trouble to look up these places.

'Anyway, the man to ask for in Musty's is Dave somebody. Ginger hair. Missing his little finger.'

I gave a vague nod of intent.

'You should, you know.'

'I know I should but I didn't. I ran out of time.'

Just what did I do? I read the newspaper and ordered another cup of tea or looked for my reflection in the passing shop windows. Names floated up from the past. Assorted paint arcana.

In paint tech we used to have a teacher we all liked because he played in a rock band at weekends. He was entirely bald, apart from a pair of rimless glasses. When he smiled it was from a position of unrealised advantage. Our paint, he liked to say, could stand up to the most testing of conditions—searing heat, freezing rain, salt winds. London's paint by comparison would turn to omelette. He said this a lot and whenever he did we would exchange triumphant smiles. *It'd all turn to omelette.* We loved saying that.

'John Ryder. That's it. I knew his name would come to me.'

Adrian looked unimpressed. He doesn't know about the paint tech side of me. When he was born I'd given up paint for trade in second-hand goods and furnishings. He looked at the dregs in his glass and drained them.

One night he said he wanted to take me clubbing. I scratched around for a reason why this wouldn't be possible. I asked where he had in mind and he said in his new way of speaking, his eyes and face angling off to new arrivals entering the bar, 'Doesn't matter where. Trust me. You'll love it.'

I ended up paying an exorbitant taxi fare. Twenty years ago it had been enough to walk everywhere, and with holes in my shoes. I didn't dream of catching a cab, anywhere. Adrian and his mates seemed unfazed. They all work in the film industry—Adrian said what they did but I can't remember; strange-sounding job descriptions, grippers, line people. They probably catch cabs every day of their lives. On the other hand I paid an amount which in my daily trade in second-hand furnishings was worth a decent sofa and maybe a mattress thrown in. But as I say, Adrian and his mates seemed so remarkably cool about it that I hated to make a fuss. Instead

I followed them through the doors manned by Nigerians in black leather jackets. They nodded at Adrian but seemed puzzled by me. I couldn't hear a thing. I gather Adie was explaining, his thumb hooked back in my direction, while the Nigerian's face hung low to catch the drift. He nodded at the floor and I passed by his uplifted red eyes. Inside it was a deafening *thump thump thump*. I had to yell for Adrian to hear.

The price of the drinks was out of this world. It was beers all round for which I paid after stupidly saying 'Let me,' which they did. I paid for another round, and another one after that, until at last they slipped off the feeding teat and disappeared into the crowd of bobbing heads. I followed the arrows to something promisingly called 'the conversation pit' where indeed I had a conversation with a black woman along the lines of, 'You're black,' to which she smiled patiently and said, 'Yes. Thank you. I know.' It wasn't so horribly gauche as that, but not all that far behind either. I asked her where she was from. She leant her head closer so as to hear and I could smell all kinds of tropical fruit smells. I said, 'Are you from Guyana?' and she shook her head and her big luscious mouth fell open; she said, 'No, darling, I'm from around here. Born here, Harry Bryant,' she said. I liked the way she said 'Harry Bryant'.

After some more fumbling of this kind we did manage a conversation. We asked about each other. We were even going to dance but we didn't in the end. Eventually I used up all my goodwill and her patience and after saying decently, 'Well Mister Mayor, it's been nice meeting you,' she moved off stylishly, holding her glass with both hands before her, a whiff of tropical breeze cutting through the thick air. Across the room of dancing shadows and shaven heads there was my son grinning back at me.

I don't remember much more of the night. That nice black Brixton woman was the last decent conversation I had. The rest of the time was filled with noise and beer. And shots of something in tiny glasses that was painless and irresistible at the time. I don't recall how we made our way back to Adie's flat; I hope there was a taxi, I hope no one drove, but that's where I woke feeling just bloody terrible, in a sickly sweat. The conversation with the nice black woman from 'round here' played endlessly back in my head with a clarity that was cruel and mocking.

I got dressed and slipped out of the flat and drifted to the nearest underground station. I rose gastrically near St James's Park to warm sunny skies. Flirted with buying a yoghurt outside a nice-looking deli and thought it best not to tempt fate. Instead I crossed the road and entered the park.

Everything looked so beautiful and I felt so shitty I could barely stay upright. I followed a path and felt my age every step of the way. As the morning grew warmer I found a nice grassy spot to lie on, and there I dozed for a pleasant few hours. At some point I woke to raised, hectic voices. It was a pick-up game of football and the goalposts—two humped jerseys— were only metres away. Twenty years ago I had joined in these sorts of games at Holland Park. I remember one game played under an early evening sky where the light actually seemed to stall and we had played on and on in a state of suspended bliss. Skills I never knew I had revealed themselves; a flashy slap of the ball off one foot then the other turned the goal-keep, a schoolteacher with a long pre-war face, and I banged in the shot past someone's shoe that was standing in for one upright of the goalposts. A man on a bike who had stopped to watch actually applauded. Funny that this man, so incidental and anonymous in every other respect, should rise in my thoughts all these years later. I seem to recall telling someone who had asked that I was from Sweden. I wanted origins more spectacular than my own to go with that drive past the shoe upright. And afterwards, on this particular night, the night of the goal by the young Swede, I went for a beer in the pub opposite the park gates—I've long forgotten its name—and remember falling in with a Nigerian officer on leave from the war in Biafra. He had a nasty gash over his forehead, and two nicks in his cheek. Here was another occasion where I was all too aware that I was speaking to a person of colour, a black man. At the same time I was also determined to give the impression that his colour was neither here nor there. But of course that was untrue. It was colour generally which had made an impression on me during my first trip to London. That new colour white I'd not seen before, and now black.

On my last night I took Adie to see *Chicago* and afterwards jammed into a forgettable Soho eaterie, then in the morning took the train out to Heathrow. I got the exit seat I asked for, in cattle class of course, and after the lunch cart came through I popped a sleeping pill.

By the time I woke, many, many hours later according to my TV monitor, we were over the Arafura Sea. And there it was, far below, flat, grey, untroubled. The smiling Singaporean cabin crew were handing out hot flannels. Coffee and croissants and something listed as a fricassee arrived over the Northern Territory. Soon we were above central Australia. In the bright morning light the plane cast a birdlike shadow for the eye to chase, and I stared at that ancient coloured floor with thoughts of my father. I imagined he was with a new woman, despite the onset of age. I haven't seen him for twenty-five years. Whenever I am forced to admit this I always find myself rushing to say it's nothing, really; the truth is, I don't feel anything. There is no anger. Whatever anger I felt at the time has well and truly passed. If I think of him at all it's usually at Christmas because that is when his annual postcard used to arrive. On one side a colour photo of a wombat or a huge fantastic-looking lizard, or a cane toad. Frank had a sense of humour at least. On the other side a few quickly scratched words—'Hope all is well, Harry. Be good. Your dad.'

The last time I saw Frank was the year after I finished high school. With my best friend, Douglas Monroe, I flew across the Tasman and took a train up to the mining town where he was working at the time. Over the years I had shared my father's postcard correspondence with Dougie, the pictures of the goanna and the Opera House and of Ayers Rock. I used to spread them over my bed and that's where Dougie had seen them. With Dougie, at least, I could talk freely about my father. For when Frank left us the effect on my mother was awful. She went through a bout of depression that all but disabled her, although I don't recall anyone using the word 'depression' to describe what was happening to her. Sometimes she appeared to freeze, and it was like she'd hit quicksand while passing from one room to another, and then she'd forgot what had brought her in there in the first place. Purpose flew out the window. She would have sunk into the ground if I hadn't been around to move up behind her at such times and give her a gentle shove to get her going again. Sometimes I'd sit her down and she'd ask for a cup of tea, 'If you don't mind, Harry.' But I didn't always know what to do. Sometimes I would hurry up the hill to bang on the door of our neighbour, Alma Martin—it seemed he was never too busy to put aside whatever he happened to be doing, to pick up his drawing gear and come down the hill with me and sketch her. It worked like a spell. My mother would fall into a dreamy state; she became serene, accepting. She became like a woman in a painting. But that was only while Alma was there. He'd pull the curtains back and encourage her to come over to the window and look out at the world. 'See how it changes? Look, Alice, the trees are budding.' Slowly, patiently, he would manage to will a smile on to my mother's face—a brittle smile, but a smile nonetheless. At some point, though, he would have to leave and the silences would return. The house became more shadowed. Now my mother took the solution into her own hands. She immersed herself in long baths. She'd lie in them with the lights out until the water turned cold. And I'd stand outside the closed door listening for sounds, anything that would reassure me that I could safely leave the house and cycle over to Douglas Monroe's house with my father's latest postcard shoved up my jersey.

Compared to ours, the Monroe house was a hub of noise and high spirits, of lives going forward. Briefly it was possible to forget about my mother soaking in brackish water and Frank off somewhere unknown. But then it would be time to cycle back home. Crossing Chinaman's Creek I'd force myself to look up at the dark windows and the gloom that awaited me. Alice hadn't thought to switch on the house lights. Over a short period, one by one, the light bulbs failed. I had to remind her to buy new ones. It was a small thing. But it was alarming to think that she hadn't noticed. More likely, she had and didn't care.

On our trip to see my father, Dougie and I spent a night in Melbourne and boarded a train the next day. The whole way there my head was turned by what was galloping past the window. I remember feeling some confusion at a landscape that didn't contain edges or rises. I remember thinking that it would be difficult to just disappear into a landscape like this one, with everything so lightly tethered, even the scrub, none of which appeared to be deeply rooted. The odd spooked tree looked like a woman's hair roller. The trouble my father had gone to in order to escape my mother and me lay outside the train window, bending into the windless distance. And yet there were also these postcards hinting at the future. Otherwise, why bother? Why would he keep up the contact?

On the train I thought back to the last day we did anything together as father and son; Frank had taken me and Dougie diving. Later I would realise he had an ulterior motive for the trip out to the coast, that he was measuring his escape route. But at the time there was no way of knowing what he had planned. I did know about the woman from Wages—that was another secret I had recently shared with Dougie, though no one else in the world knew. In the car we sat together and stared at the back of my father's head with all its walled-up life that I wasn't supposed to know about. Near the beach the wheels hit the loose metal. Clouds of white dust were sucked back past our window. Frank chopped down a gear. We had left the road now and we could hear bits of driftwood snapping at the chassis. I was aware of Dougie's extreme discomfort.

He'd never ridden in a car like this one, that did the things that this one did, or that had a hairy-shouldered driver like Frank. Doug's own father worked in sales, and NE Paints had given him a car which he washed and polished every weekend. Mr Monroe would never treat his car the way Frank was thrashing our family car across the gravel and driftwood. At this rate if he didn't stop soon we'd end up in the sea. Doug was holding on to a roof strap. His mouth dropped open, his face bailed up with unasked questions and heaving fright. There was some more snapping of wood, a final growl from the motor and we stopped. A cold-looking sea bulged and crashed ashore and my father said, 'This'll do us.'

Doug and I were in no hurry to climb into our wetsuits, though as I remember, I didn't have a wetsuit. I had surf shorts and a woollen jersey with sawn-off arms. In the chilly air we stood about hugging ourselves.

'I have news for you, boys. You have to actually go out to where the crays are. They don't come to you. Any objections. Harry?'

'Nope.'

'Doug? How about you, son?'

'Nope.'

'You sure? You don't look sure.'

'I'm sure.'

'What about you Harry? You too, sunshine? You haven't said much. We all sure about this thing?'

Down on the wet shingle there were last-minute instructions. Crays don't have ears but my father was saying that it helps to think that they do and that you want to pick them up just behind the ears. 'Just pick it up as you would a hairbrush off a dresser table.' We watched him tighten his huge lead belt. 'One last thing. This one is for you, Douglas. What colour is a cray underwater?'

'Orange.'

'Harry?'

'Red?'

'You're both wrong. A cray is kelp-coloured. Think of yourselves looking for an old black sock under your bed. You ought to know about that, Harry.'

The information was confusing: socks, hairbrushes, crustaceans with ears. 'Okay,' he said, wading forward in his flippers. 'Let's go and rob a bank.'

He was a strongly built man. He wore an armless steamer suit and I remember watching the layers of shoulder hair lift in the cold breeze off the sea. We watched him wade into the shore break and sink amphibiously into the icy water—there was no hesitation—then we followed him, kicking in a line for the reef about sixty metres out from the beach. Halfway there I lifted my head out of the water to look for Dougie—sky and water filled my mask, and there in the distance I saw Dougie climb out of the tide. I remember wishing I could be there too but knowing this was impossible I kicked on to catch up to my father. Without him I would not be out this far.

Inside the reef, the sea shifted and moved us around as easily as if we were kelp. We were in three metres of water and by now I'd started looking for hairbrushes. My father dived down and near the bottom rolled on to his back to get my attention. He was pointing to something—a hairbrush—stuck in a crevice. He wanted me to dive down for it. Between the surface and the depths were shifting pillars of light and sea dust.

I could also feel currents of trust and blind faith. I was going to have to dive down because that was what was required. The pressure in my ears increased until they were really hurting. The change in temperature was dramatic. I remember wanting to surface, to get back up to the world of light for air, when my father grabbed hold of my wrist and guided me down deeper to that crevice. Finally he released his grip and dropped his hand on the cray and lifted it from its hiding place. Together we bulleted to the surface, my father with the cray in his outstretched hand so that it was first to burst from the sea into the white light of day. Frank blew the water out of his snorkel and dropped the cray into a sack. I waited until he dived again and taking my chance I swam like hell back to the beach.

It's not much of a memory, but then you can't pick the memories you'd like to be representative of yourself. When I'm dead, I'd like to think that Adrian's memory of me will be of the time I carried him home wrapped in my raincoat in driving rain after he sprained his ankle on a tramp, or of the time I took him out to an expensive London restaurant for veal marsala, rather than a memory of looking up across that crowded nightclub to see his old man with a lean on list his points with an outstretched finger to an amused-looking black woman.

My memories are of the crays we ate on the beach around a fire of crackling driftwood, the drive home, and later the strained silence of the house. And of that night, curled up in bed, with my father rocking in the door of my bedroom, caught between wanting to be elsewhere and needing to venture forward, and for the moment unable to do either but stand there and grin perhaps at his own memory of his boy kicking in the direction of the beach for all he was worth.

It was a few days later that he left us, his footprints on the grass preserved by the first frost of the year. All morning different women came over. I sat up in a tree and watched these crabbed figures examine the footprints that the sun hadn't yet reached. The tour then moved to my parents' bedroom where my father's clothes still lay on the floor, just creases and compressed air. His car was found later in the day. It looked to everyone like he'd driven at full tilt at the sea. At low tide the car sat in water up to its windows. For a couple of days we waited for his body to wash up. At its failure to do so, people began quietly to theorise. Then it came to everyone's notice that the woman from Wages had disappeared as well. My mother waited a week before we drove out to the coast. At low tide it was possible to walk around the back end of the Holden. You could see where people had taken potshots. The windows were shattered and the paintwork was damaged where rocks had missed the more glamorous target of the windows. The sea shifted puppishly around the chassis. My mother said, 'Do you know what is so embarrassing about this, Harry? It's that anyone would go to this trouble on my behalf.' Soon after this the postcards began to arrive.

The next time I saw Frank was after Dougie and I left the train and followed the stationmaster's directions through a superhuman heat. There was a suburban iron fence, flat, unyielding and unimpressed by the oven-like heat; it was all that kept at bay the vastness of the desert, and beyond the fence stood mounds of piled soil and against them the insect-like shadows of huge mechanical diggers, all very still. Eventually we arrived at the address scribbled down on a scrap of paper I'd held in my hand as far back as the station. We put down our packs and stared at a movement in the window. We'd definitely seen it and since we hadn't seen another human being since leaving the station both our gazes stuck to the window. A moment later the door opened on a woman in calf-length slacks. She wore a white top, thin white shoulder straps, white on white, blonde hair out of a bottle, a face that once might have been pretty. She held a cigarette in her hand. Some time previously I had heard gossip that Frank and the woman from Wages had parted. But I hadn't stopped to think that there might be another woman. Over her shoulder we could see cool shadows. Now the woman pushed herself off the door jamb. She seemed curious, and then impatient. She called out to ask if we were coming in or not.

We picked up our packs and as we moved towards the door, the woman moved half into the blinding light where she stuck up a hand.

'You can stop there. I'm not running a motel. Just so you know.'

Doug asked me to check the address again. In the few paces forward it hadn't changed but now he wanted to see for himself.

The woman said, 'All right I've had enough of this. You can fry out here or pay at the door and I'll tell you right now so that you know—I'm not interested in bullshit excuses or any-thing like that. Just so you know. I'm not interested in discussions. Just so we understand ourselves.'

Clearly there was a misunderstanding of major proportions. Either I had the wrong address or she had the wrong impres-sion of what we were there for. But to check a final time I managed to ask her, 'Is this 11A?' before she snapped back with, 'No bartering, I thought I said, or stalling. Or negotiation or whatever you want to call it. And I'm not interested in standing out here and frying my arse for much longer.' She took a big steadying breath and after eyeballing us separately she said, 'Sort out who's first while I count to ten. After that the meter's running.'

That's when Doug told her, 'Harry's looking for his dad.'

The woman didn't say anything. She was staring at Dougie's face, so I was off the hook for the moment. She looked cross with what she found there.

'How old are yis?'

'Old enough,' said Dougie.

'What about him?' She meant me but she was asking Doug.

'The same.'

By now though I was craning my head back to see if there were any other 11As hidden further along the block. That's when the woman wriggled her thin hips. She smiled at Dougie. She said, 'I like you. What's your name?'

'Dougie.'

'Dougie,' she said. 'Isn't that a dog's name?'

'Must be. I'm here, aren't I?'

The woman found that funny. She gave Dougie's shoulder a friendly push. She said, 'I like you,' again. She stepped aside for Dougie to enter. But as I followed she blocked my way.

'Not you. You can bake in hell.'

That's when I told her that I thought my father lived there. I showed her the address I'd written down on the scrap of paper but she wouldn't look at it. She said, 'I don't have to look. I don't care what the damn paper says. It could say Queen Elizabeth lives here or Elizabeth Taylor. It could say George Washington himself lives here and I just fucked his bewigged brains out. I don't have to believe anything just because it's written down on a shitty piece of paper. Understood?'

And that was it, I was thinking I really was going to fry in hell when Dougie rescued the whole mission with, 'His dad's got a tattoo on his bum.' Doug saw it that time Frank was changing into his wetsuit. Then he started describing this butterfly. He had the woman hooked. But he had to ruin it by saying it was a monarch butterfly and suddenly she was shaking her head.

'I don't know anything about a monarch butterfly.'

And just like that Doug was backtracking, 'Well it may not be exactly a monarch...'

'His name is Frank,' I said. 'Frank Bryant.'

The news took the wind out of her sails. Her earlier hostility was waning and we could hear her mind ticking. She said, 'I know lots of men by that name. There's thousands of fucking Franks.'

But as she was saying it, all the conviction of what she was trying to put across seemed to lift and her face softened as if she too didn't really believe in what she was saying any more. And just like that she said we could come in but on condition that we didn't use her bathroom. She said she had water and she had beer. 'If you want beer you'll have to pay for it first. Water's free, though.'

'Water,' said Dougie, and the quickness of his reply saw the woman roll her eyes. The important thing was we'd got in out of that terrible heat. For God knows how many years I'd dreamt and fantasised of meeting up with my dad, but at that moment I'd have given it all up for a glass of water. The woman set down a jug on the kitchen table. She placed two glasses beside it. We gulped down three glasses apiece. The woman refilled the jug and we drank that too. I was gulping down the last glass when the woman said to me, 'Your father usually gets in around seven.' She said, 'I don't think I want to miss this.' Now she was looking at me in a different light, examining me, and in a voice that was slightly mesmerised, she said, 'You've got your father's eyes. You're lucky.' Then she said, 'I'm Cynthia, by the way. I've known your father for the past three years but I think I'll leave Frank to explain all that. I don't want to say anything more for the time being.'

She wound up letting us use her bathroom. It was either that or we'd have to piss in her backyard. And after that we sat around waiting for Frank to turn up. Dougie joined in the vigil too, checking his watch, staring between the whitewashed walls and the window where we first saw the shadow of Cynthia.

For the first hour with Adrian in London I'd felt skittish as we worked ourselves into our respective roles. I hadn't seen him for eighteen months and so naturally there had been some loosening of the old parental shackles. He was a young man now. Despite this and a shared desire to meet as equals, the old relationship of father and son would not lie down. It loomed over us, stalked us, at different times had either one of us tongue-tied or at the other extreme had us assertively revert to form.

With Frank I didn't know what to expect. A diving expedition; a memory of him lingering at my bedroom door. It's not much to sustain roles. I didn't feel like anyone's son. I suspect Frank felt the same, that he wasn't anyone's father. And yet while we waited for him to turn up my strongest desire was that I wouldn't be a disappointment.

Once when Cynthia went to the bathroom Doug gave me a nudge and asked me how I felt about her.

'She's all right,' I said. At least I wouldn't have to confront the woman who had made my mother's life such a misery. We heard the toilet flush. Cynthia came to the door to ask if we'd like more water. 'Or would you rather have a beer?' She said, 'Don't all speak at once.'

'Water.'

'Water,' I said.

'The beer's on me.'

'Okay, a beer,' said Doug.

'Harry?'

'The same. Thank you, Cynthia.'

'Politeness. I like that.' She gave me a meaningful nod and went off for the beer.

We stared at the windows for I don't know how long, watched them fill with darkness that when it came was sudden and without fanfare. The first time a car's headlights washed into the room Cynthia stood up. 'Frank's here.' We could hear doors opening and closing. Now the front door opened. And Cynthia called out, her voice loud, sounding gleeful.

'Frank, you have a visitor.'

It was awful. And possibly a mistake. I wondered that years of yearning and hope should lead to a moment of such banality. There was surprise. A handshake. Some chortling laughter accompanied by backslapping. Cynthia's own sense of occasion. 'Oh give him a hug, Frank. I'll go and get my hanky.'

Frank's first words to me in over seven years were, 'My God you're a big bugger.' Then there was his discovery of Dougie standing shyly by. 'Who's this then?' And Cynthia telling him, 'He's the mouthy one.'

'Dougie,' said Dougie, extending his hand, and for a moment my father stared at the hand as though he didn't know what to do with it. He was searching back through memory for something to grasp on to. 'Dougie. Dougie.' Then he remembered. He pointed a finger and Doug nodded. They'd both arrived at that awful day at the beach.

'I told him Dougie's a dog's name,' said Cynthia, and Frank laughed. For all Cynthia's obvious faults, she managed to extract from Frank an easygoing-ness that I don't ever remember seeing with my mother. He said to Cynthia, 'You're the only mouthy one I know.' And he made a grab for her. That's when I smelt the beer on him. As he fell backwards into a chair he tried to pull Cynthia on to his lap but she wasn't interested. She looked for me. She said, 'Harry, your father has greedy hands.'

'Hands are made to hold things, Cynth. Isn't that right, Harry?'

All eyes were on me. The easiest thing would have been for me to agree. New, unexpected feelings were beginning to lock into place. I was thinking, if I saw this man behaving in this way elsewhere I wouldn't like him much. That he was my father prevented any wholehearted embrace of like or dislike. He simply was what he was. Finally it was left to Cynthia to answer for me.

'Pity your hands can't ask first, Frank.'

My father snorted. He'd forgotten Dougie now that he'd placed him as that same dismal being he'd last seen shivering at the beach.

'That's Cynthia for you. She'd talk a snail out of its shell.'

Cynthia smiled. She'd heard Frank say this before was my guess, and besides, her eyes were afloat with a new subject. She said to Frank, 'I was thinking Chinese.'

'Chinese is fine with me. What about you boys?'

'Chinese is fine,' I said. I was wanting to sound upbeat and positive.

'Harry says it's fine,' said my father. And for the moment we grinned at each other.

'I'll go,' said Cynthia. 'I'll take the dog for company.'

Frank laughed, and I tried out a laugh of my own. Doug decently barked to help ease things along. Frank barked back. With that bark Dougie had grown another dimension from the useless cunt on the beach Frank had in mind.

Later when I asked Doug what he and Cynthia had talked about on their way to the Chinese takeaway he said she'd told him, 'Frank is a wonderful man, but I'd never have him as a father for my kids.' And later, riding home with the boxes of Chinese steaming through his thighs she also told him, 'As soon as I saw that boy I knew he was Frank's. He's got Frank's eyes and nose. I hope he hasn't got Frank's heart, though.' And when Doug asked me the same there wasn't much to report. After they left for the Chinese my father who I hadn't seen in years excused himself to go and shower. The whole time they were away I sat in the sitting room listening to the shower run. I had an idea Frank was hiding, and I realised I was happy for him to. I think that was the moment of release for me. His signature might be on my birth certificate but it didn't need to be scribbled all over my life.

That night we rolled out our sleeping bags in the sitting

room. Dougie fell asleep quickly. For a while I lay there in the humming dark listening to the distant murmur of voices from the bedroom. It wasn't the hale and hearty voice we'd been treated to all evening; it was low, serious, slightly menacing. Once I thought I heard my mother's name spoken. As I strained to hear more the voices fell silent as if they had just worked out that they could be heard. I must have dozed off after that. When I woke it was still dark. I heard a door open, the fly-screen door smack back, a moment later the car engine start. And in its low idling departure I fell back to sleep.

We woke late. In the kitchen there was a note from Cynthia. We were to help ourselves to whatever we could find in the fridge.

Dougie was frying eggs when I came out of the shower. He asked me if I wanted bacon.

'Nope,' I said. 'We're going.'

'Now?'

'Now. Pack up. We're going. There's a train at eleven. I rang up while you were asleep.'

'What about your dad?' asked Dougie, the fish slice in his hand, eggs sizzling away.

'What about him?' I remember enjoying that tone of voice. It sounded hard, unforgiving; I liked the effect it had.

Later, as we hurried like fugitives for the station and even as we boarded the train, and later too, with the desert flashing in the windows, all I felt was relief. None of this was planned. I wasn't after revenge. It was more self-serving than that; I'd got what I was after. I would leave London the same way in a few years' time. It was necessary to go there for all kinds of reasons to do with origins and curiosity. But none of that had to stick. None of it had to last. With Frank I felt like I'd removed a thorn from my side. I quite liked Cynthia, though once I was back home I was careful not to mention her to my mother. It would be easier on her, I thought, to tell her that Frank was living alone and had turned bitter.

I had a short wait in Sydney for the connection to Wellington. In the lounge I fell in with a young couple (he was a roofing contractor, she was a librarian) waiting for a series of flights to Murmansk where they would take delivery of two orphaned babies. What a swift change of fortune for all concerned! The roofing contractor sat in his jeans drumming his fingers over his thighs. I could see baby stuff sticking out of his wife's carry-on luggage. Those Russian babies would grow up between goalposts surrounded by hills and ocean, and in twenty years' time or so I imagined there would be a journey up to the Arctic Circle where they would arrive as foreigners but with some inside knowledge of fruit recognising its husk.

In London this time I'd come away with a sense that to be from somewhere, anywhere, was suddenly old hat. It didn't really matter any more. The faces in the street. The Italian, French and Slavic names I read in the newspapers turning out for English football clubs. The crappy food I ate in any number of so-called ethnic restaurants. London has a way of putting everything through a common strainer.

But when we flew across the Tasman in the dead of night I did feel I was from somewhere. I felt it keenly when the plane dipped its wing and seemed to take aim at a tiny cluster of lights huddling together in the immensity of the night. It was after midnight, no cars on the road, not another soul, just me and the taxi driver in his woollen v-neck, a plastic deodoriser in the form of a Hindu deity on the dash.

The thing about going away and coming back again is how much your own life has changed. It is an illusion of course, but this is what you leave the terminal with, and how little the world you left behind two weeks ago has altered. Things are out of whack. Your smile is sunnier than others'. Even the way you walk looks slightly expansive, which is to say, put on. The signs are all there. You have been out in the world.

My car was where I'd left it two weeks ago in the car park, unmarked, and with a sort of dog-like humility that was almost touching. On the back seat lay the familiar clutter. Boxes of books I hadn't had a chance to sort yet that I'd bought from the sale of an elderly woman's estate. On the passenger's seat the faxed message to the harbour master with its miraculous news of the impending visit of the cruise ship, the *Pacific Star*.

As I got in behind the wheel I could feel my old life crabbily demanding my attention.

On my mobile were twelve messages—three from Alice—so as I pulled out of the airport carpark I called up my elderly mother. The conversation went like this.

'How was Adie? Were you nice to him?'

'Of course I was nice.'

'He said you got drunk.'

'That's ridiculous.'

'And something about a black woman…'

23

2

Different people help out at the shop otherwise I'd never get away—our daughter Jess when she comes home from university; Frances when she isn't working on her jigsaw puzzles and up against a deadline. My mother, Alice, sometimes, but only if I am desperate since I also have to accept that she will give stuff away to old people, her cronies, and leave it to me to discover a hole in the stock. Usually it doesn't amount to much, an armchair or a lamp, mostly things of a practical value, heaters, light bulbs, that sort of thing, so Alice's days on are known in my books as 'charity days'. Her great friend Alma Martin is my most reliable 'staffer' though he'd scoff to be thought of in those terms. Still, it's some relief to know that he will act as a handbrake whenever my mother's largesse gets the better of her. In his time Alma has been many things—rat catcher, teacher, artist. Back in the heyday of NE Paints he was one of the better colour technicians. Most of the colours slapped on to the older houses around the district dating back to the late fifties are his creation. The popular Bush Green and Mount Aspiring Grey are but two. He is often mistakenly credited for Pacific Blue, the relief colour of choice that was all the rage around the time the walls of every house found the need to display a large butterfly. But by then he'd already fallen out with NE Paints' management over aesthetic differences. The surprise is that it had taken so long.

The great value of Alma to me is that he couldn't care less what I think. The unspoken truth is that he is infinitely more useful to me than I am to him. The tip face holds no horrors for him. I imagine he also knows that were I ever to cut him from the payroll my mother would be at my door in a flash. For as long as I can remember Alma has been in my mother's life. For nearly as long she has sat for him. There are sketches around of her pregnant with me. And even when Frank was still in our lives Alma was drawing Alice; long before then as well, when my mother was married to George Hands. He still draws—compulsively as ever. He draws the way other people breathe. Sometimes I think he is one of those people who come into the world with prior knowledge—without being told they recognise paper as paper and pencil as pencil. In a quiet moment at the shop he will drop into one of the many second-hand armchairs, pull out one of his tired notebooks which he carries everywhere, even to the tip, and draw customers. He appears to work quickly; from the counter you can hear his grunts and the rustle of paper. I've looked over his shoulder a few times. They're just sketches: a couple of vertical lines and a horizontal slash here and there. The subjects of the sketches are none the wiser. He even draws the sulky adolescent boys who come in to look at the soft porn at the back of the shop. Alma catches their blushing uncertainty as they linger around the cane fishing rods or pick up an abandoned basketball from the sporting goods section and roll it in their fingertips. The moment the phone rings or another customer enters the shop they take their chance. And I'll hear the retiring bounce of an abandoned basketball, followed by the ripple of the beaded curtain that closes off the magazine section from the mattresses.

On busy days they can get in and out without being seen. Or else I might look up in time to see a figure dart from the door. What a strange business it is. Frances wishes I'd dump the whole lot at the tip. She says it's not very becoming for a mayor. My mother says it is a disgrace. She's embarrassed, she says, that a child of her own would involve himself in that kind of thing. Frances wishes I could just stick to the 'curios' end of the market—the headhunter's knife, its hilt wrapped in human hair, for example. Or the World War One bayonet. These things are infinitely more acceptable. But it's the magazines and the endless recycling of glossy flesh that provides the cash-flow. Every time I hear a moral riff from my daughter about the exploitative aspect of these photos I am tempted to remind her of what pays her university fees. For that we have the enthusiasts to thank. They're not lepers or broken souls in filthy raincoats; all are exceedingly polite and none of them look for cover but cross the floor purposefully and without shame.

I have a degree in paint technology—it seemed a good idea when we were the 'paint capital' but now all that's gone—and my mail sits in a Victorian pisspot. For company there's the empty sofas and armchairs, the fold-up card tables, the rolled-up carpets. It's not the sort of future I once imagined for myself, but this is the reef on which I washed up more than twenty years ago, all this household stuff that men and women once argued and flogged one another over, spilt blood for, badgered

26

and exhorted promises and threats in order to have the sofa with *that* flower pattern. How important it once was. How lightly it is let go.

On my first morning back from seeing Adrian in London I had customers by the dozen and council papers to read and arrangements to make for the cruise ship visit. All morning I heard the clacking of the beaded curtains while I dealt with a long line of customers. To someone with a carton of hardbacks, hunting titles, celebrity biographies, I casually mentioned that the hospital was always on the lookout for more books. There was nothing there that I really wanted because to some extent what I buy is what I'm forced to keep company with until I flick it on. On the other hand, ours is a poor community and I try to make sure everyone leaves with something. The books belonged to an older man. When I mentioned 'hospital' he turned forlorn. He pushed the books away (I suspected them all along of being a smokescreen) and produced a lovely little thimble made in Holland at the turn of the last century. The silver engraving was exquisite—a woman sewing with a needle. He must have been holding this back in reserve, and naturally he was hoping I'd take the crummy books and he would keep this family heirloom. I paid more for it than I needed to, and gave the hospital another plug. He looked guiltily away and as he made space for someone else I saw his bushy eyebrows lift for the magazine section at the back. He was thinking about it, still thinking, and finally, with regret, no, another day perhaps.

A regular face pushed across the counter an old tin box. 'That's a World War One survival kit. Old but not used. It's amazing. Everything's there. Take a look, Harry. Fish hook. Needle. Cotton thread.'

'Thank you, Raymond.' Unshaven this morning, he stood to one side while I recorded the details in the ledger. 'Raymond B. WWI soldier's kit.'

The line moved forward: an elderly man with a back strain who winced (a touch theatrically? Perhaps...you have to be aware of these things) when he reached into his coat pocket for a pair of Victorian scissors; he was followed by a very tall man with a wooden aeroplane and a woman with a wax angel which she said shed tears. Further back, dear old Tui Brown. I happened to glance up when she swung in the door. I caught her look of surprise, and she knew that I had seen it too. As well as its descent into disappointment. She slowed half a step then decided to brazen it out. Obviously she thought Alice was still behind the counter and the tight-arsed son still in London. I will buy her plastic ice cube trays out of duty and after she's gone biff them out.

I'm making these calculations when a face I've never seen before pokes in the door. Then the rest of him follows cautiously—barefoot, torn jeans. He isn't a local. There are a number of ways of knowing this. For one thing, he doesn't know where to rest his eyes. It's the same with every newcomer. They bump their feet against porcelain cats, stumble against the hunting dogs as they sort out a passage through the jam of furnishings and ancient golf bags. As he comes nearer I pick him to be around Adrian's age. His hair is dark, fine, like Chinese hair, and his eyes are dark and liquid, more so from the effect of his pasty complexion. Jeans, barefoot as I said, thin arms flapping inside a threadbare T-shirt. It's not a survey I make of everyone who comes into the shop. But he's here to ask after Alma. 'Someone called Alma...' is what he says, and he points to the 'For Rent' notice on the board inside the door. That notice has been up for more than five years. Once in a blue moon someone asks after it but when they see Alma's old cottage on Beach Road they quickly turn and run. Alma lives on the cut I give him from whatever is on-sold from the tip. He also has a pension of some kind, a pittance I don't doubt, and my mother's lament is 'if only poor Alma could get a tenant for that God-awful dump of his out at the beach...'

It's a Monday. Mondays are a big day in this business. The tips are transformed, newly stockpiled by weekenders. And that's where Alma is, with the other tip rats, combing the weekend goodies. I'm about to give directions when I have a better idea. I have a favour to ask of Alma. I want him to paint something, maybe a mural of some kind over the vacated shop windows in town. Something more pleasing to the eye than the everyday ruin of businesses gone bust. When those people from the cruise ship come ashore I want them to see us in our Sunday best.

I offer to run the newcomer up to the tip if he'll wait a few minutes.

'I've got a car,' he says. His manner is impatient. He just wants the information and he'll be out of there.

Alma, however, is in his seventies, and these days he tends to get flustered. Alice would want me there.

'What's your name?'

He hesitates, sets his face.

'Okay. I'm Harry. Harry Bryant. The reason I ask is because Alma is an old friend of mine.'

'OK,' he nods back. 'Dean. Dean Eliot.' Some colour enters his cheeks. He looks around the shop as if expecting someone to challenge that.

'Okay, Dean. Just hang fire a moment.'

The tall man with the wooden aeroplane is getting agitated. He pushes forward. 'You probably know,' he says, 'there's only two of this model left in the country.' And so on. He doesn't have to try so hard and sound so earnest about it. I hate it when they underestimate my own knowledge of the market. And I happen to know the names of at least three collectors who will drive any number of hours through the night to buy this very model.

In the back office I write him out a cheque. He stands in the door holding his hat. I hear the woman with the wax angel cry out, 'Harry, I'm lighting the candles. You'll miss the tears!' This is one of those times when I experience the unhappy thought that what I do is not a serious job for a mayor. More often than not it is the nights that I fear. After the last house light has been switched off the New Egypt night is dark and final. You stand on the doorstep with the unpleasant feeling that you are sinking down into the earth and there is nothing to reach up and grab hold of but the glittering stars gathered around the rim of the abyss into which you are fast sinking. At such moments I have been known to cry out. Then that's it. Over. Done with. Frances will look up from her book. The mayor is experiencing another anxiety attack. Day breaks with all the answers. Someone with a pair of fire tongs to sell. Someone who wants to beat me down over an old carpet. Alma to run to the doctor. A cut has turned septic. My mother blames the tip and me but not necessarily in that order.

Dean Eliot is waiting for me. I go to the beaded curtain and clap my hands several times and the under-agers fly out like frightened quail. I am about to lock up when I see Tui Brown still standing in line. I take her plastic trays and give her a ten-dollar note which she gazes longingly at (as well she might, at this miracle the day has delivered). 'Oh, Harry,' she says. 'Isn't that a bit much?' And of course it is. Far too much. I walk her to the door. Her eyesight is not so good these days. She goes out into the day with her ten-dollar note in her hand. Her husband, Stan, is waiting across the road, by his feet his old canvas bag with its empty sherry flagon. Tui holds up the ten-dollar note. Stan takes his holstered hands out of his pockets and looks suitably awed.

About now I notice Dean Eliot's car with its human cargo. He actually has a mattress roped to the roof. I'm aware of passengers but I can't see how many because of the overlapping shadow from the mattress. Now I notice how short Dean's hair is, a white gleam of protean scalp which I find myself peering at, and in particular a scar, thin and white, as if the past movement of a worm has stilled and calcified. Dean moves his hand up there. And I decide there and then if the car contains two or three more like him I won't let Alma hand over the keys to the beach cottage.

Dean Eliot drives very slowly. In fact, there is something ingratiating about how slowly he drives; it's as if he is out to impress me and contain the Mad Max within. I actually have to slow down to a dawdle to keep him in my mirror. I still can't see who might be sitting in the passenger seat with that flapping mattress casting shadow.

The tip is one hill back from the fire-watcher's cottage which has been Alma's home for nearly forty years. His place looks down on my mother's and on the farm where I grew up. There's nothing nice to say about the tip. Except that since the closure of the paint plant the tip has sustained more of us than we like to admit in polite circles.

It's not a pleasant place to be. The air is eerily clear, still, the seagulls observant, circling, their beaked heads hanging. Far below, their view is of the bare heads roaming through the stew. I know everyone hates the sludge sticking to their shoes and the stone-eating noise of the grader with its puffs of black smoke. The same folk complain of the chemical stench. My mother doesn't know how Alma puts up with it but I suppose the simple answer to that is that he does so because I pay him to. He spends half his week stomping around in this filth, salvaging any number of household items that one person will throw out without a second thought and the next person will buy from me and wonder how anyone could have acted so hastily. Without exception all my customers beam with proud ownership over the new thing in their hand and think its last owner to be a mug.

I have my shop clothes on so I have to step carefully around the edge of the tip face. I can see the top of Alma's beanie, his denim shoulders, the stick he holds to gauge the depth of layers when he goes to place his weight. Moving across a tip is very much like crossing ice floes. You don't hurry it. He still hasn't seen me and I cough so I won't startle him. But he's distracted by his enterprise. Finally when I call down his shoulders jerk up and seeing it's me he looks a bit annoyed to have been caught out in this way.

His whiskered face with its blue eyes peers up at me. I feel sinfully safe and clean.

'Alice said you were back. How was London?'

'Good.'

'Adrian?'

'Good.'

'Alice said something about a black woman. You haven't got the clap, have you?'

'We'll talk later,' I say. 'Someone's here to see you about the cottage.'

'Jesus,' he says. He looks at the filthy gloves on his hands. 'I biked up here.'

'That's all right. I'll drive you over.'

'Thanks, Harry. Maybe in an hour.'

'No, now. It has to be now.'

'What? They're here, now?'

'As we speak.'

'Jesus,' he says again. He looks down at the footstool and a yard broom and something wrapped in a carpet—I can't tell what exactly.

Dean Eliot has parked the Datsun on the edge of the mud. The driver's side door is open and Dean is sitting while he puts on shoes. Shoes. Well, that's something. I almost report back to Alma, 'The applicant is putting on his shoes.' Now the passenger side door opens and out gets a young woman, olive-skinned, big-hipped but finely featured, youth and destiny fighting for control, part-Maori I'd say, or Greek. Thick-rooted dark hair. A wave of it spills across her face as she stoops back inside the car. From that position she gives a sideways look and a little wave. I wave back. Reaching in the back door she pulls out two babies. Babies. I hadn't thought of that—not in a thousand years. You have to wonder how they all fit in there. Dean Eliot has his shoes on now. She hands him the babies. Then she searches in the back for something. This time it is a milk bottle. And now the babies are handed back, one at a time, one for each hip; free at last Dean sets off following the dried track of the grader to where I have been taking all this in. It doesn't look quite as bad as I had thought.

Dean nods back over his shoulder. 'That's Violet,' he says, and indicating over the edge of the tip face, I say, 'Down there is Mr Martin.'

Dean cranes over at Alma squinting up in to the low afternoon sun.

'So Harry tells me you're interested in the cottage?'

'If it's available.'

'It could be. Could be.' Alma thinks about his next question. I can feel Dean dying a slow death beside me. 'Could be' has sounded such a cautioning note. Dean has been thinking it either is or it isn't available. What he can't detect of course is Alma's own thrashing angler's heart.

'Just for you, is it, Dean?'

Dean's eyes take off across the tip. How should he phrase this?

He begins to look behind for the answer but quickly has it resolved and comes back to Alma.

'For me and my family.'

Alma gives me a look. I didn't say anything about family. I shrug back as if to say this is recent news. I didn't know either until a minute ago. Now Alma reaches to grab some petrified filth for purchase. He's going to have to come up and take a look for himself.

34

On the edge of the tide of mud is the orange Datsun. Soon as he sees its tired-looking mattress I can see every instinct in Alma railing at him to say 'No' but then comes the master-stroke—from the Eliots' point of view. The young woman—she can't be any older than Jess, I think now—gets out of the car. And the scene that just a moment ago looked so alarming and desperate with that mattress slopped over the roof dissolves some of the apprehension spread across Alma's face.

For his part, new hope enters Dean's voice; it is as though at that same moment he cottoned on to his trump card. Proudly, possessively, you could say as he senses it will help his case, he says, 'That's Violet. And that's Jackson and Crystal.'

It was September, and towards the coast the land grew flat in the late afternoon sea light. I hoped for Alma's sake the Eliots were taking all this in—the shredded leaves of the cabbage trees, wind worn, bashed but hanging on, and now the vast and tilted shingle beach with its litter of driftwood. I wound down the window but the dust was worse than the chemical stench clinging to Alma. The road ended with a short run up an incline on to a scrappy lawn with sandy tyre ruts and crushed white shells scattered here and there. I switched the car engine off and we got out to wait for the Eliots. The sea drew back and slurped ashore.

Immediately the peace was broken by the throaty noise of the Eliots' exhaust and I saw Alma's thoughts shift to matters to do with risk management and liquidity.

'You can always say no,' I said.

He thought about it, nodding, the thick skin above his eyes creasing and bristling.

'Well, we'll just see, shall we?' he said.

We watched the Eliots unbuckle their babies. The young woman passed them out. Dean had shed his sneakers and was barefoot again. Now Dean handed one little bundle back to Violet and they were ready for the tour.

'As you can see. It's a little unlived in,' said Alma.

We followed him around to the front to a weatherboard porch of peeling blue paint, some white undercoat and a more distant experiment with pink. Dean sat one of the babies on the rail. From here the world opened up and in the distance a tanker appeared to sail off the line. Dean lifted the paw of Jackson and waved it at the disappearing tanker. So far, so good.

The bottom of the door caught on the sandy carpet. Alma said something about the maritime climate. One after another we filed through and were met with the stale warmth of the house.

'You hardly need electricity. The house cooks in summer,' Alma said.

That may be so, it was warm, but there is also no easy overcoming the atmosphere of an unoccupied cottage. The walls themselves actually seemed to frame and hold on to an air of deepening despair. Violet gazed at the front windows and I saw the problem. There were no curtains up and it occurred to me that I could easily donate something from the back of the shop. I passed this on to the Eliots but the offer hardly made a dent in their faces. Nor did they give any indication of how they felt towards the place. The attractive fireplace with its stone hearth and the problematic absence of a fridge were met with the same indifference, Dean blankly and Violet with the slightly more calculable expression of someone not used to giving an opinion.

The bathtub had an ugly rust mark. Everyone stared at it until Alma ushered us out again. In the bedroom he artfully placed himself in front of the mouldy wall. I think he'd made up his own mind that he could live with the Eliots as his tenants. Still, there were things he needed to ask them. I didn't like to butt in and run the show but he needed to find out how long they intended to stay. Did they have employment? References? On the other hand, I suppose he saw little point. Their silence seemed to indicate their lack of interest. Now Alma just wanted to end the tour and see the Eliots off.

He led us back to the front door and stood aside as we filed past, the young woman with a 'Thanks'. And while Alma locked up the Eliots conferred in a whisper down on the lawn.

A moment later Alma turned from the door to find Dean Eliot coming forward with a fistful of notes.

'Is a month in advance all right?' he asked.

Now the girl nudged him, her eyes lowered. 'Ask 'im, Dean.'

'Yeah, ah. The bond. Is there one?'

All four of them stared at Alma—the fledgling adults and the babies.

'No,' said Alma. 'There's no bond.' He caught my eye and we both turned and stared at the sea.

Now Dean had something else to ask.

'We were wondering,' he said. 'Is it all right if we move in now?'

The question slowed Alma down. I could see what he was thinking. If he said 'No' where would they stay the night? Curled up in the car? The Eliots were passing on their amateurish lack of organisation. I couldn't bear to look at Alma.

I heard him say, 'I don't see any reason why not,' which was possibly more generous than he really felt.

Violet smiled and kissed the cheek of the baby she was holding. Jackson or Crystal. I didn't know any more which was which; they kept swapping them. Dean put out his hand— he meant to shake on the arrangement but because Alma was slow to respond he dropped his hand back at his side. For the first time a bit of embarrassment entered his cheeks.

'Of course there's no power,' Alma told them. 'You'll have to organise that. And I don't know about the stove. There's no hot water either.' Now I could see him reconsider if it was wise for the Eliots to move in right away. 'If you were to wait a few days...'

But Violet pounced on that. 'No. No. We're fine, Mr Martin.'

She dropped her eyes; almost closed them. Her mouth drew a stubborn line. We listened to the sea puzzle its way to the shore.

'All right, I'm not going to change your minds. I can see that. It's Alma, by the way. I don't have a phone on at my place. If you want to contact me you need to call Harry at the shop. I'm there part of the time. If I'm not and there's a problem Harry can pass it on to me. I still think you should wait. Have you got candles?'

'No. But we're fine.'

'Bedding?'

As one we glanced up at the mattress slopped over the roof of the Datsun.

Alma told them, 'You could do worse, a lot worse, than poke around at Harry's. He's got enough mattresses and beds and anything else you might need.'

I chimed in with my earlier offer. They should drop around the shop and borrow whatever they needed. Then I had a thought. The cruise ship visit was less than three days away. In the back of the shop I had a carton of two hundred test tubes that needed to be filled with sea water and sand from our best beach so that the cruise ship people 'could take a little of us home with them'. It's not a big job, I told Dean. But it might be worth a few dollars if he was interested.

Dean's face twitched. He sucked his cheeks. I saw Violet give him a look. Dean should have said something by now. But you could see his problem. If he accepted it might suggest the finances were more parlous than they wished to let on. On the other hand, if he declined that was money they wouldn't see.

Finally it was left to Violet. She said brightly, 'Dean'll do it. Dean can do anything.'

Saturday morning. A huge lump of sugar, interior lit and God sent, popped up on the horizon. Later everyone had a story to tell how they had been at their window and looked up to see the cruise ship.

I drove into town around nine. Broadway was glistening and black-topped—it almost looked prosperous thanks to the over-night rain. Alma was working on the painting over the shop windows. I didn't pay close attention, just noted with some satisfaction that he was almost finished. On the corner of Railway Avenue by the port the old NE Paints band were passing around sheet music. Groups of schoolchildren were being herded in the direction of the port.

The crowd had to wait for the high tide. At eleven o'clock the harbour tug accelerated across the bar and headed off to the cruise ship lying at anchor still some distance offshore. The tug bashed its way into an opposing swell and spray lifted over the bow. At last we came around to the lee of the liner—the sides of the ship were immense.

None of the passengers got their feet wet. A quick glance told me they would have complained if they did. Thirty-five passengers in all—less than what we had planned for. A lot less. I looked up at a large porthole and saw a man in pyjamas and reading glasses sitting up in bed with a book.

I was able to greet each passenger with a flier containing information on the town they were visiting, some rainfall and sunshine figures.

The older women wore silk scarves and sunglasses. Their skin was soapy, ageless, like marble. I had the impression they were on to second and third husbands. These were older men, tanned in short-sleeved shirts, iron-coloured hair swept back, proud of their ageing virility. Americans. Germans. Canadians. An English couple held things up while they argued whether to bring jackets ashore. A final word came from the woman: 'Well if it's cold I'll blame you.'

At last the tug eased away from this gentle plaza of bottle-green water round to the exposed sea. We were running with the swell. At the first surge cameras swung out from swollen bellies and hands shot out to the nearest thing to grab hold of; each other as it turned out. The elements produced in me the usual mix of apology and pride. I let the spray settle on my face and squinted at approaching landfall, always impressive at this distance. First, the purple ranges, then the native bush and the spilling effect of wilderness. This same scene has found its way into a number of paintings, one famously by a Dutchman, which NE Paints in a civic-minded moment once produced as a calendar and is still to be found in fish-and-chip shops. The brooding ranges, the massed cloud slightly overdone in opal colour. On one level that is all there is to where we live. The rough outline of existence. You look at that painting and you think, it's as if we are still to arrive, we are still ship-bound with our flutes and wild hopes. For a month I actually owned the original painting until I sold it to the former mayor, Tommy Reece. It was a large canvas with a gilt frame. Tommy was a little guy with abnormally long arms and huge hands. I remember the way he carried the canvas from the shop; his arms spread to contain this early landscape of where we live, his unnaturally large hands gripping the rolling gilt edges, his shiny-suited mayoral figure crucified against the ranges.

The voices grouped at the rail were suitably awed and as we surged in on the back of the rolling swell the rooftops came into view. A breathy pot-bellied voice said, 'I don't see any-thing. I thought you said there was a town. I've got the bi-nocs trained on them and I tell you there's nothing.' Then the tug plunged across the bar and the same voice cried, 'Goddamn!' Fliers flew out of hands as our visitors for the day once more took hold of one another.

It was just a brief hiccup, nothing to get excited about. By the time they regained their composure the tug was gliding across the slick waters of the inner harbour. A long grassy embankment tilted up against a clear blue sky. Some black geese flew cinematically across the bow. Several cruise ship people took aim with their camcorders. As the embankment conceals the town from the harbour, a first-time visitor can wander along Broadway and never guess that a harbour with fishing boats sits over the rise at the end. The same secret applies from the port. There is no sense of what lies on the landward side of the embankment.

The expectant crowd was supposed to stay down at street level. Everyone had been briefed, I don't know how many times. Now, with horrible mistiming, they sprang up along the grassy embankment. My heart sank. Aboard the tug I felt the mood swing as attention seemed to switch from where we lived to who lived here. The Americans decently waved. The rest were quiet, some frosty faces among them and one or two with the faintest of smiles.

There must have been a crowd of about a hundred adults plus another larger group of schoolchildren in sunhats and caps. In their panting eagerness I saw the age-old affliction. *Please like us. Please say it is okay for us to live where we do and in the manner that we do.*

'Isn't that sweet, Cary?' a woman's voice said.

Cary, like several others, was reaching nervously for the sheet of information covering industry, population and climate.

Now, in ones and twos, they stepped ashore and climbed the path up the embankment to the start of the walking trail. There, our schoolchildren pressed on them bouquets of wild-flowers and the test tubes that Dean Eliot had filled with sea water and sand. I was still silently fuming as I reached the microphone. I offered a few words of welcome. This was the first time that a cruise ship had visited. We all hoped it wouldn't be the last. It was a new experience for us as no doubt this trip ashore into our borough was for them. It was a

shortened version of what I had intended to say, of what I had
so painstakingly written down in the jet-lagged hours of pre-
dawn wakefulness. At the time of composing it I hadn't given
any thought to its audience. The cruise ship was still a faceless
constituency.

It was only when I stood up to the microphone and looked
back at their dangling wrist chains and the blank tanned faces
that I sensed their boredom. A man in a navy jacket looked
around as if he had lost someone. Someone else fidgeted with
a cufflink. A woman in sunglasses and head scarf searched in
her leather bag for tissues. I wound up my welcome and led my
own applause as I stepped away from the mike.

A councillor escorted the passengers on to the bus. Heath,
who works at the garage, had been asked to fill in as driver for
the day. How ridiculous he looked in his peaked cap! I stood
in the crowd waving up at the bewildered faces that lined the
windows of the bus. Then at the last moment I skipped aboard,
the doors thankfully closing as the band started up with
'Georgia on My Mind'. Out at sea the sleek white cruise ship
lay at anchor; along Broadway grumbled the wheezing old
paint factory bus with its belches of black smoke. After two
hundred metres the bus stopped outside Angie's Koffee Kafe.
Angie stood beaming at the bottom of the step like the former
flight attendant she professes to be. That's when for the
first time I actually began to feel a little sorry for the cruise
ship people.

Under the leaking roof of the abandoned paint factory they
congregated around the edges of a large puddle and listened
politely while I recited the story of NE Paints and its long and
fruitful association with the town. '*Any* paints, we used to say.'

The Canadian woman chuckled and I concentrated in her direction for the next minute. A can of paint with the NE logo carried a premium. Our paint knew local conditions. It would not blister or fade. We were famously known as 'the paint capital'. I led them through the management area and we crowded into Felix Sampson's office with its second floor view over the rooftops of New Egypt. I deliberately stood beneath a large black-and-white portrait of Felix with his white goatee and customary long white shirtsleeves. With casual modesty I let it be known the boy in the photo with Felix was me. I am still in the sack from the NE Paints picnic sack race. My face flushed with the exhilaration of having won it.

'So what happened to the paint factory?' It was Cary.

We were screwed. Bought up and spat out. That's the truth of it. More politely, though, I explained how NE Paints was bought by a big international concern which promptly closed down the plant and shifted its operations to an Asian country. And Cary nodded like he knew that story.

Frances and I had just married when things turned to dust. I remember how the town scrambled around to make things right again. A group of people seized on tourism. Tommy Reece, who'd enjoyed the entire span of the NE Paints era of prosperity, naturally looked for a paint solution. Both were right and in an unexpected way they converged when Tommy came up with the idea to colour-code the town and rename the streets, strip them of their explorer names and slap on the names of colours from the old company paint chart. But it was a lost hope and poor Tommy was lurching around with a death rattle in his throat. People did what people always do in those situations—they moved out. Kids I competed with in the

NE Paints picnic sack race took themselves off to Queensland and Sydney. Whole streets emptied out. The frosty white oxalis sprung up in abandoned gardens. My friend Douglas Monroe and his wife, Diane, went into a venture painting desert scenes on to the sides of old paint cans to sell as plant holders. They painted camels, date trees, seascapes, rocky shores. None of them sold (well, Diane's mum took as many she could deal with) and in a black mood Doug gave up the camels and painted the words 'paint can' and to his surprise, and it was depressing too in a way, these cans began to sell. Doug would later buy the Albion. A terrible mistake. Even at its fire sale price. Everyone said so. It was like seeing an accident happen before your eyes.

With my own redundancy Frances and I bought Pre-Loved Furnishings & Other Curios from Alice's first husband, George, and his second wife, Victoria. As the town emptied out we picked up some great bargains. Things that cannot fit into the boot of a car or an aeroplane—sofas, bed frames, mattresses, TV sets. Money wasn't an issue, either. I'd been worried about having to barter and drive hard bargains with old friends. But everyone was so eager to leave they didn't care. They might have brooded on the decision for months, then in a single night they made up their minds and cleared out. Several days would go by, and this happened a lot, then a neighbour would hear a dog wailing. Once someone opened a front door and a whole menagerie of budgies flew out. One item was common to all: don't ask me why, but people left their lawnmowers. They stood in their back sheds, oiled and cared for up to the last moment, the handles next to the rake handle and the catcher with its oil spots and grey mould. In the backyard would be a cheap plastic slide, an old tractor tyre filled with sand, a half-buried doll, its pink plastic arm flung up like that of a drowning person. You found yourself closing the eyes on the doll or picking a cricket bat up out of the long grass. These small and simple acts helped us along. You stood a cricket bat against the side of a house and you felt like you were restoring possibility. You were also removing the traces of abandonment, and this was vital, because in those years and ever since really the challenge has been for the rest of us who stayed to find a way to live in a place so riddled with rejection.

It always takes someone else to truly tell us how wretched we look, and the cruise ship people didn't disappoint in that regard. The visit to the paint factory was as good as it got. Afterwards they filed on to the bus to visit the historic cemetery. But they weren't interested. They drifted around the blackened headstones. One woman tried to call someone in Toronto on her mobile phone. They weren't generally as fascinated as we had hoped they would be. When it started to spit they all rushed back to the bus. Heath wondered if it was the creepy feeling of the spongy grass; when he said that we both fell silent at the sound of the nearby creek water running beneath the graves.

They were more excited at the sight of a chicken walking along a footpath. A cry went up, 'A chicken! Look!' and the cruise ship people rushed to that side of the bus. At the commotion Heath looked up in his mirror. A woman yelled at her husband to roll on more film. Heath wrestled with the gear stick to change down but I waved him on.

After the chicken highlight I sat back and let the town drift by my elevated window. I thought back to that black woman at the nightclub Adrian had taken me to. I remember telling her I was the mayor. I have an awful feeling I might have also said it in a boastful manner. It was after she said her name was Ophelia. But is anyone really called that? Ophelia from 'around here' had half-mockingly said, 'Well Mister Mayor, are you going to buy me a drink?' I do wish I hadn't told her she was black, though; for all that I don't think she minded much. She seemed to be the forgiving type. I amused her. When I told her I was the Mayor her eyes lifted and I think it genuinely surprised her. I didn't tell her about Pre-Loved Furnishings & Other Curios. I didn't think she needed to know about the tip, either. I let her hang on to her vision of mayoral chains.

A mayor tends to know his town in an unique way. A visitor, Ophelia say, will see trees, a handsome welcome from Rotary, arrows pointing to the beach. A more bleak vista greets the mayor, a more troublesome one in terms of expenditure covering sewage, landfills, potholes. You see it in terms of what remains to be done rather than what has been accomplished. It is forever a work in progress. From the bus window, however, we had looked even more desperate than the records show. It was embarrassing and heartbreaking too, in a way, to see everyone stand so stiffly by their pie warmers and vege stalls after the cruise ship people left Angie's. How politely we averted our eyes as they pecked away among our arts and crafts. We are not London or Rome where for every customer put out by yet another half-arse meal and mediocre service another customer crowds the doorway. Our chance to impress is our only chance.

I had some other stops scheduled but I decided to pass them up. The cruise ship people were already tired of getting on and off the bus. When I looked up in Heath's mirror I could see them stifling yawns, glancing at wristwatches. Now they began to speak of other places they had visited, of other voyages, other cruise ships. Travel tips passed up and down the aisle. As Heath slowed down for one of our natural wonders, a rock formation which from a certain angle looks like a giant lion's head, the cruise ship people leant in to the aisle to hear the Englishwoman describe the wonderful colours of the fishing boats in Zanzibar. The bus dropped down another gear. Heath leant his head back for instructions. I waved him on. 'We won't worry about Lion's Head, Heath.' And that was that. I settled back to listen to the cruise ship people talk of restaurants with fish tanks and iced water. Opinions on last night's meal out at sea were exchanged and with a surprising depth of feeling that had been notably absent from all the other conversations I'd listened in to. Their voices seemed to rise another octave. A rumour swept the bus that they would be served lobster tonight—and one elderly man who had hardly moved a facial muscle from the time he arrived on the tug boat suddenly shot out of his seat, his eyes blinking wildly, as he sought out the source of the rumour.

On Beach Road we carried on as far as Big Bay where only half of the cruise ship people left the bus. The Englishwoman was one of them. Her husband slumped back in his seat, his sports jacket flung back over his head so he could sleep. When I stood outside the bus and looked up at the windows I thought all the other tilted faces were asleep. Most as it turned out were reading.

I led the party of stragglers down to the beach. The fur seal nursery is about a hundred and fifty metres from the car park.

After five minutes the complaints started. The shelf was too steep. Shingle kept getting in their shoes. In grim silence we soldiered on, until the Englishwoman piped up. She said somewhat discouragingly that she had been to the Galapagos Islands where she had seen over five hundred fur seals. Five hundred! I was simply hoping old Bess would be there to save the day, a scarred veteran of the sea with an obliging manner and a vanity for having her photo taken. The rain returned and that sent everyone running for the bus.

On their way back to the port everybody came alive. One older woman actually began to clap her hands. They were on their way back to the cruise ship, back to civilisation and maybe even lobster. Hereafter, everything smacked of haste. Their swift exit from the bus. The quick handshakes. The words that held no meaning given between the gritted teeth of a smile. *Yeah, nice to meetcha. You bet. Hang on in there.* They didn't want to know us. From their great balustrade they hardly noticed us in our cramped lifeboat waving our white handkerchiefs.

That evening was to be our surprise, our crowning effort, our big hurrah. As the *Pacific Star* sounded her foghorn, along Beach Road in dozens and dozens of parked cars we tooted our horns. We tooted and tooted until the white sugar lump melted into the pale horizon.

Along the beach fires were kicked out. People began to move away. Cars started up. To the last there were a few drunken toots, then all was quiet. The night reared up. We heard a wave roll up the beach and the pebbles roll over.

The next day the fliers with their flora and fauna information floated soggily across the bar. A few days after that the first of Dean Eliot's test tubes of saltwater and fresh air were washed ashore. We were back to life as we had known it before the visit of the cruise ship. We were back to our gaudy selves and that would have been that, put it all down to experience, had not a strange thing happened.

The night the cruise ship put out to sea and for several nights after that, along Broadway, they arrived like moths in the night—women my mother's age, a few younger ones as well, come to find themselves in Alma's crowd scene painted over the derelict shop windows.

The portraits were based on sketches Alma had done more than forty years earlier. There was one of my mother sitting on a set of porch steps. She looked so young. Painfully young. She must have been in her twenties. In those days she was married to George. In addition to my mother I counted twenty-five other faces. Now the original sitters of these paintings wrapped themselves up against the night and walked slowly with their faces turned to Alma's portraits. Some who had already spotted themselves in previous visits went directly to that section of the crowd. It was a big mural; as I've said, I'd asked him to produce something that would stretch over three shop windows. During the following days the paintings drew a lot of attention and comment. I watched from my shop door. It was fun to observe those women who were seeing it for the first time; the way they crawled along the pavement with a deliberate shopper's eye. Some had to dig around for their glasses. These women would lean closer and try on different faces. It was like someone rifling through a lost property box. Word must have spread far and wide because people who had moved away from the district years ago turned up out of the blue. Celia Merchant was one. She arrived in a late-model car, lined up her younger self with a camera flash and ran back to the car and drove off.

When I reported this to Alice she said in a critical voice, 'That's Celia.' Then she asked, 'Who else has been down there?'

I said, 'Hilary Phillips,' and she answered, 'Poor Hilary.'

Hilary was the only woman who could put up with the shamelessness of staring at herself in broad daylight and not give a damn. There were people who refused to believe that this large, unhealthy-looking woman with emphysema and tiny screwed-up eyes was the same person as the alert face leaning forward from the crowd of painted women, a fresh face on the end of a delicate neck seeking engagement. Even the older Hilary looked doubtful at times. She could even look like she was cross with that young person. Sometimes you actually heard her talk back to the young woman on the window. Once I saw her rock back on her heels with laughter at a shared joke. Hilary didn't care that anyone was watching. She didn't give a toss for what people might think of her. She was past that, and yet when I saw her stand before her younger self she could look puzzled and worried as though that younger face belonged to a scrupulous bank clerk with news that she didn't have as much money in her bank account as she had thought.

For these women in whom youth had already passed there was a pleasant and exhilarating feeling of resurrection. Now—and come to think of it, it wasn't just Hilary, I'd noticed other women doing this—Hilary turned her face very slowly from the painted one in the window. The thought was there, so long as she didn't rush it or make too sudden a movement, she might take that younger face off into the world with her.

During the day men in farm vehicles pulled over and got out to saunter up to the painted shop windows and search for certain faces known to them. Family members, obviously, sons, daughters, grandchildren in tow. I caught myself doing the same thing. If no one was in the shop I found myself wandering across the street to stare at the portrait of my mother sitting on that set of porch steps. Here, she is not yet my mother. She is a woman whose history is still mostly in front of her. In the portrait she is at least fifteen years younger than the son staring back at her.

A week passed, then another. Yet there was no good reason to take the portraits down. For one thing, Alma had waited nearly forty years for this exhibition. For another, the portraits were beginning to attract out-of-town interest. Who were these women? How had the portraits come into being?

3

In the years 1941 to 1943, Alma painted a whole community of women. He had completed thirty-seven portraits by the time the men came back from the war, and another five hundred and eighty sketches of my mother, Alice Hands, as she was known then.

I suppose the sketches amount to slices of life. Hurried drawings of women on all fours as they weed and tend to their gardens, of them hanging up the washing or idling at a window alone with their thoughts. Their tinkering inquisitiveness, as they lift the lid on the letterbox, hope fading. On occasion he liked to employ props. His explanation was that certain accessories extract a look that would not otherwise avail itself. The mere touch of something precious and a face will come alive. Place a teapot in a woman's hands and look at how it heightens the shoulders and drops the head. And yet as much as he sketched the women of the district in their everyday activities, more often than not it was the formal pose that they requested. They were impatient with the three-quarter perspective where one eye is half concealed by the bridge of the nose. They wanted to be looked at, which is hardly surprising, I suppose, since their men were away at the war. Innocently, Alma did not imagine any reciprocal joy until Hilary James told him, 'You know something, Alma, when you are drawing I feel like you're touching me.' The shining, earnest look in Hilary's eyes scared him into laying down his pencil. He told her, 'I can stop if you like, Hil?' But, of course this is not what she meant or wished to hear.

Not all the men went off to war. Some of them stayed back, men of a certain age, let's say, together with those who were wedded to the land, some of whom were deemed crucial to the wartime economy. Not only farmers but also bushmen who no one kept tabs on. The first category lived on remote farms the way others occupy distant countries. They and the bushmen rarely entered the women's lives.

After the men in the district went off to fight the women were left with the potholes of their old existence—farm machinery, trucks, a rusting idleness. Horses stood in paddocks awaiting their riders. Grass grew over the cricket pitches. When the crossbar fell off the goalposts in a storm no one fixed it. The doors to the hotel in town grew sullen and the bars ever gloomier.

Soon the women forgot to lower their eyes. Bashfulness slipped from their skin. They showed up in town hatless and laughing. With the younger ones, though, a dullness spread across their faces. At times it looked like a sheet of disappointment, as if they were asking, *Is this all there is?* In their wondering...well, they could not see the edges of their wondering. Certain gestures and intuitions came naturally but they were less sure of what they were connected to. Smiles of vanity tend to leave faint traces around the reach of the nostril and in the corner of the eye. On the inside they create an almost mindless sunburst which the outer features struggle to contain. Such a smile disappeared during those years of the war.

On the beach as well a freer spirit ruled. One low tide Alma happened to venture around a point that is inaccessible during high water and there he came upon two women sunbathing without a stitch on. Alice was sure Alma had seen her and Victoria. He had looked and then looked quickly away. At thirty-seven Victoria was ten years older than Alice. My mother sat up and pulled a towel around herself. Victoria didn't bother. What was the point, after all? Alma had already looked.

And besides, Alma was regarded as harmless. For a man just turned thirty this is not especially flattering. But it was known that his life had been touched by tragedy. Alma had lost a young wife in a train accident. His decision to live alone seemed both sad and honourable, as though having tried that other life which had ended so badly, from now on he would tread more carefully. For another thing, his interest, this near-obsession with drawing, made Alma seem a less-than-dangerous male. A male without horns. He was also the local teacher out at the country school with a roll of half a dozen farm kids. Five miles from town or in those days thirty minutes on a bike. Today the school is a café and the surrounding countryside has been swallowed up by the explosion of suburbia in the sixties, the rich years of NE Paints, the tip, and the new bypass. Everything considered, if a man had to stumble upon my mother and her friend sunbathing in the nude you couldn't go past Alma, a man in an old straw hat who carried his flat tin case of pencils along with his ratter's gear in a canvas knapsack.

In the summer of '42 there was a rat infestation on an unprecedented scale. In broad daylight rats were seen running up trees and crossing the road. Houses and barns were overrun. School finished in December and didn't resume until February. Over the intervening period Alma was out every day on ratting business. He would sprinkle his blue trails of poison and return the next day to pick up the corpses. It was not exactly glamorous work but there are few things he says he's done in life that were appreciated as much.

A dead rat is a slightly worse spectacle than a live one. A dead rat conjures up the bubonic plague, bodies piled into carts hauled up medieval streets. And while a live rat is little more than an insult to our idea of civilised space, an infestation is something else again. The only information my mother gleaned from her own mother leading up to her marriage with George Hands were tips on keeping a house clean. Cleanliness and wifeliness went hand in hand. The sight of unhurried rats inside the house struck at the moral heart of what my mother and her generation thought important.

She remembered what George had told her to do. Get hold of Alma. In those days he was the nearest neighbour for miles around, though she still hadn't visited him at home. She left a note in his letterbox.

Alma came down the hill that evening and laid his poison. He was back in the morning to collect the corpses. There wasn't a room without a dead rat. The most Alice had heard was some scratching noises behind walls and out at the kitchen at night. She thought Alma might catch one or two but never these dozens. As he stood there with brown paper bags filled with dead rats she tried to pay him. But he wouldn't hear of it.

So she offered to bake him a cake. A banana cake, she said upping the ante. He dithered but in the end decided no, he couldn't accept that either. 'I would Alice, a smart man doesn't ordinarily turn down banana cake, but I don't want to establish a precedent, if you know what I mean.'

He said, 'I can only eat so many cakes.'

'Well, that may be so, but I still want to give you something.'

'You could sit for me,' he said. 'I'd like to draw you, if you're comfortable with that.'

My mother was lost for a reply. Although Alma had caught her by surprise it wasn't like he was asking her out, though it was close, very close indeed. To be drawn is to be singled out.

Alma must have sensed her inner conflict because he pressed his lips together thoughtfully and said, 'I was thinking in lieu of payment.' It was the gentlest pressure he applied. My mother noticed his smile. It was a nice smile. *In lieu of payment.* There was obviously nothing threatening about it. Other men spoke loudly, as if they wanted a third party to hear and mark them for wittiness. They stumbled over kindness of course, wiped a kind remark from their mouths like it was spittle. So when Alma said 'in lieu of' there was just the gentlest hint of—of what exactly? Services rendered? She didn't know Alma well enough to judge. She'd been married for little over a year when George signed up with the armed forces. Over that time George had had the most to do with Alma. There was that one time before he left for overseas that they'd had Alma down for a card evening. He'd shown no guile at cards. He didn't know how to be tricky—not like George with a cigarette stuck in his mouth. Still, she had to beat out all the usual bush fires thinking he might mean something extra. Now she rounded that bend of suspicion she came into a more generous understanding. This was Alma, a man who had lost his wife and his memory, and of whom George had said, 'For God's sake, if anything goes wrong get hold of Alma. He knows the drill and I've told him to expect a call from time to time.'

She caught a glimpse of herself in the sitting-room mirror; she was touching her hair and blushing.

'I'd have to wash my hair first,' she said.

That seemed to amuse him; again the warm smile pegged to that creased line over his forehead.

About now she thought to look down at her bare feet. She'd been outside collecting cowshit for the garden.

'Look at me!' she said.

'That's what I'm asking to do,' he replied.

The next morning Alma showed up with his tin case of pencils and his sketchbooks. She showed him through to the sitting room. She had an idea that a sitting was a formal occasion and in preparation had gone around the room straightening cushions and pulling off furnishing covers. She had dressed herself up in her Sunday best, a black skirt and red blouse. She had been toying with putting a flower in her hair when Alma turned up.

It is hard to know what to do with yourself the first time you sit. You are suddenly aware of your arms and legs, too aware, and as soon as that awareness slips into place it's as if those limbs were never really an integral part of you at all, but clumsy add-ons. My mother had expected some direction from Alma but he just stood there looking at her, moving a pencil back and forth across his chin. He might have been taking an interest in the view outside the window or gazing at a slow-moving river. A river is unconsciously what it is. It does not know how to be anything else. A river does not suffer embarrassment. My mother didn't know what to do with her arms. They had never felt so alien. She tried folding them. Now she unfolded them. She felt herself grow clumsy before Alma's gaze. 'Just relax,' he told her now. 'We're not in a hurry.' She told him she felt silly. But it was as if he hadn't heard.

He had his tin case open on his knee and was sorting through his pencils. A beast lowed in the paddock outside the window. She wished she was out there. She said apologetically, 'This doesn't seem to be working, does it.' Again Alma didn't answer. She said, 'If I'm no good just say. I don't want to waste your time.' He said, 'You're not,' but he didn't tell her what to do either. He glanced back at the window, and remarked casually, 'Looks like rain.'

This mention of the weather switched her thoughts to the drainage canals that still needed to be dug in the far paddock. She might have asked Alma to help if she hadn't used up all her favours with the rat business. If she didn't ask, she could at least make a start. She knew that she would be visible from his cottage up on the hill and that he'd let her swing on the end of a shovel for no more than half an hour before he'd race down the hill. She was thinking about that swamp. She was thinking about that shovelling. She was only dimly aware of Alma. She could hear him breathing—now she couldn't as she dropped back to a place deep within, back from the flashing exterior of the world. The erotic experience Hilary reported would come later.

That summer every poisoned rat in the district decided to make life hell for Alma. The rats chose out-of-the-way places to die. He had to dig a passage under two houses and feel around in the cobwebbed dark. There were walls to lever open. Women screamed at their children to get away from where he was working. A need to quench a terrible thirst is the last act of a dying rat and usually they will crawl under a water tank to die.

At Victoria's house he arrived to a terrible stench. It wasn't a hot day but every window in the house had been thrown open. Vengeful rats like this one of Victoria's will crawl inside walls where they fester and rot.

Alma tied on his ratter's scarf. Sure enough, he found what he was after down by the skirting of the wall that contained the open fireplace. In a worst-case scenario he would have to pull a wall of scrim apart, but on a day when luck and skill are equally favoured what he preferred was to make a small hole in the wall, just large enough to poke his hand through. With a deft angler's wrist movement he could flick a leadline with a hook and reel in a decomposed rat. But Victoria's was one of those houses where nothing had ever gone easy—not the portraits that came later or the recovery of this corpse. After five or six failed attempts the stench stuck in his throat. He told Victoria he would take that glass of water now.

They went out to the garden where they could breathe. He cleared his lungs and after the break he found he was getting better length and a few minutes was all it needed before he had his corpse. Alma took it outside to bury in the patch of weeds. Victoria was embarrassed about that too. Her late husband had always been the gardener.

Now they went back inside the house and checked in all the rooms. They sniffed the air in each before returning to the sitting room. More adventurously, Victoria took herself over to the wall where the rat had crawled inside to die. She sniffed. She sniffed again, and smiled with relief.

She opened her purse to offer a payment. Alma told her it wasn't necessary.

'But Alma, I couldn't sleep while that thing was in the house. You smelt it. You have to take something.'

'Well, there is something,' he told her.

Everyone whom Alma was to sketch or paint can thank the rat epidemic for bringing him into their lives. The sitter's payment was negotiated for Mrs Swain, Mrs Long, Meg Wyatt, Meri Thorn, Mrs Black, Jill Christophers, Beryl Knight, the Hasler girls, Tui Brown, Ginette Fields, Gracie Brewer, her mother Augusta, the Healy sisters Joan and Kate, Bronwyn Rapson, June Fairly and her daughter Joyce, and Hilary Phillips.

He didn't get to Hilary's until a few days before Christmas. Hilary was vague. She thought she'd heard telltale noises in her bedroom ceiling. Alma poked around and couldn't find anything. He lowered himself down on to the steps she was holding.

'False alarm,' he told her.

'Are you sure?' she asked.

'Pretty sure.'

'But I saw one,' she said, and this news pricked his interest. She hadn't said so earlier. She hadn't said she had actually seen one.

'Yesterday' she said. 'Yesterday morning. It ran across the kitchen floor. A huge brown grey black thing.'

Alma followed her into the kitchen. He looked behind the stove. There were no droppings that he could see. He searched through the pantry—nothing there. By now he was shaking his head. She'd led him on a wild goose chase. To oblige her he checked along the skirting but he was simply pretending. For whatever reason, Hilary's place was the only one in the district to escape the infestation. Alma told her she should feel lucky. She didn't look lucky. She looked disappointed to hear that, as if she wanted rats, wanted them verified so she could be part of things, part of the infestation. It didn't make any sense. In the end he told her he'd lay a trail, 'Just to be on the safe side. Just to be sure.'

'Yes, definitely,' she said, her face lighting up. 'I know I heard something and isn't it best to be on the safe side, as you say, Alma?'

Hilary's cottage was set at the end of a finger of sand on the town side of the estuary, separating off the wharf area. She had all the windows open to the glittery view of the sea. If the rats hadn't found her cottage by now Alma was sure they wouldn't but he laid the poison that Hilary so desperately seemed to want.

As he began to pack up his gear he was aware of Hilary standing over him. She had something in her hand and without looking up he knew what it was.

'There's no cost involved, Hilary,' he said.

'Well, I still need to pay you, Alma. You can't come all this way for nothing.'

He told her she could pay him when he caught something and not before.

'No. I'm going to pay you now.' She sounded firm. But then as she opened her purse she seemed to linger as if she had forgotten why she'd opened it. She raised her eyes and gave him a hopeful look and the penny dropped. Alma smiled.

'There is another way,' he said.

Hilary's was one of two portraits he could never get right. She couldn't wait to see what he'd drawn. She couldn't wait to find out what he had seen. Her brimming eagerness made him rush. Then he wouldn't show her. Together they'd arrive at a decision to start over and for her to sit back in her chair a little more and think of Jimmy or vanilla ice cream.

In the case of Victoria she complained that her body lacked figure, that her dress bulged in all the wrong places. She said she looked like she was made of mattresses or armchair stuffing and that bits of twine had been pulled tight in all the wrong places. Two weeks after Alma finished and presented her with her portrait he was around there on another rat job when he noticed she had taken down the painting above the hearth. Its absence was puzzling. They had spent a pleasant hour deciding where to hang it and Victoria had been excited at the time. Now the blank space on the wall made him question the accuracy of his memory. They skirted the subject, but after a while their eyes kept returning to the emptiness above the hearth and finally Victoria told him, 'Alma, I had to. You gave me no choice after I saw what poor company I make...that downturned mouth, those grumpy eyes.'

And as was their habit in those days the conversation stopped there. Then they both heard it—a scratchy sound behind the skirting. Alma told her, 'Victoria, let this one be on me.'

As far as the rest of the women in the district were concerned, to be looked at or observed was as rare as sugar or chocolate. They could have looked in the mirror, of course.

But there is nothing like another's eyes to set us alight, to make our nerves stand on end, to tell us, in effect, who we are.

A long period of fine weather put further distance between their lives and the war in Europe. When you walked outside you saw dragonflies. You saw waxeyes in their upside-down efforts to get the nectar of the flax flowers. You saw the great unhurried parade of clouds. You breathed in and forgot the war until you picked up that day's newspaper off the lawn, or a letter arrived, and then the local imagination crept into areas of the map previously unknown. When a name such as *Tobruk* arrived in a letter a face would go slack, like sailcloth.

With the men away some things continued as they had before. The sound of tennis balls smacking against the wooden volley-board, balls kissing the net, only it was women playing women. Like at the dance at New Year's Eve, the hall decorated as it had always been with streamers, flowers, trestles sagging under sponges, music, the same old dances, but no men.

In 1942 the last of the married men were called up and with these men gone the altered world was more or less complete. Every second or third day Alice found something to ask Alma's help with. The beehives. Thistle to dig out of the paddock. Those drainage canals that had been bugging her. For a farmer's daughter she didn't have much of a stomach for blood so Alma did the butchering, and when he grabbed a chook and smacked it down on the saw horse, its neck stretched, she made sure her head was turned or better that she was inside so she wouldn't hear the light splatter of chicken blood. Once when a neighbour's bull tore a boundary fence down Alma helped fix that. There were also the rats, of course.

By now she was so used to his being around they dropped

certain formalities. When he turned up at the door she no longer headed for the sitting room to perch on the edge of the stuffed armchairs. While the hot weather lasted the door was open day and night, and to the extent that Alma was part of the outside world there was no attempt to hold him at bay.

In those days there stood a hill about a hundred metres from the farmhouse. When Alice's parents had lived there her mother complained endlessly about the hill blocking the sea view. Various sheep tracks wound to the top. Every morning Alice would walk up the hill until she could see the rooftops of town and the blue ocean. When she was very small, before she could talk or walk, her father used to pop her in his fishing net and drop her over the gunwale then drag her back and forth through the top layer of warm ocean, curled up like a trout in her father's net, her gummy mouth wide with laughter, or so it is told in family lore.

From her father she inherited this love of the sea. And on those days she decided a swim was in order she'd run down the hill tracks, cornering like a vehicle, her hips moving like swing doors. But on days when it was too rough or windy she would raise her elbows and let the breeze fan her; and maybe she'd turn and look the other way, follow the ridge up to Alma's cottage on the hill. Maybe then she'd see a movement beneath the guttering of the rat catcher's cottage, and she would smile at the thought that Alma had been watching.

4

After that first sitting my mother was naturally curious to discover what Alma had found in her that she could not see for herself in the mirror. At first he was evasive and put her off. He made up excuses why now wasn't the right time. He glanced at his watch. He tried to change the subject. My mother wouldn't give up.

'It's just a drawing Alma, no one will go to jail.'

Eventually he relented, unhappily it has to be said, and she saw what he had been trying to hold back from her, what she now saw for herself, some strange inclination on her part to present herself to the world as an eager-to-please shop assistant. It wasn't her—so how did that look get there. Where did that person, that stiff-looking shop assistant come from? It wasn't how she thought of herself. But Alma must have seen something to come up with that. And maybe he wasn't entirely wrong. But it wasn't all of her either—not the whole story. Not the representative self she wished to be seen out in the world.

The next time she met him at the door and asked where he

wanted her, he looked down at the porch, used his foot to shift an old boot to one side, and said, 'Here's good.'

It was to become a favourite pose that turned up in a number of paintings. My mother leans against the door jamb; there's the glare of her bare legs and feet, the lazy angle of her head. Thoughts to the soft pillowing sea. The eager-to-please shop assistant had been sent packing.

It was progress. And it was progress that prised her from the house, a bit at a time, until one afternoon after weeks of wondering if she should ask first or just go without invitation, she walked up Alma's dirt hill road. In quick time the surrounding farmland revealed itself, straw coloured, the black flecks of telegraph poles; and on the far edge of everything stood the ranges, in shadow at this time of the day, but their jaws dropped open in the February heat. At the top of the drive where it levelled out to a half-kept lawn and the start of Alma's porch she was alarmed at how much of her life was on show—the red roof of the farmhouse, the washing line; she could even see scored into the paddock the track she took each day to the top of the hill.

She knocked timidly on the door and Alma called out, 'Door's open!' which made her wonder if he'd seen her lurking around his letter box trying to force herself up the hill. She pushed on the door. Alma was standing at a bench filling a kettle. He didn't seem at all surprised to see her. Pleased though, his mouth buttoned down, some pleasure seeping out despite his efforts, but hardly surprised. 'Just in time for some chai,' he said.

While he busied himself with that task she looked around. The rat catcher's cottage was basic. One large room crowded with drawings and canvases, none of them framed. All the work was pinned to a back wall. There was a door to the bedroom which Alma kicked shut on his way to closing the door behind her. A coal range stood at one end, a potbelly at the other; a pile of chopped wood climbed the end wall.

My mother passed along the wall with the drawings. She picked out faces, identified names. Victoria—grimly captive. Hilary's face crammed with smiles; knees pressed together, like a schoolgirl about to sit a piano exam. Some of the women had settled for the chaste expression of someone asleep. Sadness was another subject. In two or three cases the eyes stirred with times long gone, opportunities once theirs for the taking; or else they showed confusion at the turn the world had taken, or were commiserative for the fish that once swam by so elegantly and was now the white skeleton lying on the sea bed.

Now she arrived at the series of the life that my mother feared Alma had seen far too much of—sketches of her pegging up the washing; standing at the letterbox; walking back to the house with folded arms, containing herself rather than cold; sitting on the porch, back to the door frame. She was disappointed to see that in every sketch he hadn't bothered with the detail of her face—instead it was represented by a crosshatch of lines, a loose scribble, a wool ball of light and shadow. She was better represented by gesture—the working struts of her arms as she reaches up to the washing line, the sag of her shoulders, her domestic solemnity as she chops the carrots.

There was one she almost missed. She was sure Alma would have removed it had he known in advance of her plan to visit. The sketch was of two figures sitting on the beach—a few dashed-off lines is all they get yet there is no doubt who they are. The more fully worked figure leans into her knees. There is the heavy fall of her breasts; one pigtail falls over her front shoulder; in the raised face there is a sharp look of annoyance. Alma has just waded around the point past the nude sunbathing women. One of them has sounded the alarm and at once the other has sat up. And already Alma is looking away with what he saw. The sketch is a commemorative in which my mother's breasts feature prominently.

This was the first of many visits up to Alma's cottage. It was on the second visit that he talked a little about himself for the first time. It was prompted by her glimpse of a tattoo on his arm, another portrait as it turned out. It was a gorgeous sunny day so they were sitting outside on the porch; it was as Alma reached for his cup that his shirt sleeve rode up his forearm and she saw it, a bluish oval shape already faded away beneath fine blond hair.

Alma quickly noticed my mother's interest.

'That's Claire,' he said.

It was the first time Alma had mentioned his wife. He excused himself and disappeared inside. A few minutes later he returned with a photograph of his wife, his only photo of her, but this version was no clearer. Blonde hair fading into an overexposed white background. A young pale face staring out of the middle. They were on their way to a new life when the train plunged into the river. Alma lost Claire and the baby she was carrying.

It begins with a weather system, thereafter a steady aggregation of detail ending up in tragedy. Heavy rains, a slip, the railway tracks shifting. Lives are jolted. Lives end. And the next day, as Alma hears later, people place wreaths over the mud slip. Others throw wreaths into the river. A man who lost his nine-year-old son nails up a white cross.

Into that river plunged Alma Martin's old life. A lengthy period of convalescence follows. He's taken some head injuries. Obtrusions. Concussion. Bruising around the eyes. There is other internal damage that is harder to gauge. For one thing, he can't recall anything of his immediate life. He can't think why he and Claire had boarded the train in the first place. He can't explain for himself where they were headed or what they intended to do when they got there. Relatives might have filled in the missing spaces, but Alma's parents are dead. His one sibling is in Australia. Some strangers professing to be second cousins come in to see him; he has no idea who they are and is glad when they leave. Each morning a man in a white coat approaches his bedside and shines a torch into his eyes. He asks questions which is silly because even if he knows the answers Alma can't reply. His jaw is broken and wired up.

He drifts off; when he wakes it is dark. He can hear crying from another part of the ward. But in the dark nearby is the heavy breath of someone asleep. His bed must be parked up alongside another patient. He dozes off again. When he wakes a face he's never seen before hovers over him. There is news to digest. His wife is dead. Sorry. A needle punctures his arm and he drifts off.

Eventually the time he is awake increases and soon he is able to sit up in bed. He has been told to expect a certain amount of memory blackout. The brain is a mysterious organ. He is encouraged to think of it as a castle with as many rooms and entrances as a honeycomb; a castle with its own inclinations to open this door and close another. The doctor has asked him to think of it in this way, to think of different bits and pieces of himself residing behind different doors. Some of those doors are opening; others remain stuck. In short, the whack to his head has created a spectacular erasure, a white flash across the blackened detail of the life lived so far.

As part of his rehabilitation the doctor recommends he try drawing. There are classes available at the hospital. And why not? He can't talk. He might as well draw pictures. Someone from the WEA visits every day. Others in the class hobble in on crutches, with bandaged heads, in wheelchairs. The teacher tells the assembled class, 'What I want you to know is there's no such thing as a mistake. I call it a starting point. If it doesn't work, it doesn't matter. It'll work its way out in the end. After that you'll be content to call it texture.' Mostly though they hear about technique. The geometry of the head, its various partitions of vertical and horizontal lines, the downward weight of a body at rest, the shifting compass of the body's disposition.

He draws every day. He draws for hours on end. Whole mornings and afternoons disappear in this way—slabs of time previously marked by the *tick tock* of a wall clock and the squeaking progress of the meal cart up the corridor.

It is a slow passage back into the world. When people ask about his wife Alma casts around for the photo, and since it is also an illustrative story he might roll up his sleeve.

He told my mother that when he looked at the photo of his wife he was struck by how little he could say about her. He had read somewhere about the ability of the great French painter, Pierre Bonnard, to paint from memory. Bonnard was able to get down accurately every movement of his wife getting in and out of the bath.

Whereas, Alma has to stop and concentrate hard to remember whether he had ever seen Claire in a bath. He must have, he thinks, but can't recall it. He has an idea that she had also gardened—again, it isn't information based on memory. And obviously she must have walked as well. But that is back in a life when he simply told himself, Claire is gardening or Claire is walking. He hadn't looked carefully enough to see how she did either.

My mother has an interesting thesis. She believes Alma decided to build a picture of his late wife from the bits and pieces of the women in the district that caught his eye. It's an appealing idea, bolstered by the fact that the tattooed portrait had already started to fade; it no longer resembled anyone but looked more like a net or a mesh. If he was fishing for attractive features, my mother thought he would find Victoria's drawn mouth attractive and Hilary's youth a source of vibrancy; Tui Brown, stalwart of the tennis club, had a nice figure, and so on. It was just an idea.

He loved Bonnard. For hours he would talk about the painter's life with my mother. He showed her a photo once. The man's eyes stood out. They bulged. She said he looked like someone under threat of being struck blind who was taking a final look around at the world. My mother didn't think much of him—Bonnard, the man. He didn't look like a man participating in the cut and thrust of life. She couldn't imagine him mending a fence or waiting at a bus stop or taking his place at the back of the line for tickets to a film. She liked the portraits she saw in the library books, however.

Alma was a regular visitor to the library. My mother would often see him push his bike up the hill, a heavy book of colour plates in the bike carrier. When they made plans for a last swim at Easter he smiled at his 'water baby'. He told my mother she was like Marthe, Bonnard's wife and model.

'You both have water in common. She spent her life in a bathtub. In her husband's sketches she is forever getting in and out of the bath. She was devoted to cleaning herself, and Pierre was devoted to capturing her cleaning herself. Do you know how they met?' It was no longer necessary to answer, because Alma would tell her whether or not she wanted to hear, but as he talked on my mother was besieged by the thought that here was a man who must have once told his wife he loved her, and who had known her intimately, and yet couldn't begin to tell you about her breasts, how she tasted or what she felt like. And in startling succession came this thought, and not without a shudder of responsibility, that the woman Alma was coming to know best in this world was herself.

Alma Martin once told my mother a story that Matisse had Madame Cézanne in mind when he painted his own wife, and that Amélie was said to have wept for the 'lost image'. My mother and Alma were looking at Bonnard's bath series at the time, and she was beginning to think that if it was good enough for Matisse to strip Madame Cézanne into his wife's painting then maybe, just maybe, she would pose nude for Alma in order to help him flesh out his memory of his lost wife. It took my mother some time before she raised the courage to propose the idea, but eventually she did, and Alma took a slow sip of his tea. For the moment neither could shift their eyes off Bonnard's painting. 'Well, let's just think about it for now,' she said.

At Easter they went for their final sea swim. They waded around the point at low tide and arrived at the beach where a year earlier Alma had looked up and seen my mother and her friend nude sunbathing. Seeing Alma glance up the beach to that same place my mother said, 'I'm still thinking about it.'

That winter the women's club hosted a series of talks. Weather permitting my mother tried to get to as many of these talks as possible. It was the war years and everything was in short supply—including stimulation. Like plankton eaters they sat with their mouths and minds wide open. Alma sometimes came along. He would double my mother on George's bike. Within view of the town lights he would stop pedalling Alice to dismount and to hide the bike in the bushes. Whereupon my mother would start walking and after a pause of five minutes Alma would follow her, in case their arriving together caused tongues to wag.

Victoria helped to organise these talks in the large space above the Plunket Rooms. She asked Alma to give a talk on drawing, or maybe his favourite artist. 'Or ratting,' she said by way of another option.

In September he was due to give his ratter's talk but was troubled by what to wear. My mother went to George's wardrobe and found a white shirt, and while Alma sat in the kitchen in his singlet she ironed her husband's white shirt. In all sorts of ways Alma was replacing George. He rode his bike. Wore his shirts. Wore his gloves when he tore out the blackberry threatening to smother the bridge over Chinaman's Creek.

The rat talk drew a large crowd. There were questions at the end, some discussion. Its success encouraged him to give a talk the following month. This one on Pierre Bonnard and his wife, Marthe, was less well attended but still a success. Much of it my mother had heard before. Marthe's obsession with water and personal hygiene. Pierre the eager chronicler in close attendance.

Later they picked the bike out of the bushes. It was a warm night. A white moon hung in the clouds. Instead of mounting the bike they walked along beside it. My mother had a question she'd been bursting to put to him ever since leaving the talk. She warned him first that she had something private to ask. And Alma smiled, 'Not too private, I hope.' He stopped wheeling the bike and waited, and my mother said to him, 'Tell me honestly, can you remember what your wife looked like undressed?'

For a moment he looked up at the trees. She saw him begin to frame an answer. She saw the upward roll of his eyes, a taut drawing of his cheeks that warned her to expect an untruthful answer. Then he looked at her and his eyes rolled back; the face reluctantly recomposed itself. He shook his head. 'No, Alice,' he said. 'I can't.'

'In that case I'll do it,' she said.

To look at the nudes of my mother is to know what the painter is thinking. She is some sun-kissed landscape sitting at his feet. Horizontal lines cut across her knees like surveyor's pegs indicating where future heaviness may lie.

The Saturday after Alma's talk my mother wore a raincoat up to his cottage. As she said, when the objective is to remove them no clothes seem more appropriate than others. Up at Alma's when the time came to take off the coat she said she felt as naked as a shelled pea. It was a warm day, sunny. They moved out to the porch. While Alma set up his easel he hummed some tuneless melody. He never usually hummed. He fussed with the gear. Without looking up he asked her if she had heard from George, and she said, 'George would blow his brains out if he could see me now.'

'Well, George is in North Africa,' he said. Now, at last, he raised his eyes and looked at my mother. 'Alice, let's have you lean up against the door jamb and just hang your arms, and maybe cross your legs. Let your head drop and just let everything flop back.'

She asked if she could close her eyes and he said if she wanted to.

'George had better not ever find out about this.'

'Cross my heart and hope to die.'

'Oh you will, Alma. He'd shoot both of us.'

'I'll bear that in mind,' he said.

'I'm sorry, Alma. I'm not very professional, am I? I'm probably not what you're used to.'

'You're fine but I need to concentrate now, Alice,' he said.

When a sitter begins to talk the pose loses all its binding; arms and legs fall away, the mouth widens, the tongue waggles, a sense of form withers. By now my mother was aware of this and so shut up. She held the pose for twenty minutes, the whole time with her eyes closed. And the whole time she didn't hear him draw. There was none of the usual scuff on paper or the punctuated breathing.

They stopped twice for breaks. Alice didn't bother with putting on her raincoat. There was nothing left to hide. So she stood on Alma's porch completely naked except for an enamel cup of tea in her hand. Across the valley floor people were doing the normal Saturday things, mainly women of course, removing the heads of chickens, bringing wood inside their kitchens, shifting cattle across paddocks. How far and apart their lives seemed.

For all the nervousness surrounding the exercise, in this series of nudes my mother looks happy. Someone has just told a great joke on the big screen and she is looking up at it.

The session was interrupted once when a kingfisher mistaking Alma's blue carpet for a pond flew into the window. The blue-crested bird flew a garden-sized circle to show it wasn't hurt or embarrassed, but its tiny fast-blinking eye knew. It knew. It had known all along. Until the next time they heard it fly into the same window. Temptation is tireless and forgetful in that way.

Two other nude paintings completed that November and December are from Alma's sketches of my mother down at the river. They have walked along the shingle in the hot and dusty blackberry air, swaying like drunks, bumping into each other. Along the riverbank all the way up to the pools they hold branches back for each other to pass through. The pools are high with water off the tops; their bloated surface swirls with twigs and brown water.

My mother didn't bother to change behind a bush. She hadn't brought anything to change into anyway. In one painting that as far as I know no one else in the world has seen, thank God, she is scrambling over the white boulders for the top pool. Alma has caught up with my mother's womanhood— a rear view, what in the painting is made to look like a small purse; the delicate line is the colour of watermelon. In the second painting she is a fish in water—a streak of white bone in the depths.

There is one other painting from that summer. This is my mother's favourite and it was the one Alma made a mistake in giving her.

Here, she is fully clothed. From the window seat at home she leans forward—she is the kingfisher who has just glimpsed the blue promised land.

I have made it sound like it was all one-way traffic; endless women for prey, notably my mother, Alma in pursuit with his drawing materials. But there were times when observation flowed in the other direction. At the pools she trod water, her eyes sparkling out of goose-pimply flesh, taunting him to come and join her. Alma will swim in the sea at the drop of the hat but lakes and rivers fill him with dread. So did changing out of his clothes in front of my mother.

Slowly he unbuttons his shirt. He is in no hurry. My mother slips over on to her back and lies there gazing up at the bits of sky suspended from an overhanging tree. Alma is a shy man, that much is obvious. The way he carefully stuffs his socks back into his shoes and starts for the water only for my mother to roar back at him, 'For God's sake, Alma, you still have your underpants on!' His face burns. The whole damn world must have heard that. Now he looks down at himself, at this over-sight—he will pretend it is. My mother, happy as a frog, yells out once more loud enough for the world to hear. 'Take them off!' Slowly he starts back for his clothes. He is going to have to take off his underpants and my mother hasn't seen him this unhappy in months, not since a dying rat outwitted his best attempts to recover it behind the hot water tank. But as she is about to discover, there is no elegant or interesting way for a man to take off his underpants. As he lifts one foot, and now the other, he looks like a man getting ready for his own funeral. There is just this final thing to attend to—the folding of under-pants which peculiarly reminds Alice of Alma's finicky arrangement of his tubes of paint.

As he began his sad procession to the water she performed a duck dive to give him the privacy he so obviously craved and by the time she surfaced he was standing up to his midriff, shivering behind his folded arms, looking disgruntled. She laughed and swam gleefully towards him.

She wasn't given time to fall in love with Alma Martin. Before Christmas there was a phone call. She didn't catch the man's name but it didn't matter anyway. The news he had for her was so astounding. George's battalion would be home in the New Year. There was some other information she didn't pay attention to, and there was also the sense that she hadn't sounded quite as excited and heartened as the voice at the other end was used to hearing. She thanked him, and after replacing the phone she went about the house opening windows and chasing out traces of the neighbour up the road.

It was time to meet Alma and walk to the river in that delicious smell of blackberry air. Now as she left the house she walked right past the towel hanging on the clothesline. Alma was waiting for her on the other side of Chinaman's Creek, a white towel slung over his shoulder. As she approached he looked up with a smile. She could see he had no notion that the world was about to change. She had an idea he was thinking of something clever to say so she came right out with it.

'George's battalion is coming home after Christmas.'

She saw Alma's face fold up and look off in half a dozen directions at once.

'Jesus,' he said.

'I just got word.'

'I don't know what to say, Alice. I just don't know what... except I suppose what I should say...' She waited, but it seems he wasn't about to say that.

They found themselves shaking hands, but that just felt silly. And so, out there on the road in plain view, they hugged. They kissed briefly, and parted. There was nothing else to say. No rules to make for the future. They held hands until my mother drew her hand away, her fingers drawing through his, regret trailing Alma's mouth. Already my mother and Alma Martin were falling back from each other, and as Alma took the towel off his shoulder and bunched it up in his hand, my mother said he looked at it as if to ask what in God's name use had he for this thing.

5

Throughout the month of January the men arrived back in the district at different hours of the day and night. They left the troopship and ran from one another back to their old lives. They disappeared inside their homes and didn't come out for two or three days. There was some catching up to do. Some anxious smiles to cross the room. Some misunderstandings to come to grips with. And a lot of starting over. Favourite chairs, favourite meals, peculiar mannerisms, sayings, affections, ways of being—all had to be unscrambled from memory. No one was unaffected, and of course sadder stories began to leak out.

Alma's sketches of Victoria reveal a mother worrying about her son. All his failings list in her face. Dean was no good at sport. He walked away from games; the shrieks of delight came from other boys. They were like scampering monkeys whereas Dean held himself like a delicately built adult. He fell out of a tree once and broke his arm. Other boys faced with the same swift change of circumstance somehow manage to break their fall or make a grab for a branch and swing to safety. But Dean wasn't like that. He fell with the heavy resignation of a human being that knows it is not supposed to be airborne and so must face the consequences.

Victoria received some warning. She was told to meet her boy in Wellington. She stood in the crowd down on the wharf, wearing her new hat, her hand placed against her chest to conceal the missing button on her coat. She kept smiling bravely. Teeth and wind—hoping for the best. She wasn't sure what to expect. Soon the crowd began to thin and she was able to move closer. Now, at the top of the gangway, a number of naval ratings juggled a stretcher. It was halfway down the gangway before Dean raised his pale face—so much paler than she remembered. She wondered if he was sick. He was always coming down with a stomach bug; always first in the street to catch a cold. There he was, coming down the steps, clearly without the use of his legs. It was hard to know how a mother should look and conduct herself under these circumstances. It was hard to know whether to rush forward or to hold her place as you do on a platform for the train to come properly to a halt.

Dean raised his pale face and smiled weakly. 'Hallo, Mum.' The men carrying him stood waiting like removal men. She hadn't come prepared for this. She hadn't even thought to have a taxi waiting. She looked around the wharf and pointed to where a number of pigeons were pecking the asphalt by the iron rail. She held Dean's hand and walked alongside. After they lowered him on to the asphalt she reached into her purse and gave Dean a chocolate bar she'd bought off a man in a monkey suit in town.

It was yet another story about luck. Dean had been in a lorry that clipped a landmine. Others lost their lives. Dean was only paralysed from the waist down. Well, that counted as good luck. What did you say to those who had lost their loved ones?

With the men back, the world was a noisier and busier place. Up at Alma's cottage the view had more detail vying for his attention. It used to be he'd notice a cow get up and change direction and sit down again on a farm two miles away. Now, over the same expanse, he saw men walk out of their farmhouses and stand in a paddock; cigarette smoke kite-tailing across farmland. He could see George wandering the property below.

Used to smaller places, old habits continued as the men took over corners of rooms, disappeared inside sheds, sat on upended apple cases.

Machinery that hadn't sparked for two or three years now tore fields up into irrigation ditches. The trembling white apple blossom and the roar of machinery and the dogs! How can it be that the dogs barked more—my mother is certain they did. The dogs barked and howled into the night, setting one another off from one farm to the next.

By winter of that year there were more pregnant women in the district than at any other time in its history. The younger women tottered around on swollen ankles. They strained to recover clothes pegs from around their feet while the men gazed away into the distance with thought to the next project.

It was a time of confusion, of great change. A motorised tractor and a horse-drawn plough were often seen working the same paddock. Changes came to Alma's life as well. A letter from a firm of solicitors in Melbourne brought news of a modest inheritance. The money was forwarded to a solicitor in Nelson, and this man sat Alma down and advised him to buy something. Until that money was cabled he hadn't given a moment's thought to owning anything. That all changed when the money went into his account. Suddenly he was a rat on a raft looking for the nearest landfall. Of all the houses he could have bought he ended up buying the place Hilary and her soldier husband, Jimmy, were renting. Money did seem to change one's view of the world. Until it came up for sale he realised he hadn't properly looked at Hilary's cottage. He had known it the way a rat knows a cottage, a collection of cupboards, dusty hard-to-get-to corners, stuffy ceilings. He knew the kitchen—most of their drawing sessions had been conducted in there. And if someone was to hold a gun to his head he could probably remember the blue-and-white patterned curtains and walnut grain of the chairs. But the rest of the house in its full-bodied self? He couldn't have told you what colour it was. Now it was up for sale he suddenly noticed the defect in the chimney that leaked smoke, the sand in the carpet, the sloping pitch of the sitting-room floor to the corner of the cottage most desperate for re-piling. For all that the house had a pleasant kind of lean, as if it was meant to be. What is commonly condemned as derelict when inland has by the sea a knack of acquiring character. Some strain told on the window panes—a tension where the floor went one way and the windows another; it was an arrangement that made the ordinary blue sky sing in the way glass achieves in chapels and courtrooms. He signed for the house and kept Hilary and Jimmy on at the same rent.

On the afternoon George was due back, my mother happened to glance up at a portrait still on the wall of the bedroom. In her hurry to get it off she pulled the pins out with it and as she rolled up the canvas a pin stabbed her finger. A small pin-prick of blood appeared and dropped onto the canvas. She rubbed it away into the timbered foreground of Alma's deck by her bare feet. A stubbed toe she could always explain. The only place she could think to hide the canvas was in her underwear drawer.

She spent the rest of the afternoon on the window seat waiting for George to turn up. Sometimes a vehicle travelling up the valley saw her get up and walk expectantly to the far window. It was a little like the first times she sat for Alma Martin. Questions of how to present herself preoccupied her.

Soon the shadows of the hill had spread from the bottom paddock across the house to reach the road. My mother wasn't feeling nervous any more. She was fed up with waiting and considering going to bed when she heard something. She looked up at a flash in the window. She heard a motorbike roar off. This time when she went to the window she thought she saw George. It was George. He had crossed the bridge and had stopped to look back at the house. There was a large bag by his feet, a lit match, a bowed head. The George she remembered and the one out there juggled and worked into each other. The waiting was over. As he moved she smiled at his slightly bow-legged walk, and the way he held his hands up to his chest as though he was playing with twine, eyes and mouth shaping for pleasant surprise.

She closed the fly-screen quietly behind her so he wouldn't hear. George didn't see her until she was well away from the house. And as she went to hug him his first words to her were, 'You'll have to excuse me, Alice, sweet. I'm sweating like an Arab.'

The physical changes are more easily dealt with. His hair seemed both coarser and thinner, darker at the roots. The skin over his face was heavier. The dark rings under his eyes were new. And there was a cloudy quality there, unknown for the moment, the sad droop of things seen and stored.

They walked to the house hand in hand. George set his bag down in the kitchen. My mother saw him throw a wary look in the direction of the bedroom. He didn't unpack. She made him a cup of tea, then another, until he asked if there was anything stronger. For hours they sat at the kitchen table, talking. She held George's hands in her own. And when it was time for bed they dressed as if they were going out, taking their time to button up pyjama tops and smooth down nighties. They went to different sides of the bed and climbed in and my mother switched off the lamp.

This isn't an area to dwell on. For one thing, George wouldn't appreciate the world knowing what happened between him and my mother beneath the bedsheets. But I will say this—the earlier observation about memory and reality making for mismatched partners holds here—and I'll leave it at that.

In the days after George's return Alma kept his distance. George had to be given a chance to slot back into his old life. My mother welcomed that space as well. After all, a flower can bend only to one source of light.

Early on, the signs pointed to future difficulties. Once when Alice was in the sitting room and George came in looking for something he apologised and actually said, 'Sorry.' She told him he didn't have to say that—this was his home as well. 'Right,' he said, not at her. He nodded at the window and as he left the room he mumbled, 'Sorry,' again. He seemed troubled by something. He fell into long silences. More than once my mother suggested they go out, or if he preferred George could go off by himself, cycle into town to the pub.

On the second Saturday he was back she was preparing dinner when she looked up and saw a match flare in the darkness of the window. Across the yard light from a lantern swayed in the open door of the barn.

She saw George, and there was someone else. She could make out a shoulder, and now Alma's shirtsleeve. She moved away to the oven. George hadn't said anything about Alma coming down the hill. When she checked again she could see Alma sitting on an apple box that was too low to the ground for him. George had the sawhorse. She saw him stand up to get at his tobacco. He got out his papers and wet one with the tip of his tongue. When he did that he drew his tongue along the paper and sometimes he sent his eyes in the same direction. My mother hopped out of the way. An hour passed before George came into the house. She said, 'I thought I saw you out there with Alma Martin,' careful to refer to Alma in full.

'You were right,' he said. 'Came down to talk about those rats causing merry hell.'

The next day George cycled into town. As soon as he was gone Alma showed at the door and my mother learned the gist of the conversation that had occurred out in the barn.

Alma said George had come at everything in a roundabout way. As he wet his paper he'd glanced down and said, 'You seem happy, Alma.'

Alma told George he wasn't unhappy.

'That's what I mean. You seem all right.'

'Then I must be all right.'

'I'm not trying to be tricky, Alma. It's just an observation.'

George looked jumpy though. He shook a box of matches in his hand. His gaze was restless. He said, 'So, how does Alice seem to you?'

He snuck that one in while lighting a match.

'Oh, she seems fine,' said Alma.

George lowered his eyes and grunted.

'Terrible about Dean.'

'God yes. Awful.'

Now George pointed with his cigarette to the house.

'She wrote lots of course but what does a letter tell you, really? I'd say they leave out more than what they tell.'

'Dear Johns?' asked Alma.

George nodded and drew on his cigarette. 'I know of one man who had his hands blown off ask a mate to read out one of those. You can imagine.'

That's when another light came on in the house and they had both looked out across the darkened yard.

'So, Alma, nothing took place as far as you know?'

'Nope, nothing as far as I know,' he said.

'Not as far as you know.' George seemed to find that problematic, worthy of closer interrogation. Alma's glass caught his eye. 'Tide's out.'

As he poured from a flagon George said he had something he wanted to show Alma. A painting, he said. 'A very good one it is too. You have a talent, Alma, no doubt about that.' He carefully screwed the top back on the flagon. He was taking his time. Alma watched him walk across to a large old leather suitcase. And as Alma watched George unbuckle the straps he

88

wondered if he was getting something other than a painting. But in a few seconds he smelt the paint. He stood up from the apple box. George nodded to the light switch behind his head. Alma got that, then helped George to unroll the portrait of my mother reclined on his deck; clothed, he was relieved to find. But there were things he'd missed the first time around. Looking at this portrait of my mother with her husband in attendance he was unsettled by the residual traces of pleasure in Alice's face and figure. If you had to give the portrait a title you might have called it *Contentment*. George looked like he was trying to see right through the paint to the scene on the other side. He let his bottom hand go and the painting rolled up.

'It's a nice painting, Alma. Don't get me wrong.'

As he said that he dropped the painting into the suitcase and attended to the straps. What was he doing? Why would anyone lock up a portrait?

Once more George asked his earlier question—how things had been.

'You know, quiet, George. A lot of time left over. If I wasn't drawing I don't know what I would have done.'

'That's what I hear,' George said. He nodded as if he was hearing it all over again. Then he said, 'Guess where I found the painting? I'll give you a hint. It wasn't on a wall. I found it in her underwear drawer. Strange, don't you think?'

Alma folded his legs and tried to look for the answer out in the yard, as though this was a puzzle to share.

'Now why would she roll up a painting and stick it in her underwear drawer? You see how you are forced to ask yourself that question, Alma? I mean, anywhere else in the house and a painting is just a painting. But in an underwear drawer…a woman's underwear drawer. My wife's. You see how the news just gets worse, don't you?'

Thankfully at that moment he noticed Alma's empty glass and lost his thread. Alma let him reach for the flagon; he waited, then stuck his hand over his glass. He didn't want anything to slip out while his guard was down.

George smiled and refilled his own glass. 'Down the hatch.' He emptied it in one gulp. He swirled the foam while he thought what to say next.

'I was away nearly two years. It's automatic to think certain what-have-yous. Well cheers, Alma.'

He put down his glass and screwed the cap back on the flagon. 'Okay,' he said. 'Let's hear about the rats. What am I being hit for?'

'Well, I'd say there's a nest or two under the floor of the kitchen, judging by what you've told me.'

'Why aren't I surprised to hear that?'

Alma told him, 'I can do you my day rate or we can take it by the head.'

'Whatever. If they end up inside the house Alice will bitch. What's your bitch rate?'

'Same as my daily.'

'In that case, let's say per head otherwise you'll clean me out.'

Then as Alma stood to leave, George said, 'I was in Franklin's today. Dennis is selling mousetraps. Did you know that?'

'That won't stop a rat.'

'Maybe, maybe not. I just thought I'd mention it. Everything is changing, Alma. These are changing times.'

'A trap might slow down a brown rat. That's if you're lucky. But honestly, George, a trap won't clean out a population.'

'I'll pass that on to Alice.'

At that moment, according to Alma, as he told my mother, they both looked across the yard to the lit window.

'Anyway,' George said. 'Loyalty's got to be worth something.'

'Definitely,' Alma was quick to agree. 'Loyalty is all there is.' It had come out more passionately than he intended, and that caught George's interest.

'Don't get me wrong about the mousetraps. I was just pointing to them as an example of changing times. I'm not griping about your rates.'

Alma moved to the door. He was anxious to leave.

It was early evening of the next day when my mother heard Alma slide himself under the floor of the house. Muffled effort carried through the floorboards and now and then there was a sound like a hammer.

She was trying to put the fact of Alma's presence out of her mind because once more George had brought the painting into the house from wherever he was hiding it. He held down the corners with a small Bible and a brass alligator doorstop and an empty beer bottle.

'There,' he said, and with his finger stabbed in the area of my mother's painted face. 'Who is that person, Alice? That one with love shining out of her eyes?'

It was the same old song-and-dance routine with George in the prosecuting role and my mother bluffing it out. She told him he was acting nuts. It was just a painting. She couldn't help how she came across. She couldn't help what another human being saw. Then she stopped. She could hear the scuffling noise of Alma sliding out from under the house. George heard it too and swore an oath at the rats overrunning the place.

George wouldn't let go of the controversial painting, what it represented, what was being held back from him. It drove him crazy. He lay awake with it at night, dreaming up new angles of investigation. He moved into a testing phase and began to make suggestions and watch for her reaction, such as when a few nights later he told her he'd invited Alma down for cards.

At the card table no one mentioned the painting of course, their eyes lowered around their hands. They were playing twenty-one and George was banker. Cards, and games generally, brought out a side of him my mother didn't much care for.

'I hear you're doing good deeds at Victoria's,' George said to Alma at one point.

'If you mean putting a pencil in Dean's hand is a good deed.' Alma was trying out a certain voice. After their conversation in the barn he had gone away feeling he'd been too defensive. He'd allowed George to get away with too much.

George grunted; his interest had returned to their respective hands. This was the part he liked best. He said, 'I have a feeling Alma's bluffing and Alice, dear, dear Alice, bless her, has underestimated. I'll pay over nineteen.'

They showed their cards and George smiled to himself, got that cocky look my mother didn't like, and swept the pennies to his side of the table.

'Alma, why don't I lend you some pennies.'

'I'll make do thanks George.'

'All right. It's no skin off my nose. Alice?'

She said, 'The same,' and stole a quick glance at Alma but immediately George was there to pick that up. He said, 'Anything else I can lend you, Alma?'

That night my mother moved into the spare room.

Three days later she is standing at the sitting-room window with its sweeping view of hill and paddock when George comes staggering into view.

There is the day in the high part of the window in all its giddy indifference. Cloud. Sky. And there is George like he is acting the goat. Stumbling around like that. Throwing his arms up. Bees lifting and falling over him. Masses of bees. A dark cluster forming and re-forming. Some banging against the window behind which she stands.

Later when George was to ask her where she was when she saw him she would tell him she happened to be passing the window—not standing in the window which is a position too removed, too chillingly neutral. Still, it had taken a moment to register, to distil this unlikely fact of George covered in a swarm of bees. What it meant exactly. It had taken a moment to awaken from the slumber of everydayness to this surprising new thing. Even now she didn't rush. She walked quickly.

There was a hose at the side of the house. My mother turned on the tap and trained the nozzle on George. Clusters of bees rose until George's pinched face was revealed, then for reasons known only to himself he lurched back in the direction of the hives.

Here was another job for Alma. He would know what to do. What she should have done was get out the smoker. On this point Alma was mildly reprimanding. 'A little bit of fuel and newspaper or a damp rag and a match. The smoke does the rest...' He spoke in a cool brisk way as they hurried down the hill. 'Bees hate smoke. I'm surprised that George hasn't told you that...'

Some survival instinct must have stirred in George because as they crossed Chinaman's Creek they saw him below, half-submerged in the water. He lay on his side, his raised hip and shoulder exposed. When they pulled him out he was barely conscious. His pulse was faint. George's face a swollen mess. His eyes were slits.

My mother fumed over him. 'What a crazy thing to do, George. Crazy. Crazy.' Some layer of being an inch beneath George's swollen red skin seemed to acknowledge this point. His eyes shifted wider. His chest rose.

It was another hour before they heard the doctor's Wolseley bump across the creek bridge. He climbed out of the uphol-stered car in his tennis gear, a middle-aged schoolboy with a shining flop of brown hair. His white legs waded in large white shorts and white canvas sandshoes. He didn't bother with intro-ducing himself. When he got out of the car he simply looked dimly in the direction of the house. 'In there, is he?'

He took George's pulse. He rolled back his eyelids. George's pupils were fishy and dull. He said George was in toxic shock. Obviously George had a strong ticker. But the doctor was confused. Why would a man rush into a hoard of bees and dance around like a drunk at a fairground? It made no sense unless you knew what my mother knew, that George had been looking for a gesture. Once, years before, when they were going out and she had showed some interest in another boy George had deliberately crashed his Indian motorbike to make her look his way again.

In a few days George was well enough to sit up at the kitchen table in his dressing gown. My mother was still angry with him.

'You could have been killed and then what...?'

George got up and walked over to the sink to pour himself a glass of water. He finished his water and put the glass down.

'The bee thing is over. I don't want to talk about it, Alice.'

Silence was George's solution to most things. Now a new layer of silence fell over their lives, this one more heavy and suffocating than any before. George spent his days in his dressing-gown. Some days he shaved. On those days he forgot to or couldn't be bothered he looked like a figure of ruin. The dressing-gown. The dark stubble. His idleness. He was content to sit and watch Alice cook and feed the chickens. She put meals in front of him which he picked at. He spent a good deal of his time looking out the window at the clouds. He'd sit until dusk, smoking and gazing at the dark shifting patterns of the starlings rising in the sky. How did they know when to make a turn? How was it communicated? He smoked his cigarette and drifted. He was so quiet at times it was easy for my mother to forget he was there. Once he stuck out his hand and tried to squeeze her. It gave her such a fright she cried out and he let go. George stood up and tightened his dressing-gown cord and moved shamefully into the other bedroom.

Over this period of convalescence, he dressed only once and that was when Alice's mother visited.

She came over for lunch one Sunday. After listening politely to the account of George's brush with death she turned the conversation to memories of when she and her husband used to live on this same farm. While my mother got on with making the lunch George sat in the sitting room listening to Alice's mother talk up the qualities of Alice's father—which is to say his unstinting dedication to her. How he would pick the hair out of her hairbrushes and combs and bring her a cup of tea in bed before disappearing out to the farm for the day with his cold mutton sandwiches. The hill must have caught her eye in the window because she remembered the day Alice's father had made her climb to the top. 'You don't want to die without seeing the view.'

'Oh but it was exhausting!' she told George and twice, she said, she had fallen; there was no neat and winding track like today, and what's more, she told him, twice Alice's father had pulled some loose skin from the balls of his own feet to cover her watery blisters.

This information had a stunning effect on George. He sat back and stared at this small woman with the non-stop mouth.

'Really though, George, Alice's father was a saint when it came to the small things. I've mentioned my blisters, my hairbrushes. But if I'm honest, truly honest, then I have to say he wasn't one to move mountains. How often did he promise to get rid of that bloody hill?'

At that moment they both looked out the window. There it stood. George and Alice's mother picked up their teacups and stared at it.

Over the following week George often appeared distracted or lost in thought. He'd sit scratching his chin, brooding, thinking, scheming. The swelling had left his face. It was a good sign. His blood was kicking out the toxins. Now he began to draw up plans. There was no hint of what he was planning until Alice found a list on the back of an envelope.

Paint the house.

Turn the bottom paddock into orchard (pears and apple).

Dig another well.

Double the size of the chicken run.

Under '5.' he had written 'hill—get rid of it', circled it, and marked the circle with a big tick.

6

The morning George made a start on the hill Alice was still in bed. She didn't hear her husband get up and make himself breakfast and slip out of the house. Alma Martin, however, claims he was on hand to see the first spadeful. He was up on his deck with a cup of tea watching the new day spread across the plain when his eye picked up George down in the paddock still stuck in shadow. He had a shovel and a wheelbarrow at the base of the hill. He must have filled the barrow already because now he picked up the handles and walked the load to the edge of a large depression another hundred yards away. There he tipped up the barrow, shook out the last of the soil and started back to the base of the hill where he went about filling another.

Alma sipped his tea. It still didn't seem strange or out of the ordinary. There were any number of explanations. George was after topsoil. Or he had made a start on back-filling that area of swamp which was a good thing to do and finish ahead of winter if he could manage it. More importantly, it looked like old George was back on his feet again and swinging into action. Alma drained his cup and went inside.

It was much later in the morning that he suddenly remembered George. He stopped everything, put down his brushes and went outside for a look. This time he caught up with George over at the swamp; he was carrying a long scaffolding plank over his shoulder. At the base of the hill Alma could make out a bald spot where George had been shovelling.

My mother was watching this same scene from the back window of the house. The natural thing would have been for her to wander outside and ask George what he was up to but she was reluctant to break the spell of his industry lest he turn back into that forlorn and hopeless dressing-gowned figure. She also had a horrible idea of what he was up to, however far-fetched and extravagant it might seem. She had an idea George had taken to heart her mother's comments about that 'bloody hill'.

She watched him as he approached the paddock with the cow. George put down his barrow to open the gate. The cow stood up—George waved his hand—and the cow sat down again. Now he lifted the handles of his barrow and went through. There was a patch of paddock where heavy rain tended to collect. It wouldn't drain. Hoof traffic quickly turned it into quagmire. That's where George had laid a number of planks. He ran the barrow up, jogged to the end and tipped the load out.

Throughout the rest of the day my mother and Alma checked on George's progress from their respective positions. George didn't stop shovelling until dark. There was nothing especially alarming about that—from Alma Martin's point view, that is. A man in his singlet pushing a wheelbarrow is hardly an unusual sight; even a man casting the sharp end of a shovel into the side of a hill, no matter how much it might remind the casual observer of a gnat biting a rhinoceros on the bum.

That night George spoke of back-filling the swamp. He didn't mention the hill. For the first time in weeks he ate with a healthy appetite. His face, neck and shoulders were red. After clearing his dishes he ran a bath. My mother was in bed when she heard the door next to her room close.

The next day, however, what had looked perfectly ordinary the day before changed into something else.

Up on the hill Alma woke to roosters sounding across the valley floor. Bits of cloud shuffled across the top part of his window. He dragged himself from bed and wandered in his underpants out to the porch where he stretched and yawned; away in the distant paddock at the bottom of the hill there was George and his wheelbarrow. He had stopped to light a cigarette which suggested he had been up for some time already. The heifers stood in a line watching him. Never before had the heifers looked so sane.

Over the following days the same pattern established itself. The early morning rise. The repeated journey between hill and swamp. The mindless application which George brought to the awesome task of eliminating the hill.

One afternoon towards the end of that week my mother waited for Alma at the bottom of his drive by the letter box. These times they got to themselves were so rare that she tended to come quickly to the point.

'First the bees, now this mad thing with the hill,' she said. 'He says he wants to make me happy.'

'Well that's not a mystery, is it? George isn't motivated by engineering. He wants you to admire him. That's what this is all about.'

My mother shook her head. In her own mind things couldn't get worse than this.

'What a situation. I'm married but I don't have a husband. I have a...' Here she caught herself. What was Alma Martin to her, exactly? A friend? An intimate?

Alma gazed off in to neutral territory

'It's unusual. I'll grant you that,' he said.

'No, it's a mess,' replied my mother. She tried to find Alma, tried to look around him and make eye contact. She said, 'I don't know what to do, Alma.'

This time Alma raised his head and aimed his attention over her right shoulder. He thought for a moment, then shook his head.

'There's nothing to do, Alice. Your husband is back. That doesn't leave a lot of room for us, now, does it?'

That could have spelt the end of everything between my mother and Alma Martin. It is my mother's view that he didn't mean to say it quite like that. The same thought must have occured to Alma. Now, as if to make up for it, he raised his arms and pulled her into him. It was a brazen thing to do under the circumstances. Over Alice's shoulder Alma would have seen a tiny figure in a white singlet run a wheelbarrow around the base of a hill which he aimed to remove as a token of his love for the woman Alma happened to hold in his arms. And had George laid down his shovel and looked back in this direction he'd have seen the whole story laid out before his eyes.

More positively, George had a goal to work towards now. He had turned himself into a draught horse. From now on, his love for his wife could be measured in pints of sweat. It would boast geographical proportions. One day he would be able to look my mother in the eye, and say, 'Alice, look what I've done for you. I moved a mountain.'

There are precedents. Kings building palaces for their mistresses. Ship-owners naming ships after their wives. Poets dedicating their books. Explorers naming channels and landforms after their absent spouses. Youths with penknives carefully, lovingly cutting the name of the girl with the shy eyes into the bark of the tree.

On a more practical note, once George removed the hill Alice would have only as far as the bottom paddock to walk in order to see all the way to the ocean. From the paddock with the cow, the valley tends to roll downwards to the town—soon to provide the illusory but deeply satisfying neat rule of a shoreline.

Word of George's enterprise quickly got around the district. Within a week sightseers began to drive out to take a look for themselves. Cars, small trucks, delivery vehicles, the odd tractor parked in the long grass along the verge. A man sat in a harvester with his hand resting on his knee, squinting across the paddock. Others hung off the fence, smoking. More embarrassing as far as Alice was concerned, a pub sweepstake had started, and the men along the fence spoke authoritatively, some in a boastful, knowing voice.

At the pub, you put in your money and were invited to pick a number from a hat kept behind the bar. None of the numbers were below one hundred. No one in his right mind thought George would move the hill in less than one hundred days. The highest number was five hundred. Most of the wizened faces who had swung on the end of a shovel reckoned it should take George around three hundred days to shovel and wheelbarrow the hill from where it stood to where he was dumping it in the swamp.

By mid-February, some progress was evident. Alice could see a new hill rise in the sitting-room window, while in another place the old hill was being lowered. The view across to the ranges was slowly erased and this gave the house an odd sinking feeling. When George came in at night his eyes were half-closed with fatigue. Every bit of muscular effort had been drained from him. But Alice heard no complaint. She was hoping that once he realised the immensity of the undertaking he would give it up of his own accord. For now, though, there was still no sign of that happening as he plonked himself down in his evening bath. Once after a particularly gruelling day, George fell asleep in the bath and my mother had to reach down and find the plug between his ankles and drain the water around George's sleeping torso in case he drowned in his dreams.

He was never too tired to eat. He wolfed down whatever she put in front of him. Afterwards he would sit back in a glow of satisfaction and watch Alice clear away the dishes. As she set a cup of tea before him he might say, 'A hundred and forty-eight barrow loads today, Alice.'

My mother would have to try and remember the previous day's figure.

'That's thirty more than yesterday.'

She'd realise her mistake as George smiled modestly down at his tobacco pouch.

'Actually, it's forty more.'

The time to have spoken out and insist he drop this insane project was at the beginning. My mother had taken him too lightly at his word. Only once in passing did she manage to say, 'Honestly George, I don't mind the hill the way it is...' but he hadn't responded. Perhaps he didn't hear in that way megalomania is said to be indifferent to dissenting voices.

Already it was March, and too late to stop him. Too many yards of soil had already been shifted on Alice's account. Between this calendar month and George shrugging off his invalid's dressing-gown, people had died, others had been born. A man raking his hair with a steel comb had been struck by lightning. Throughout it all George chewed away at the hill. And it has to be said, as George's defenders claimed, at times it felt like there was just too much seriousness in the air.

There is something to the idea that idleness has its season. Standing in long wet roadside grass is not conducive to watching a man wheelbarrow a hill away. In June and July, as the days shortened and rain fell with grey urgency, the crowd along the fence line dropped away.

A great-uncle of George turned up for a brief stay. He was a heavy man who hobbled around on bad hips and wore an office shirt tucked into farm trousers. The uncle had made a strong impression on George as a small boy. The older man had taught him how to fish and, on family visits, would slip George a small glass of beer. The same loud boisterous figure kept him up long after his mother said it was time to go to bed. Now it was the turn of the favourite uncle to persuade George to lay down his shovel and leave the damn hill alone.

Others had tried, well-wishers, friends of the extended family. They just ended up walking beside George and his barrow between the old hill and the new one. George couldn't just stop for any old chit-chat. With new hope my mother stood at the sitting-room window and watched George's uncle pad across the paddock with a chair he'd taken from the kitchen. No one had done that before. There was an innovative air about George's uncle that was promising. He didn't look the kind to give up easily. Alice watched him park his chair and arrange his tobacco and tea flask. Obviously he was there for the long haul.

The uncle had told my mother that what he had to say to George was perhaps best kept to themselves. He did indicate, however, that he wasn't one to stride into lecturing mode. Rather, his style was to let the words fall about George and soften him up like persistent rain. 'Trust me, Alice,' he told her. 'Nagging doesn't work. It just turns a man's head, if you see what I mean.'

Across the paddock Alice saw George hesitate with his implements—there had been no advance notice of the uncle's visit—there was a handshake, some words, the uncle good-naturedly waving him on. George seemed to give a grateful nod before hurling himself at the hillside. The uncle turned round and gave a nod in the direction of the house.

Throughout the day, whenever Alice checked at the window, the scene was the same. Persistent rain, she reminded herself, and to be patient. George was shovelling and running, with new vigour if anything, back and forth between the old hill and the new one. Every now and then the uncle uncrossed his legs to reach down for his tea flask or tobacco. It was getting on for dusk when she thought she'd check once more. This time there was George with his barrow moving at a spry trot towards the open gate, the fat uncle trailing behind, his hand raised as if to make another point. Alice fell back from the window, discouraged.

The uncle drank a lot that night. He'd brought his own whisky. At dinner he told stories and risqué jokes. The talk seemed to provoke his appetite, and gloss over his failure. After he'd cleaned off the roasting dish he started on Alice's leftovers. George didn't say a lot. He kept his uncle going with a word here and there. Otherwise he sat up like a polite child who knows that if he keeps his head down he will pass unnoticed. At a certain point he looked over at the window covered with night and condensation. He moved a hand to his mouth as he yawned and excused himself from the table. He had a big day starting in the morning. He smiled at his favourite uncle and winked at Alice and took himself off to bed.

Later, while my mother was doing the dishes, the uncle came up behind her and pinched her bottom. She leapt from her daydream; a cup and saucer flew up in the air and broke over the floor. George's adventurous uncle backed away with his hands raised, his remorseful eyes shifting to the end of the house where George was already tucked up in bed.

In the morning Alice heard George get up and shuffle about. It was very early—still dark. She got up and went to the window in time to see George walk his barrow across the paddock and disappear into a thick mist. She let the curtain go and went back to bed. Another two hours passed before she got up and returned to the window, this time to see the uncle totter out, this time without a kitchen chair. She'd put out some breakfast but he must have passed it up. She had an idea he was on his way to say goodbye to his nephew. At least she hoped that was so; she didn't want to see him again. She locked herself in the bathroom and sat on the toilet with a cigarette, staring at the peeling blue paint. In another ten minutes she heard the uncle's car start up.

Late August. A lightness in the sky. Signs that winter was passing. If you stopped absolutely still and held your breath you could feel the sun crawl and settle over your face, neck, arms. A passing milk truck driver mulling on these things wouldn't have given it another thought at that hour, a barefoot woman in a raincoat standing in the middle of a paddock, a line of heifers looking on between the woman and where a man was shovelling. The heifers seemed to be waiting for George to turn around and discover his wife. A mob of sheep in the next paddock looked as one along their grubby flanks at the woman. The sun moved serenely behind cloud and a huge shadow spread like a stain over the half-bitten hill; when the sun re-emerged it was brighter and more dazzling than before. There was a dark flash of shadow against the hill as George speared the shovel head. He picked up the handles of his barrow and balanced his way along the planks to the new hill site. He had only to turn his head a little to the left and he would have seen what the heifers and the sheep and the line of birds on the pylon could see. If only he'd put his calculations to one side for a moment.

From his deck Alma Martin saw George lay down his barrow. He thought, here we go, George boy, your day is about to turn. But no, what does George do? He brings his tobacco out of his back pocket. The heifers, his wife, the sheep, the birds and the rest of the world wait patiently while he rolls a cigarette and then stoops to pick up the handles and run the barrow the rest of the way to the tip face. The large heads of the heifers were the only ones to turn when George came back the other way with his empty barrow—they did so in a neat choreographed line as he ran back and picked up his shovel to resume his battle with the hill.

The woman in the raincoat turned up at Alma's door a few minutes later. She was unbuttoning her coat as she came through the door, and as Alma had guessed, she was wearing nothing underneath it.

It wasn't the same as it had been. It wasn't like when George and the others were away at the war, when it felt like they were the only two inhabitants left in the world. Now they were like compatriots who meet in a foreign place to share memories of how things used to be. They talked a lot about earlier times. And then in the way it always did these days, talk would turn back to George.

By the end of September he had made such inroads that they began to talk about the end of the project, and what would happen then. My mother was resigned that one day it would come to that—she had begun to imagine the moment when George would fling down his shovel, wipe his forehead and turn to her with a look of sweaty accomplishment. And then what? What would she say? 'Thanks very much, George'?

My mother would have left George had Alma Martin asked her to. She'd have given up the farm for the fire-watcher's cottage on the hill. There was plenty of opportunity for Alma to take the bull by the horns and propose something. But inertia is Alma's failing. His way is to respond rather than to initiate. And for all his sharp observation and dedication he failed to see my mother's gradual slide away from him.

In the sketches of her during this period, the heightened eyebrow betrays irritation that Alma should think to sketch at a time such as this. She could well believe he had just sat in his seat as the train left the tracks.

7

What is important in life? If you ask a man without the use of his legs he will answer—legs. The same question asked of a legless man with a pencil and paper in his hands will produce a different answer. He wishes only to see more clearly. This was Alma's idea—his hope for Dean's salvation from immobility.

These days when Victoria left Dean drawing he didn't seem to notice her tip-toe departure. Mind you, Victoria would say Dean didn't seem overly aware of her presence in the first place. Pencil, eyes focused to an almost mean-spirited extent, he looked prepared to be surprised by what he was drawing—in this instance, a lemon tree—in case it turned out to be not what he thought it was. Victoria, on the other hand, didn't have time to discover that a lemon tree, as it turns out, is, by the way, a lemon tree. And there it is on paper, more or less how it looks in the garden. It was such an idle and pointless discovery when elsewhere around the house there was work to be done, rat carcasses to dispose of. Still, it was better this way. She didn't mind leaving him when he was so engrossed in what he was drawing. It was preferable that he stare at that lemon tree than lie back in bed translating damp areas over the ceiling into various countries. She could leave him to draw, mount her bike and move out into the world.

But then Alma had to get Dean on to portraiture. And now along with being Dean's legs, Victoria had become his sitter and this captivity was the worst she had known. Eventually Alma was to see the problem. He told Dean it was time for a history lesson.

The woman in Cézanne's life was a comely woman with piled brunette hair. The artist stared at her more than he did at the sky or the family or the moon or the sailboat on the blue horizon. She was his constant subject—forty-four portraits in all. That's a lot of staring. But give credit where it's due. That's also a lot of patient sitting. In the portraits hers is a face worn by silence. She sits as one would sit in the dark. Her face is closed down. She begins to look fed up. She looks like she would rather be out dancing. She looks like the nineteen-year-old she was when she and Cézanne first met, someone who knows it is time for something else but who is unable to rise from the chair.

Here too is Victoria's predicament. She is stuck in her chair. She sits and sits. Then at a rogue thought her shoulders might find occasion to drop as she sighs, and Dean will look up with annoyance when he sees that she has shifted her expression. He tells her that it's like trying to nail a fast-moving cloud to the one spot in the sky. 'Hopeless if the sky is moving about too.'

For hours on end she sits for her invalid son to draw her, a hostage to Dean's needs—she already washes his clothes, washes him, holds him up over the bowl so he can piss. It is excruciating for them both. A grown man with legs of jelly writhing inside her strong arms. The stern sound of Dean's piss against the porcelain bowl. 'Are we there yet, Dean?'

There are certain things that Alma could congratulate Dean for achieving in his sketches but perhaps they have been achieved too well. His mother's misery is not something he wants to draw attention to. It's time for a change of plan.

'Dean,' Alma said, easing forward on his chair. 'I think it's time we gave landscape a go.'

They were sitting outside and Victoria had cleared Dean's drawing materials from the card table to make room for the teapot and cake.

'Landscape,' said Dean, his lip curling up at the thought. The freckles on his pale face made him look for the moment more simple and ordinary than he really was.

That's when Alma noticed the long grass part in the direction of the house. Now another line broke for the house. And another. Victoria looked hard at her plate. She stabbed at a piece of leftover lettuce. Dean also tried to find somewhere to park his eyes. Separately and together their glances intercepted Alma's.

He knew what he had to do, and funnily enough he had come prepared for this moment. He dabbed his mouth with a serviette and stood up to reach in his vest pocket for one of Franklin's mousetraps. He handed it across to Victoria who had the good grace to look doubtful. To his own surprise, as he would later tell my mother, he found himself talking up its virtues.

'The great benefit of these things, Victoria, is that you get to choose where the rat dies. It will only slow down a big one but most of them will sit tamely through to the moment of death. Then what you do is simple enough. You take a paper bag, drop in the corpse and bang it in the rubbish bin.'

Alma sat down; mother and son were quiet, contemplative, each of them picturing the procedure whereby Dean would cling to his mother's back in the manner of a marsupial and poor Victoria, her eyes shut against the grim prospect, would have to bend at the waist for Dean to reach over and pick up the rat by its tail and drop it in the paper bag. Around the table, all three opened their eyes as if they'd just completed a prayer.

'Well only if you think they're worth a try,' said Victoria.

Over the next week Alma built a cart out of planks. In Victoria's back shed he found a length of steel rod which he sawed in two for axles. He discovered Dean's childhood pram in the long grass out by the incinerator, stripped the wheels off and fitted them to the axles. With some fencing staples he attached the wooden chassis then looped a rope through a screw hook an inch or two from Dean's sprawled feet and tied it to his bike carrier.

It was a fine spring morning, chilly though. A vapour of white breath trailed Dean's mouth. His pale cheeks turned pink. His bare knuckles froze and it wasn't all that comfortable; clearly Alma wasn't much of a builder, but Dean wasn't about to complain. He was back out in the world.

They stopped once for Dean to take a piss. Alma had to hold him up against the fence-line while Dean aimed into the long grass. In an attempt at easy conversation Dean asked Alma if they were near the Hands' property.

'Another fifteen minutes or so.'

'This'll be worth seeing,' Dean said.

'Oh so you've heard. From who?'

'Mum.'

'And what did Victoria say?'

'What everyone says. That George is carting off a hill to please his wife.'

'I see. So everyone says that, do they?'

'Mum said…'

'Mum's the expert, is she?'

Dean shut up after that and concentrated on buttoning up his fly. Alma didn't try to explain. He was sick and tired of people theorising about George. He was weary of the talk and he'd heard all the jokes. These days he found himself feeling protective of Alice's husband.

As the vandalised hill came into view there was a stifled 'Jesus!' from Dean and Alma told him, 'You can speak freely, Dean. I'm not going to chew your ear off.' They cycled across Chinaman's Creek and as they came around the side of the house Dean discovered the new hill. He saw it for what it was: raw, unpleasant to look at, and wrong; it screamed out for cover, for grass or some such softening effect that nature is good at providing. The only word you could attach to it was 'endeavour'.

The ground was heavy. Alma had to dismount and push his bike across the paddock. Dean's cart bounced over the cow pats and bumped towards the singleted figure swinging on the end of the shovel. Alma called out ahead, 'I've brought you a visitor, George.' George turned his unshaven face from his work; he looked annoyed to be interrupted but seeing it was Dean he brightened up and javelined the shovel into the loose bank of soil and came forward wiping his hands on his trousers.

'I see you've got wheels now, Dean.'

'They don't help me piss though. Ask Alma.'

George laughed; and Alma thought he looked happy about that and that he might well have looked happier still had Dean told him he pissed over his shoes. Still, he put the thought to one side. He said, 'Dean's got the drawing bug. He wants to tackle some landscape.'

George set his hands on his hips and squinted across the paddock. He said, 'We've got the new hill going up over there. We've got this one coming down here. Take your pick.'

Dean couldn't decide. In the end Alma made the comment, 'There's some nice shadow effect happening on the new hill, Dean.' To George he said, 'We'll try not to get in your way.'

He had to pull Dean along on his cart as far as the fence-line. As soon as they were out of earshot, Dean made the obvious remark, 'Earthmoving machinery would make quicker work of it.' He had missed the point, but Alma didn't feel like explaining that this was George's thing—the physical effort was his art. *That* was the point. It could be measured, evaluated, tallied. Here finally was the answer to that dodgy question: how great is my love? I will not say, but I will demonstrate with my barrow and shovel.

Alma didn't voice any of this. Instead he allowed, 'Possibly.'

He set up Dean and wandered back to within range of George. What Alice had said about George's flesh falling off him was true. His clothes looked loose. His eyes seemed too large. The bone of his eye socket leapt from his face. His forearms were muscled, sinewy. None of this was all that surprising. But up this close, with the smell of dirt and endeavour so prominent, Alma felt a grudging admiration. There was George's balance and his rhythm with the shovel. His huge heart. The outsized vision. As far as gestures went, it didn't seem so mad any more. It wasn't as mad as, say, inviting a swarm of bees to settle over your skin.

George looked up just once and it was to say, 'Sorry I can't stop to chat, Alma.'

Every Saturday that spring Alma cycled and towed Dean out to my mother's place for landscape drawing. In the end it wasn't landscape that captured Dean. Perhaps it was just too large and free-ranging. Too much itself—sky, hill. His eye and hand stalled in the search for smaller details. In the end he found it in the magpies.

No one is able to say with any certainty when the magpies arrived from Australia. One day there was the soft lump of George's hill and pasture rolling away to the farmhouse. The next day, or so it seems to my mother in recollection, black-and-white baubles covered the same area.

Think of Churchill dressed as Noel Coward and there you have the magpie. The generous undercarriage, broad in the beam; joined by a short neck to a cantankerous head. And those eyes! Cross with everything! Opposed to everything in general—even their own young.

Older farmers recall the arrival of the myna birds—'small sketchy things' that liked to hop about on the backs of cows. First there had been the mynas, and then they were gone, by which time there were the magpies. It was simply the measure of things coming and going. Mynas, and now magpies. This was the sequence of events. Bush to pasture, tree line to bare hilltop, bush song to wind, mynas to the squawking and delinquent magpies.

It must have been Dean's absolute stillness, his legless

immobility, that encouraged the magpies to come closer. It is just like a magpie to spot an advantage. The magpies held their heads at a proud angle reminiscent of the busts of famous people. The first time he noticed them Dean lay down his pencil and submitted himself to their presence. What were they doing? They didn't appear to be doing anything. The sheep were at least eating. Back in the other direction George Hands was swinging his shovel, and a short distance further away was Alma Martin with his sketchpad on his knee. Even the clouds were moving in careful lines across the sky. The magpies, by contrast, lacked a purpose. They were, Dean happily concluded, a bit like himself. Feathered cripples outside of the natural bird order. The other birds were in the trees. But here were the magpies pretending to be sheep, rolling their shoulders, their beaks lowered as if grazing. When the sheep looked up they seemed put out, hurt, as if they too were aware that the piss was being taken at their expense. Now the magpies did the same, blinking innocence. Then in the next moment they were back to being birds. As far as Dean could see there was no intervening moment—none of that shifting experimentation of, say, a seagull, which will flap its wings while staying put on a sea wall.

One afternoon an entire flock of magpies flew up around him. They were so close he felt the draught of their feathers. They reached a spot in the sky and all at once there seemed to occur a communal thought of, Hell, let's forget this, and they dropped back to earth and moved about as in an open market, worms dribbling from their beaks.

Here begins Dean's magpie period. A storm. A fallen pine tree sprawled across the road. A massive foundation of roots in the shape of a muddy fist wrenched violently from the earth.

From his cart Dean leant forward reaching over the top of his knees to touch a greener branch; it was sticky with gum. As he pulled it back his eye fell upon a magpie's nest sitting deeper in the tree, shaped like a mixing bowl. Twigs, grass, bits of wire. Instead of the eggs he expected to find he came across a red golf tee, a blue plastic ID tag that farmers clipped on to the ears of their dairy herds, the wrinkled skin of a burst red balloon, a small double-happy fire cracker and a postage stamp depicting a tui.

Magpies, he read, were tireless collectors. They were also excellent mimics. They could imitate fire engines. Meow like cats. Bark like dogs. They could even hold a human melody. Some were able to discern and express a preference for certain composers—a Beethoven sonata, for example, whereas the same magpies appeared to be stone deaf to Bach. 'Interestingly, they show little interest in Donizetti or Verdi...'

Soon Victoria was complaining to Alma about the state of Dean's room. It stank. What's more, whenever she poked her head in there she had the creepy feeling of having entered an enclosure, something to do with the light. Dean had stopped drawing back his curtains. And there was so much stuff he accumulated, most of it rubbish. Strange and useless things such as silver foil bottle tops, broken reading glasses—she had no idea where he'd stolen those from—a plastic clothes peg, shirt buttons, postcards, strange bits and pieces which on their own made no sense; nor did they add up to a whole. She worried about the rats returning, a new infestation, finding in Dean's squalor a desired haven.

Mothers are stuck with the first vision of their child. No matter what they become—prime minister, rapist, drunkard, schoolteacher, mayor, trapeze artist—they can't fool their mothers to the same extent as they might hoodwink the paying public because in their mother's eyes they can never shake free of the time they wore napkins and their bare bum was sprinkled with talcum powder. Victoria was the same as any other mother who sees what they want to see and therefore remain blind to what is unfolding before their very eyes. This is their failure. And Victoria could not see the magpie that her son had turned himself into.

But then what were the chances of her picking such a random and remote thing as a magpie to bloom inside the soul of her son? Clues? There was the disgusting state of his room. His new interest in collecting. The way he pawed at the window to raise himself in order to see out. But those signs don't necessarily lead you along the trail to magpies. It could just as well be girls, for example.

Anyway, for the moment other things consumed Victoria. She stared back at herself in the mirror. She picked up a strand of hair and pulled it across her cheek. Her face was pudgier. How did that happen? She grimaced at herself and cleared her thoughts to make room for a far more pressing matter. Dean's money had come through—a lot of money. They had enough to do something with it. She thought they had enough to buy a dairy. If not a dairy, then a shop of some kind. She could park Dean behind the counter and he would run the till and make himself useful. She had tried to excite him about this idea. She had tried to get him to start thinking along the same lines. Mostly it ended with her talking to herself and Dean concentrating on his bottle top collection.

Then, as these things tend to happen, out of the blue came

an opportunity to buy a second-hand shop, Pre-Loved Furnishings & Other Curios.

The instant Victoria pushed Dean's new wheelchair through the door he was won over by the shambolic order. The light was dim. It took a moment for their eyes to adjust, but gradually the different lumps of shadow revealed themselves as cloaks of armour, medieval swords, old stuffed armchairs, stag heads, tiny stuffed animals such as ferrets trapped inside glass domes, Victorian dolls. A number of stuffed birds swooped down from the ceiling on invisible line. There were small models of vintage cars and yachts, black-faced garden gnomes, rakes, lawnmowers, shovels and coal bins, some with bronze lids engraved with hunting scenes. On top of a pile of magazines was a cover of a modern woman with a can of fly spray. There were no walls as far as Dean could see, just clutter, shafts of light, brilliant dust particles. It produced in him a cosseted feeling, something close to a nest you could say, and without any of the boring and drowsiness-inducing logic of smart furniture placement. As Victoria was frowning at the dust mark her fingertip left on top of a chest of drawers, thinking to herself what a shame it was that people let things go, Dean was saying, more emphatically to himself, and now to his mother, 'Yes, this is it. This is it.'

8

In the late spring of that year, the view from my mother's sitting room slowly enlarged. The sky seemed to reach down further, bending at the shoulder. There was a day in November when for the first time she could see the sunny clay base of the coastal hills curling northwards. The promised sea view from the window was still to reveal itself but in the crystallised light hovering on the edge of the farmland there was a hint of things to come.

If we are to call this George's composition then we can think of my mother as the sitter, the bored sitter, and like Cézanne's model, showing signs of falling from her perch. Signs even of going a little mad.

She found herself taking issue with the sun. From where she stood, the sun seemed to be playing favourites. It was clearly on George's side, the way it would sit on his shoulder as he ran his barrow along the planks. It may seem a stupid thing to resent but not if you thought, as Alice did, that the sun actually liked George. It liked George more than it did her. The way it sat so companionably on George's shoulder compared to the way it spoke to my mother at the window: 'See what an idle life you lead, Alice. Look at George!'

But who looked after the chickens? Who had shifted the heifers? Who looked after the sheep? And who washed George's bloody clothes and looked after the damn house and cooked the meals?

George could quietly point to two things as his daily contribution. The gradual elimination of one hill, and the creation of another. As pointless as washing clothes in order to get them dirty again, you could argue. And while the new hill obliterated the swamp, to the naked eye it didn't look right. Part of the problem lay in knowing how it had come into being. Even the sheep couldn't be fooled. They wandered around its base, raising their black snouts at it, but that is as far as it went. They weren't about to be conned into climbing its sides. The cow lay in the paddock patiently waiting for the hill to leave and for things to return to what they used to be. The magpies never landed on it either. Cows for the day, the magpies stood in the paddock trying to stare the hill down. Even the wind-blown rain refused alternatives and tried to land where it had always fallen, which is to say on the swampy paddock that now lay buried under a mountain of relocated dirt.

My mother was back to thinking about the future. She had started to contemplate that defining moment of completion when the finished work would slip in like the new day. She imagined the moment—stooping to pick up one of George's socks from the carpet, there in the window she would find a glittering blue line with a white sailing boat at the edge of the bottom paddock. More optimistically she saw George hanging up his shovel and resuming his farm duties. They would be outwardly happy, of course, because that would be part of the deal. Officially she would be obliged to show joy because look at what George had done for her. Other women would make admiring noises and complain about their lazy bastards of husbands. That was one option. To share her life with Alma Martin was another. A third and completely unforeseen option availed itself that spring.

My mother was in town on her way to Franklin's to pick up some mousetraps. Around the pub she ran into some upgrading work to the footpaths. The area was roped off and she was obliged to detour along boards that were still wet from earlier rain when she slipped and was about to fall as a hand reached out and steadied her.

'Oops, caught you,' said the man.

Meeting our life partner often results from such a trifling incident. Tui Brown née Waverley was standing at the end of the wharf when a gust of wind lifted the hat off her head and blew it out to sea. Stan Brown saw the whole thing happen from the beach. Next thing, Tui sees Stan rowing out in a dingy to where the woollen hat floated soggily just beneath the surface, like a purple jellyfish. At a dance Jimmy shouldered his way across a crowded floor until he reached Hilary, and there he remained, silent but smiling hard, waiting to be discovered which he duly was.

Frank Bryant's good points are all neatly congregated into that singular moment where he sticks out his hand to prevent my mother's fall. Frank's grasp was firm and sure of itself. Once she regained her balance Alice noticed he had nice brown eyes. They regarded her back with surprise. Just that morning Frank Bryant had picked up a coin from the footpath, and now this.

'I was just about to pour a cuppa,' he said.

So he was quietly confident around the opposite sex. That appealed to my mother. She followed him to his truck. In the cab he got out a thermos. He had an extra cup which prompted her to say, 'So you were expecting me?' And he said jokingly, 'I always carry an extra cup just in case.'

So he could play along. Pick up the thread of a line. She liked that, too. He had enough milk only for himself but when he learned that she also took milk he happily forfeited his share. While they drank their tea my mother asked Frank Bryant a few questions about himself.

She'd already guessed he wasn't from around here. At least she hadn't seen him before. 'The Hokianga,' he said, and he hooked his thumb in a certain northwards direction. 'I was sent down to Ardmore to learn to fly, then the war ended, and so here I am. Just in time, it would seem.'

His smile was a handsome one.

'Well Mr Bryant, I owe you two thanks.'

'Frank,' he said.

'Frank, *frankly...*'

'People say that too.'

So he wasn't without wit.

'Thank you for saving me from my fall and thank you for the tea.'

He gave a military salute and my mother replied with a girlish curtsy and off she went. A man who caught her knew how to fly. It was an attractive package. And later as Alice was leaving town, whose truck should quietly rumble up behind but Frank's. He must have watched in his rear mirror and noted the direction she took; it was a pleasing thought. Now he leant across the gear lever to offer her a lift. Over the noise of the engine she fibbed and said she was expecting someone along any minute. She was sure Frank would have heard about George's epic undertaking. She didn't want him to know that the quest to shift the hill was for her benefit, that she was the woman whom people presumably spoke of, when in fact, as she was happy to discover and surprised too she would later say, she was quite pleased for Frank to think of her as unattached for the moment.

Frank drove off and she walked on with a smile. Soon she reached the farm. Across the paddock there was the stick figure in a black singlet running a barrow-load of soil along a network of boards. The hill was in two sections now. George had bored right through the middle to create two smaller termite-like crags. He was on the homeward leg to completion. My mother says she can remember stopping at the bottom of Alma Martin's drive and thinking she could go up there and maybe he could draw her; maybe he might even run away with her. And without consciously deciding one thing or another she found she'd moved on. By the time she crossed Chinaman's Creek her thoughts were filled with Frank Bryant, his handsome brown face, his simple eyes. He was obviously not too set in his ways either. After all, he could lay concrete and fly. The other thing about this man who had caught her when she slipped was that he actually looked at her with desire. That was the thing about Alma. Too often Alice was left with the empty feeling that he was seeking only information. She might as well be the night sky with Alma's eye fixed to the end of a telescope. Or else she was a bowl of fruit, interesting to look at in all its shape and configuration. Whereas Alma would draw it, she had a feeling Frank Bryant would want to reach for the fruit and take a bite.

She stopped at the back door and looked dejectedly across the wet grass. There was the washing she still needed to bring in—George's digging singlets and socks, and the white blouses Alma liked her to wear when she sat for him. She found herself thinking of the time Stan Brown dropped his cigarette and ground it out in the sand before picking up someone else's dinghy and carrying it like a beetle on his back to the water's edge. Where was her hat? Where was that helpful gust of wind that would give shape to the future? This impatience of my mother's is responsible for giving direction to everything that happened thereafter.

The day after she met Frank Bryant she thought to bring him a bottle of milk for his tea and other eventualities. Now the story had two strands that they would enjoy telling to each other. The time the young flying ace had flung out a hand to catch her, and the time she brought him a pint of milk just a minute after he realised he'd run out. The spirit of reciprocity was cementing itself, and before long Frank was holding my mother's hand on secretly taken walks around Big Bay to that end of the shingle beach where famously the fur seals clamber ashore for summer.

Once in a tipsy moment my mother told me Frank wasn't much as a lover. In her opinion he was too practical. He was the kind of man for whom elaborate directions for putting up a tent bring a certain joyless satisfaction. She didn't like his dirty fingernails either. The other thing about Frank was, frankly, his limitations.

They were sitting on the shingle beach at Big Bay laughing

as they told one another yet again the story of how she had tripped and he had caught her by the hand. Of course it wasn't as if their own chance encounter lacked for precedents, and one immediately sprang to mind—Bonnard and Marthe, the point at which they are still strangers nudging towards each other in the crowd waiting to cross the busy Boulevard Haussmann.

'Haussmann,' said Frank. He picked up a pebble and flung it past the toe of his workman's boot.

This was the first time she properly noted the bristling of his eyebrows.

'Paris, Frank. This happened in Paris, France.'

With a glimmer of exasperation Frank's face closed down in the understanding that this wasn't something he had to know after all. At the same time my mother sighed as one who recognises she has just entered a cul-de-sac, and perhaps a life with Frank required some reconsideration.

'Bonnard was the artist,' she explained, but Frank had been distracted by something he'd just noticed floating in the tide. His face came alive. He rose to his feet with a handful of stones, and for the next few minutes he took pot-shots at the bobbing log. The stones pocked the sea around the dark log until at last there was a wooden sound—Frank let out a whoop and raised his arms in triumph.

A slip on the pavement planks had brought them together. Now a story about a famous artist and his wife was about to draw them apart.

As soon as he sat down from throwing stones into the sea Frank seemed to realise that something was deeply wrong, that something was vitally changed.

'I should be getting back,' said my mother.

On the drive into town Frank didn't know what to do about my mother's silence.

'I feel like I've said something,' he ventured.

My mother didn't see any point in explaining. Why feign interest after such a demonstration of indifference? It wasn't right. It was a mistake. When she got down out of the truck she thought she was saying goodbye for the last time.

She walked slowly home, taking the alley by the hardware shop that leads across the playing fields—just in case Frank was of a mind to follow. She claims she felt relieved. She was sorry for Frank, though. It hadn't turned out so well for him. She was the firefly that had caught his eye and now he was left clutching thin air. Well, too bad, she thought. It's always best to find out these things early in the piece.

Within days she was back to gazing across the paddock to the flying elbows of George; the still back of the cow, the slavish wheelbarrow which just that morning in the stillness of dawn had woken her with its creaking wheels. She took out a compact mirror and searched her face for anything that Frank might have left on her. She noticed a few grey hairs and that another wrinkle had joined the others crowding the corner of her eye. She was a changing vista. She was landscape in the making. Alma Martin couldn't remember his wife. This was how all this business had started in the first place. Now she wondered if George had a mental picture of her as he toiled away, and if he did which one it was. If she was to die tomorrow, which version would pop in to his thoughts and make him smile in the shower?

The question forced her to consider the last time they had had fun together. The eve of his departure when they'd made love all through the night? Then on his return, amongst the resentment and hurt, there had been one fine day when they'd gone to the beach and swum out beyond the buoys to way over their heads, and George had swum underwater pretending he was a shark, and she'd squealed deliriously in anticipation of the shark's teeth biting into her bum—which is exactly what George had in mind when he dived down.

It was heartbreaking for her to watch George slog his guts out, move an entire hill in the mistaken belief it would declare his love over and above any normal human exchange such as sharing breakfast together, or a bath, or even a bed. And she thought maybe just a small thing had to happen, something as small as this time it being George who slipped on the wet planks and her hand taking *his* hand. But even as she was thinking these thoughts the die was cast. My mother's future was more or less decided. She didn't know it right then, at that moment she stood in the window watching George battle the hill. But she would know a month later when she would discover she was pregnant to the man she thought she'd already successfully shaken off.

9

Alma Martin was witness to my mother's sly departure. Frank's truck bumped across Chinaman's Creek. The screen door at the house opened and my mother backed out dragging a bag after her. At this stage Alma didn't know about Frank, and while he didn't know what to make of what he'd just seen down at the house he didn't think any more of it. His mind was on other things. He drained his cup and went inside to resume work on his painting of Alice standing by the curtains at the back window of the house.

My mother couldn't face George. She couldn't tell him in person; she would rather die than see his face crumple and him sit down in the long grass from the force of this unforeseen blow. In the truck, my mother said, there were two contrasting moods. She felt she was on her way to a funeral while Frank was off to a wedding. There was no thought of her immediately moving in with him; she wasn't up for creating more scandal. There was a spare room at the Browns'. Tui invited her to use that while she took stock of her life and thought what to do next.

Two days later Tui got Alma over on the pretence of asking his advice on house colour. It was a waste of time because she knew Stan would never budge from white. But she thought Alma might have some ideas around the window areas. Some highlighter could be used to good effect. Alma had told her to think of the house as a face—hair, eyes, nose and mouth had their corresponding features in roof, window, door and porch. He told her the door would look good in brick red.

'Brick red's good,' she agreed. She told him any ideas would be appreciated. 'You're the authority. I won't pretend other-wise. But on the subject of faces,' she said, 'it's all very well being noticed but you don't want people tripping over them-selves on the pavement.'

'A quieter colour. I've got it.'

Tui snuck a look at her watch. The man who had invented house butterflies was coming to dinner. Stan was keen on exploring an idea to develop a range of exclusive butterflies to go with the NE Paint colour range. She needed to get the meal on. And besides, suddenly there was nothing left to talk about. My mother had ventured out to the porch. And Alma had stopped listening. Tui Brown excused herself as Alice came down the steps slowly, one at a time, her arms folded, a wan smile. Alma thought she looked more beautiful than ever.

My mother said she would have hugged him if Tui Brown wasn't watching from the window.

'Come on, we'll walk up the street a bit,' Alma said.

For the moment they talked about everything but the burning issue. The monotony of the houses, this new neat rule used to carve up the farmland. The bone-white colour that Stan was sold on. The street came to a T-junction. They could go left or right. After looking in both directions my mother felt Alma tip her elbow.

'Come on, let's go back.'

They walked slowly, and this time Alma brought her up to date with George.

He told her he'd seen the truck and had even seen her with the bag backing out the fly-screen and still not thought anything about it. But in the middle of the night he had woken with a start. It had nothing to do with any noise; just a powerful sense that something was wrong. He told my mother he had got up out of bed and walked outside. The night was dark except down at the bottom of the hill the farmhouse had every light turned on. One or two lights can be passed over as forgetfulness but the house blazed with light. He had wondered if he should go down the hill and make sure that everything was all right. But he didn't; it was too cold and so much easier to go back to bed.

In the morning he returned outside with his mug of tea. He couldn't tell if the house lights were on. As usual, his eyes took the well-worn course across the paddock to the hillside. The wheelbarrow was there, the shovel stuck in the ground. Usually George would be out by now. It was then that Alma saw what he'd missed—fifty yards back a lone figure sat on a canvas chair.

The paddock was heavy from the overnight rain. George would have heard the squelching footsteps of someone approaching. Only the cow looked back over its shoulder. George stayed slumped. Perhaps he was sleeping? Then, Alma said, as he came up from behind he saw what George was looking at: the sunrise over the ocean. The view was still not quite there. There was still a section of hill to clear in order to widen the frame. But nonetheless contact had been made, and here was something to celebrate.

Without turning his head George said, 'She's gone.'

'Gone where, George?'

'She's pregnant.'

Thinking that congratulations were in order—and here as Alma was relating this my mother felt a pinch of guilt at the darkness she sensed Alma was scrambling out of, the different points he was forced to connect and at the same time stay calm in the face of revelation—Alma opened his mouth to speak, and again George filled in the blank spaces.

He said, 'Not to me. Another bloke.' He held up the letter my mother had left on the kitchen table under the salt shaker.

As she was hearing Alma retell this she could only imagine the impact of the news on him, and yet, according to his account, it seems he had switched into a practical mode. He told George he'd go inside the house and make a cup of tea. He said, 'You can follow me in or I can bring it out here.'

For the first time George raised his bloodshot eyes. His mouth was unshaven and broken-looking. 'Somebody by the name of Frank Bryant. If you happen to know him, Alma, tell him I plan to shoot him. But not today. I'm too friggin' tired for it right now. Tomorrow I imagine will be a different story.'

Alma told my mother that he had left him there out in the paddock and walked back to the house. In each room he had to turn off the light switch. He didn't know what had possessed George to turn on all the lights. In the sitting room he stopped at the window and looked out. George, he said, had looked like a man hurtling through space, his hair every which way, his eyes focused on a point set at a tremendous distance inside of himself.

At the Browns' that night, my mother was bad company. She sat opposite the butterfly man, a small serious-minded fellow, listening to the manufactured varieties of butterflies, to confident pronouncements about the future. Listening but not really hearing. She couldn't tear herself away from the picture of George sitting in that canvas chair. In the end she had to apologise and excuse herself from the table.

Later that night from her borrowed bed she listened to the low male rumbling talk of Stan and the butterfly man, and at a very late hour she heard the two men outside her bedroom window. Both of them were pissing into Tui's bed of roses. The butterfly man was doing all the talking and Stan was assenting.

To shoot another takes more anger than George could summon. He wasn't the hothead type who later regret their action from the dock. George was more of a melancholic and so naturally he veered towards self-pity and drink.

By that Christmas, George was one of the regulars in the Albion, one of the after-hours patrons who led the other drunks in song. It would be easy to think that this would forever be his lot—a fast-spreading bum on a bar stool or worse, a rumpled drunk found asleep on someone else's lawn next to the newspaper delivery.

It would be easy to leave him there alone to deal with his pounding head, except for this: it was the lawn directly outside the Anglican Church. Any moment now the first parishioners would turn up. Victoria was rostered on to morning tea which is why she had turned up so early. Here is another story to file under 'accidental encounter'. She walked over to where George lay asleep. He looked like he might in bed, his right arm folded up beneath his head, except for the fact that he was in his clothes and shoes. His tied laces gave the impression of fastidiousness and for a moment Victoria wondered if she had a heart attack or stroke victim on her hands. She crouched to feel his pulse. His breath was sour. She called his name quietly then insistently, and after that, irritably.

'Come on, George. You can't sleep here.'

Eventually one eye opened to the world in all its brilliant angles.

'It's me, Victoria,' she said.

She told him he couldn't lie there in full view of the congregation due any moment to file in the door. *Congregation*. The word induced deeper sleep. She shook him awake again. 'George!' She raised his arm and slipped her own underneath it. She was strong from hauling Dean around the place and George was still whippet-like from months and months of his labour on the hill. She was able to walk him along the road to her house. It wasn't so far. She had to help him up the front steps.

George was complaining of his head now. She told him, 'The door's open, and the bathroom's the one at the end of the hall.'

Victoria watched George stagger up the hall, a steadying hand against the wall, head dropped between his shoulders. She was late. She supposed she could leave George in the bathroom and still get over to the church and take care of the morning tea before services started. In the end she decided to wait and see. George might not be able to cope. He might slip and fall and bang his head against the bathtub. Anything could happen with him in that state.

When he emerged his face and hair were slicked clean. His skin shone with health. He looked so transformed, and all it had taken was a basin of cold water. And later, years later, she would surprise my mother with, 'He had the most wonderful teeth and he was smiling.'

The teeth had done it. But water was the transforming element. Not paint.

10

In 1967, a young surveyor turned up at Alma's door with a district plan. He'd come up the hill for a better view of the surrounding landscape, a boyish-looking fellow with a mop of blond hair and a struggling moustache that he was perhaps too proud of, angled sideburns, shorts, walk socks. The world had sprung a surprise. According to the contour map, the hill down on the Hands' property shouldn't be where it was.

'Oh, you mean George's hill.'

The surveyor raised his dull face. He obviously didn't know what Alma was referring to; and Alma found himself annoyed by the young man's moustache on its joint quest for maleness and officialdom.

'You don't know about George's hill?'

The surveyor preferred to consult his plans than to hear what Alma had to say. With Alma's permission he spread them over the deck and knelt down to peer at the alphabet of squiggly lines and land titles. For the moment, Alma was content to let the surveyor search for the missing bit of landscape. He wasn't sure if he could be bothered with explaining. Eventually the young man stood up and walked to the edge of the deck and squinted down at the deceiving landscape. The new hill was clothed in grass. A new generation of sheep which had no reason to think the hill hadn't been there forever trailed over its grassy bumps.

Alma came and stood behind him.

'The hill moved, if you must know.'

The young man smirked.

'Hills don't move,' he said.

Alma told him, 'I don't know if I can be bothered with this, but you had better believe me when I say that this one did.'

The surveyor thought he was talking to an old fool. Alma could see that and didn't like it. He reached up and grabbed his shaving mirror that hung from a rusty nail. He told the surveyor to take a look at himself. The surveyor looked around.

'It's all right. It's just us.'

The surveyor held up the mirror and stared at his blushing face. 'Now what?' he said.

'Well let's talk about that moustache of yours. Correct me if I'm wrong, but I'm going to suggest that five years ago it wasn't there. And that, there, that crease, that frowning line that just lit across your forehead, that wasn't there when you were crawling bare-arsed over your parents' sitting-room floor.'

The surveyor dropped the hand that held the mirror.

'So what's your point?'

'My point,' sighed Alma. He felt like showing the surveyor the road. 'My point is this. The hill you're looking at, for example. Why should it be where a map twenty years out of date says it is?'

The surveyor scratched the back of his neck. This was proving more difficult than he had expected.

'I see. So what should I tell my boss, Mr Martin? He will want to know. Did the hill just pick itself up in the night and go out for a walk—as hills do, of course—and got lost and couldn't find its way back to the exact spot?'

'That sort of tone won't help you. I was going to tell you but I don't think I will now.'

The visit of the surveyor is the closest occasion to the story of Alma's portraits getting out before now. I'm aware that various people will have different versions, but that is the history I more or less caught the tail end of.

I grew up with the neighbour always down at our house drawing my mother. I must have been very young the first time I ever saw my mother sit with the sort of patience I would later see on the closed-down faces of people waiting at bus stops.

I can remember coming across a box of old sketches. These ones were done at an earlier time. My mother is back in the house and pregnant with me. Frank is by now working at the paint factory like everyone else. George is with Victoria and Dean, newly established behind the counter of Pre-Loved Furnishings & Other Curios. And I am curled up in my mother's womb waiting to come out to the world I have just described.

As far as Frank went, my mother says he and Alma Martin never hit it off. Alma's mind was made up early in the piece when he saw Frank wander out one morning across the paddock with a shovel over his shoulder. All that remained of the original hill was a small mound of dirt, a morning's work, probably not much more. Frank was still some distance short of George's old site when he stopped and swung the shovel head down; he tapped the earth in front of him in the manner of a cricketer patting down a rough patch on the pitch, then shouldered the shovel and turned back to the house. It is unfair to dislike a man for perhaps not being in the mood right there and then but that was the moment Alma made up his mind that he didn't care for Frank. It's the oldest story around—the artist falling for his favourite model. And for years after, whenever the subject of Frank came up Alma would drop his eyes and wait until the malignancy of the subject had passed.

For his part, my father, Frank Bryant, appears to have taken a more generous view of the neighbour always hanging about in my mother's life. Alma drew my mother throughout her pregnancy. She leans back in the armchair, that immense belly, her hands resting on top. The point of her chin seems to sit another mile or two back in sunny exile.

There are plenty of other examples of this kind of arrangement.

Rembrandt accompanied his favourite model, his wife, Saskia, right to her deathbed with sketchpad in hand. Chagall and his wife, Bella, are another example. Bella flies from the hand of the artist, though *Double Portrait* is more relevant here. In this painting, Bella sits at his knee in a wedding dress and watches his work in progress. Her life is being drawn as she lives it. She lives as she is being drawn. She lives to be drawn. All three probably describe the arrangement between Alma Martin and my mother.

In the earliest years of her marriage to Frank Bryant, Alma didn't like to intrude for the long periods of time it took for a proper drawing session, and instead would take his chances as they turned up and snatch at whatever lay to hand for purposes of a quickie—the back of an invoice slip, old envelopes, in the margins of the sports pages, once on the back of a matinee ticket when the film broke down and they had to wait twenty-five minutes (Frank was doing overtime at the plant). Once, memorably, he drew on the back of an egg carton—tiny miniatures of my mother crowning each cardboard bump, a class of desk-bound Alices.

Frank couldn't talk to Alma, and Alma couldn't talk to Frank. They were like two dogs who come around a blind bend, stop and regard each other just long enough to register the futility of further engagement and move on past each other. Whenever talk turned to matters of paint, of the kind that ends up on canvas, Frank was up out of his chair and reaching for his hat. On house paint, Frank might have offered an opinion. But it never came up.

I was thirteen when I discovered his secret. A woman walked at the edge of the sea, a shoe in each hand, her blonde hair grainy with sunlight. She may have been smiling. She was too far away for me to tell.

This was during the NE Paints picnic. A group of us kids are sitting in the sandhills. Kath Wheeler. Douglas Monroe. Guy Stuart. Raymond Pierce. Diane Huxley. In the near distance a group of men stand around the side of the hangi pit. Kath's dad. Dougie's with the soggy smoke. Kath's is the smaller wiry man checking the time on his watch. Frank is there but not really part of proceedings. He has a leather flap on his watch and he's holding it open like time is a secret and slightly scientific thing to manage. It turns out that Frank and Kath's dad are comparing the time.

From our hollow in the sand dunes we study these strangers who are our fathers and who conform to some rough notion of themselves, approximate and fumbling.

Now Frank comes sauntering over the dunes, larger than life in his NE Paints-issue overalls. A good-looking man— that's what I hear everyone say, and never in a tone of approval but with the voice people use to warn of a rip. I can smell Old Spice, sweat and various tinctures from the mixing bay of the paint factory. Frank's boots are covered in limonite used to make yellow paint. It spills off his white overalls, a powder as fine as sulphur.

'Harry boy,' he says. 'Where's ya mum, mate?'

'Haven't seen her,' I say.

The other kids are watching Frank, the way he's raised his head to look around. He looks testy but it's hard to tell. Frank could be about to pat me on the head or tick me off.

'Having a good time?' he asks.

'It's all right.'

'Good,' says Frank, and now he looks around for another face to ask the same question of.

'What about you, Kath my girl?'

'Yep, fine Mr Bryant. Thanks,' she says.

Then the rest of them.

'Yep.'

'Yep.'

'Yep.'

'Dougie, what about you, son?'

'Yep,' says Dougie, staring at the sand and swallowing hard.

'Well, that's good isn't it?'

Now he rises to his full height and looks down the beach as far as the rocky point. His gaze pokes around in that direction. Smoke and ash drift from his fingertips.

'That's good,' he says once more. He draws on his cigarette, holds the smoke in and removes the cigarette which he turns in his fingers, studying it. He releases the smoke. He says, 'I hope none of you kids have snuck down here for a smoke.'

'Nope,' we say quickly.

'Harry?'

'Nope.'

'Because if you have it'll rot your lungs. You do realise that, don't you? Smoking's a mug's game.'

With that he drops the cigarette in the sand. The other kids look away so they won't have to see my father littering.

There's some activity over at the hangi pit now. The other fathers are hauling up the wire baskets of food. The steam is thick and figures in overalls ghost in and out of the steam and sunlight, some coughing as they laugh.

My mother has been handing out wet towels. Now she has one towel left. She looks around for someone to give it to and there is Alma Martin. He must have said something funny, maybe possibly even shocking, because my mother puts a hand to her mouth as Mr Martin drops down a sandhill with a pleased look on his face. About now my mother spots us and starts over.

'Harry, I see your father has done his disappearing act again just as we're about to eat. Hallo Dougie. Kath. Raymond. Diane. Guy.'

'Hallo Mrs Bryant,' they chant back.

'Harry go and find Frank, will you.'

I don't know where he is. But I know how to find him. That's easy. I follow the trail of limonite through the sandhills. Now there are yellow sprinklings on the flat stony part of the beach. Blackened sea necklace dried to a crisp has the same yellow dusting. In an area of hard sand I catch up with a footprint made from a pair of NE Paints-issue boots. The trail of limonite peters out on the rocks, but all arrows seem to point to the cave entrance and as I come around the corner I am stunned to see the bare buttocks of my father with his paint-splattered overalls gathered around his ankles, and without fully seeing who she is, I remember the woman I saw walking along the shoreline with a shoe in each hand.

The tip opened the same year as Frank ran off with the woman from Wages.

It was through the tip that I came to work for George. The tip was in the vee of the hill one around from the farm, and George paid me for a few hours after school each day to comb the tip for other people's discards—doing much what I pay Alma to do today.

Sometimes, and without advance notice, George would turn up at the tip for a few hours and the two of us would call to each other like fishermen on either end of a dragnet whenever we pulled something of interest from the smouldering layers of disintegrating filth. There was a lot of *rubbish* rubbish, there's no denying that, but there was a lot of good stuff as well, and the status of some things moved between those two points of assessment. A tossed-out vase turned into something precious in George's hands. He used his spit to rub away the grime, and it is through George that I first came to develop a contempt for those who would shun and discard so carelessly.

You can see the rub of the pre-loved in everything if you look hard enough. What tends to happen is this. It gets a little shiny, develops signs of wear—a rip appears, and it's on the scrap heap. The very thing you wrapped your arms around and just loved to pieces is shown the door and tossed unceremoniously on the back of the ute destined for the tip. Well, you tell yourself, the stuffing was coming out, the fabric had worn. It was depressing to look at. It made the room look shabby. It made you feel shabby. And yet, once you strip away the old worn fabric more often than not the innersprings of the pre-loved object and what we might call here new love—if that isn't too cute—are much the same. In the case of an armchair a spring might need tightening. Maybe a new protective layer is called for.

After Frank left, it didn't take more than a slight adjustment to think that together with household stuff, you could lump the household, you could lump the family, the wife, the kid.

Still, if Frank is good for something, perhaps it is this. His vote-catching smile was to pass on to me. I've always had this ability to appear like I was smiling at some deep thought which any moment soon I would stun the world with. It has served me well at endless council meetings. Ophelia at that London club had commented on my smile. 'You have nice eyes, Harry Bryant.' Though that was before she twisted out of the corner I had baled her up in and disappeared into the crowd with her drink. And on the tug bringing the people ashore from the *Pacific Star* I believe it was this same expression of mine that had had a calming effect on everyone when we rolled and pitched over the bar.

11

My mother wouldn't let Alma near the tip while the newspaper people were here for the story on the portraits. It would be undignified, and she was right to point out that Alma was the hero of the moment. He alone had managed to attract out-of-town coverage, a goal we spend most of our winter months in council pursuing, dreaming up new schemes, plans to bring people here. What if we were to have a treasure hunt and fill a paint can with silver coins? What if we were to open a paint museum? It's always been a struggle to see our way past paint, and even the interest in Alma's portraits wasn't such a distant cousin to those other schemes we thought up.

The problem continues to be one of geography. The road south passes away under our sills. It careens away from us in polite horror. You see the small cars of tourists bobbing into a head wind; usually it will be a retired couple, him or her with the map spread over their knees. You see them slow down and glance up, wondering. Is this it? Have we arrived? We smile back and shift to one side of the window sills. Just our short-haired dogs stare back. We wait to one side of our curtains until we hear through our thin walls their jumpy foot on the pedal followed by a tinny burst of acceleration.

When people come here to live, like the Eliots, it means they've reached the end of the line. There is nothing after this. When they wonder how they got here, by what road, they find themselves thinking, surely not that meagre two-lane broken-up strip? How and at what point did the glorious highway they were on downsize to such a narrow strip?

I'd spoken with the reporter on the phone. Sally somebody. I saw them pull up outside the store. Nervous expectation hung off the ends of her eyelashes. She saw me and pointed with her finger, 'You are...?'

'Yes,' I nodded back.

I'd done a bit of ringing around on the newspaper's behalf. I wanted everything to be easy for them. No hiccups. The newspaper's idea was to have the sitters by now well advanced in age to pose next to the portraits of their younger selves. A caption story—and that would be nice; it would put the town up in lights. Something positive for a change instead of the usual casualty stories.

At first glance, though, I wouldn't have blamed the news-paper people for thinking Alma Martin was one. His clothes were old and patched. His hair is grey but in some mad and desperate bid to recapture something of the past, perhaps in anticipation of the newspaper interest, he'd tried out a sachet of dye he'd found in a perfectly good toilet bag tossed out at the tip, and now his hair featured a raccoon strip down the middle and over his right temple. If you looked closely you saw that the dye had stained the tops of his ears. It invited all kinds of comment that could not politely be said aloud. Alma did not look the kind of human being who speaks lovingly on end about Pierre Bonnard.

When it came time to organise the group portrait Hilary proved to be difficult. The others waited while my mother spoke with her. Nervous glances were sent in the direction of the newspaper people. We didn't want them to give up on us. Finally my mother got Hilary up from her bench and pushed and sweet-talked her across the street to the painted shop windows. But, as soon as the photographer tried to place her in the group, she bolted. My mother shrugged and looked at Alma.

'All right,' he said. 'I'll give it a go.'

We watched him limp across the road—in bad light at the tip the night before his foot had gone right through a sofa he was standing on to get at an expensive-looking leather bag. We saw him crouch down and speak with Hilary. He was like that for a few minutes before he stuck up his hand and waved over my mother. She crossed the road, spoke briefly with him, and went over to his bicycle and opened a saddlebag. She got out his drawing gear and hurried back with it. For the next ten or fifteen minutes the group of the original sitters and the newspaper people stood whispering among themselves while Alma sketched Hilary. In a way it was nice for the newspaper people to see this, that Alma's portraits weren't just a thing of the past.

Hilary was the perfect sitter. She did not see the world off to the sides—she looked ahead into the window of a former paint shop where her reflection was broken up by shop lettering.

Alma finished and we saw Hilary hold out a chubby hand

for the sketchpad. She would have seen the elaborate arrangement of folds in her dress, the high-lit arches and splintered shadows; and little sign of the filthy cotton dress covering her knees. Alma let her have the drawings, and the next time I saw her in town she had pinned one of the sketches to her dress, as if to invite passers-by to make up their own mind on which version they preferred. Once we could have believed that she had turned herself into a public wall that a dog might piss up against, but now here was a picture. Here was another version. Here was a reason to look twice and wonder.

There is still another version of Hilary, and it's this one I prefer, her reddish brown hair on fire from the sunshine splashing in the classroom windows.

She has been talking about first impressions, the folly of allowing first impressions to rule our judgment. To make her point she has told us about a Russian explorer who while passing our coast in the 1800s wrote of 'a frozen sea, inland'. He would have seen snow-capped mountains and thus concluded. We did not think of ourselves as living in a cold place. We shifted uneasily in our seats while Mrs Phillips wrote the name Bellinghausen up on the blackboard. It was the longest name any of us had seen—it stretched spectacularly across the blackboard in that Russian way.

Bellinghausen, Hilary went on to say, had come within a whisker of discovering the great white continent only to tragically mistake the distant ice shelf for fog. Comically, he changed course to avoid contact with what he was looking for. He had seen one thing and thought the other. He'd made the mistake of seeing what he expected to see, what he was used to seeing.

At this point a gap opened up between what Hilary wished to share and the ability of the class to hear and comprehend what she was saying. So Hilary had fallen back on some quirky detail to crank up our interest. She spoke of Bellinghausen's stop in England and his efforts to recruit some of Captain Cook's key men, especially, Joseph Banks, the botanist. These days his is the face on our banknotes as well as the name of an investment bank ('wealth begins with a seed'), but back then he was a man whose gifted eye might have seen the ice shelf for what it was and known the difference between that and fog.

Bellinghausen couldn't persuade Banks to join the voyage and all the Russian managed to leave England with were tins of pea soup, then a new invention crucial to the future exploration of the great white continent.

Canned soup. It seems so contemporary; so hard to place with wooden sailing ships. On my way home I tried to remember what Mrs Phillips had to say about can-openers. Did she even mention openers? Or was I on to a question to stun the class with?

There are always going to be different levels of appreciation. Hilary's was more intimate. She could become breathless at times, for example, when reading aloud to the class from a novel that she got caught up in. She was like that with the new and unexpected subject of Bellinghausen. She spoke softly as if to underline privileged access. 'The facts speak for themselves. One third of the world was known when Bellinghausen set out across that vast tract of lined ocean, one popularly imagined to contain serpents and sea monsters, but also one that a reasoned mind concludes must wash up somewhere. It didn't just stop there like a ruled line in space.'

We all snorted to show our sophistication.

'If the ocean washed up on a northern shore it must naturally follow that a shore existed to the south in order to hold
the ocean. Think of a shopping bag.'

We thought of a shopping bag.

'Well,' she said, strolling between the blackboard and the
windows, 'containment is important to any notion of space. A
painting needs a frame. God Almighty holds all existence in
the palm of his hand. One enclosure,' she said, 'follows another.'
Furthermore, for the sake of tidiness and notions to do with
beauty there has to be two of everything.

'It's written in the Bible, remember?'

No one did. Our eyes scratched the floorboards between the
rows of desks.

'Two of everything,' Hilary repeated.

The dark side and the lit side, she went on to say. The
proportions of a face neatly measured up by a vertical line. (I'm
more or less paraphrasing now I don't remember her exact
words.) The same applied to any understanding of land mass.
A mighty continent such as Russia must have its companion
piece to the south. In the mirrored rooms of the Russian
Admiralty all this made sense, but in New Egypt primary
school Hilary's class sat dazed.

That night when Frank asked me in his usual perfunctory
way what I'd learned at school that day I was able to tell him,
'A Russian explorer once described our place as a "frozen sea".'

'Right,' he said. He got up with his plate and walked to the
sink. He said as casually as he could, a disarming flight of
words over his left shoulder as he rinsed off his plate, 'I left
something at the plant. I'll be back in an hour.'

My mother didn't ask what he'd left; she closed her eyes and clung on to a faint smile.

The next day Hilary led the class down to the beach where we stood in readiness to spot on the horizon a wooden sailing ship bobbing south past this 'frozen sea'. Hilary rose on her toes. She held back a strand of hair that kept falling across her face. And as she strained to see over the tops of the swell falling against the horizon I shifted to a spot behind her where I could see around the sides of her face a line curving into a tiny pit of regret etched at the corners of her mouth. It was a look so closely approaching sadness that I wondered if she really had expected to see Bellinghausen's ship.

On our way back to school a man got out of a car parked near the school gates. I was pretty sure this was Jimmy Phillips. As we got closer we could see his car packed with things. Cartons, pillows. It was impossible to walk up Endeavour Street and miss the car or the man and yet Hilary gave exactly that impression. It may have been that her mind was on other things, that she might even be considering becoming a gymnast or a vet or maybe she was wondering if Persico's fish and chip shop would be open by the time she finished marking our homework later in the day. Jimmy didn't stop grinning.

At the school gates things took their inevitable turn. Hilary stood to one side as we filed through. She told us to go to the classroom and wait there.

We did what she asked, some of us with backward glances. In the class we moved as one to the windows. By then Jimmy had placed his hands on our teacher's shoulders. Now she placed her face against his chest. We understood this to be a farewell. No one spoke until Jimmy crossed the road to get in his car; the way Hilary's arms had fallen at her side was the saddest thing and one little girl at the window said, 'He's leaving her.'

When I passed all this on at home and reached the part where Jimmy drove off, there was a sustained silence and it was left to Frank to think of something to say.

'What kind of car was Jimmy in?'

I couldn't remember the make. 'A blue one,' I thought.

'Probably the Cambridge I saw him in last week.'

Without a word my mother got up and left the room. Frank's sigh of relief was audible as it was long.

Questions were posted over the blackboard.

What kind of man becomes an explorer? What qualities might a man (or woman) need? Why would a man give up one life for another that didn't necessarily promise anything better?

We heard later that Jimmy had gone to work on one of the big hydro projects.

He was never gone for long, as I recall. Soon we got used to seeing the blue Cambridge car parked outside the school with no one in it—a kind of calling card that made Hilary smile. Jimmy was home again.

It was obvious she never knew when he'd be back; the decision was his alone.

There is nothing like longing to wear down the insides. In the absence of Jimmy, Hilary's interest switched to Mrs Bellinghausen. Now we heard about the white nights of Leningrad, and how neat and composed the world will appear when in fact it is completely at odds with itself: she invited us to imagine, outside the window on our burnt playing field, a crust of snow; below that, ice; and beneath the cracks the shiftiness of water.

School broke for summer and we forgot about Bellinghausen. Instead there were farm chores, days at the beach, and at home the sad figure of my mother. I longed to tell her about Frank and the woman from Wages, of what I'd seen. There was no way of knowing if she already knew; and if she did, then I'd make things worse. If she didn't know, well I wasn't sure that I wanted to be responsible for what then might follow. Some bleak survival instinct told me that a gloomy household was better than no household at all. And I didn't want to be responsible for things getting worse than they already were. The only thing to do was to pretend that I didn't know anything.

When school resumed the appearance of Hilary was a shock. Her face had grown flabby and despite it being summer her skin was pale. Her eyes were red. She looked like someone who had been up all night three days running. When she brushed by our desks we smelt the nicotine. Her hair was untended. She'd always been fluent, and as I've indicated, excitable when a subject aroused her. But now she lost the drift of what she set out to say. In silent reading we heard her crying very softly at her desk. No one dared look up.

The headmaster who I remember as a fair-minded man with two vertical lines folding the skin between his eyes had shown patience with his star teacher. Maybe he'd been aware of a problem before the rest of us because now there was a definite sense of Hilary being on report.

What had happened was this. One of Jimmy's absences had been unexpectedly long. He had meant to be home for Christmas, then at the last moment sent word that he wouldn't be. Something had come up. Over the summer break Hilary responded by contriving to put on weight. Some will have issue with the word 'contrived'—it sounds a bit strong, as if she knew what she was doing. In retrospect though I believe this to be the case. Hilary ate fearlessly, and this fearlessness of hers grew into an amazing appetite. Even in class she had food on her desk. She ate when marking our homework. On lunch duty she patrolled the playground with a paper bag of sandwiches and cakes. With the benefit of hindsight her plan becomes more clear. If Jimmy could remove himself from her life and distance himself whenever he so willed, then she would do the same. She would bury the person Jimmy knew inside a roll of fat. She would place that person Jimmy had once known and loved right back on the edge of memory. She would teach Jimmy what it felt like whenever he willy-nilly removed himself from her life.

There was that final absence and that was it. Jimmy forgot to return. And eventually we would forget the man with the long legs who used to lounge up against the blue Cambridge outside the school gates. Hilary had grown to such a size she couldn't fit her swollen feet into shoes any more. She had to make do with rubber jandals in all weather. She carried a string bag for her groceries. She wore a shapeless cotton dress that angled out from her enormously flabby arms like a pup tent. And because of the great depths at which she had buried herself she seemed indifferent to cold or rain.

She wasn't up to teaching any more. We heard it said she had lost her mind. When Alma finally had to get her out of the cottage he found a chair-bound woman surrounded by a pile of rubbish that seemed to pour like the tide down from the walls to her bare toes.

There was a time at high school when those of us who were lucky enough to once have had Hilary as a teacher would stop to talk to her. But that time passed. We had grown and changed ourselves and our old teacher, we hoped to God, would no longer recognise us. She sat on the bench muttering to herself, the rain pouring off her red face. She wore a plastic see-through coat that she couldn't button up. The weather lashed at her bare legs. She had become just too embarrassing to recognise any more.

12

It was nice to see Alma and the women in the newspaper. The 'old and new fruit' headline was a bit unfortunate. Alice wanted to write a letter but I stopped her. The important thing was the photo. It showed that we were alive and well, still kicking. It was timely because as usual, after the *Pacific Star* fiasco, I was feeling down in the dumps and as it does on such occasions, the thought came to me that maybe Tommy Reece hadn't done such a bad job after all. Down at council during the review of the ship's visit I had to look up at Tommy's sober black-and-white portrait and when I thought of the frilly soft porn I'd pulled from the tip that day and cleaned up with a damp cloth for resale, it was hard to resist the thought that all mayoral dignity had drained away with Tommy's death.

There are times when I wish I could stand in the door of the shop and gaze down the street and find a canyon of office buildings with lines of yellow cabs double- and triple-parked for women to step out of like spoilt pelicans into expensive department stores. There are times when everything here is just insufficient and everywhere else is better. I must admit when I get down like this I tend to pop through to the section behind the beaded curtain and pull something off the shelf to lift the spirits.

That morning I found myself staring at the vulva of someone called Robyn, admiring its gentle rise and the sunlit ends of her pubes. There is something deeply unserious about blonde pubic hair. There was not a single wrinkle on her face. I had an idea it would be like marzipan to touch. Her mouth was heavily painted to the point where it didn't really look real. The lips didn't even look fit for talking. I couldn't imagine them biting into an apple or slobbering with curry. And her skin really was too glossy. The shop lights are over the counter but even when I shifted the magazine around, the page would not lose its shining reflectiveness. It's like when you try and lock your eyes on something bobbing out to sea on one of those summer days of dazzling white light. You squint. But instead of this bringing the object closer, it disintegrates into bloodshot blurriness.

Her bottom though was perfect, architecturally speaking. In a smaller photo she sat cross-legged, dressed only in thick black reading glasses. Presumably the book in her lap was proof of 'reading' listed under 'hobbies'. In the full-page spread she looks ridiculous. She holds the reins of her favourite horse. She's wearing a black equestrian helmet and nothing else. Her vulva has gone back under cover, it's just polite fringe, almost sexless really. Over the page and we're back to a full-face shot where Robyn—and not the horse—is climbing one of the equestrian hurdles. Her left foot is raised—the camera gazes admiringly, longingly it's fair to say. Isn't it extraordinary to think of men in warm baths all over the globe right at this minute thinking about Robyn, her name more recallable than the Pope's or Neil Armstrong's, her interest in 'the environment' and 'reading' noted but not really taken that seriously?

I would have lingered longer with Robyn had not some old friend of my mother's, deaf to the point of hopelessness, come in to ask if I would buy his dog. I told him we don't do dogs but on he went deafly listing Chester's qualities—his loyalty, his obedience. Then he ran through his pedigree, by which time I'd actually written a sign. 'We don't do dogs.' This took him by surprise and I wonder if the dog read the message before he did, because suddenly Chester was wagging his tail and feeling better about the day's prospects.

Possibly I was also feeling a bit down because our friends Kath and Guy Stuart were off to Caloundra. Yet another export to Australia. I'd sat on the same school mat as them. We'd stood on the shore looking for Bellinghausen's ship with Hilary. Alma had painted our faces for the NE Paints picnic. I remember Guy and Kath squabbling back then. Kath said she was a zebra. Guy said she was a bee.

I was thinking about this as I drove over to their house. Bee or zebra. You think of these things and remind yourself, hang on, I'm forty-four, I'm the mayor and I'm thinking about face painting when I should be thinking about drainage. There are days when I question my ability to do the job. I am not a grave man; not nearly grave and serious enough for the office of mayor. Tommy Reece never smiled; there must be something in that—he was returned as mayor a record number of times. I should be thinking up ways of saving New Egypt. I should be thinking sewage. Rates. Or even the slightly more awkward matter of pricing Kath and Guy's household stuff. This was going to be tricky. This was going to be awful in fact.

As I pull up the drive the Stuart kids aged eight and ten are playing out front. There is something staged about the kids' play, I don't know, it is like they've been sent outside in anticipation of my visit. I suppose Kath and Guy are just being good parents. Who wants their kids to see their life's goods picked over by a man with a clipboard?

I switch off the van and stay put for a moment. On the other hand, it is possible Guy and Kath have not mentioned anything to their kids about the move across the ditch. I make a note to be careful what I say to them, although when I get out of the van I see something akin to upheaval register in their eyes. After that I don't think there is any doubt that they know their world is about to change.

The girl clings to a well-thumbed Harry Potter book. The boy with his kid-sized cricket bat plays a cover drive over the buttercups. That is interesting—Guy has let the grass grow. The task of the lawns has been handed on. Emotionally the Stuarts are already on that plane.

I pat the boy's head, say hallo to the girl and look up at the house in time to see a shadow move behind the door glass. I am relieved it is Kath who comes out to the porch. On his own Guy can be hard work. With Guy you have to make the conversational running and be prepared to shift and move with his long silences, cruise them, enjoy them even, but resist the panic to fill in the silence with a rush of whatever comes into your head. That just makes Guy blink faster. At the shop I have a class photo of us all at primary school. As far back as all those years ago the tension rising in Guy's shoulders is plain to see; a feeling that whatever is happening will soon pass and be replaced by something worse. Now he shows up behind Kath and places his big hand on her shoulder. In the same photo Kath is the little girl with the pigtails and missing teeth sitting in the front row. Thirty years later she is also the good-looking barefoot woman in jeans smiling at her boy practising the cover drive.

'He lives for it. He's his father's son to a tee.'

Guy's face goes all rubbery and turns bright red.

'Right,' he says and brings his hands together with a forced cheerfulness. 'I'll put the kettle on, shall I?'

I have an idea I will catch up with Guy when it comes time to look over the toolshed.

For starters we begin in the master bedroom. I follow Kath to the window where we find the Stuart kids out front staring back, concern on their faces, wondering why their parents are acting so weirdly. Why is their father so eager to please and at the same time quick to remove himself? And what is the man from Pre-Loved Furnishings & Other Curios doing inside their house with that clipboard?

'I told them the mayor was coming around,' she says. This is the most hilarious thing she can think to say. *I told them the mayor was coming around.* She starts laughing then.

'I hope they're not too disappointed?'

'No. I told them what to expect.'

'Thanks, Kath.'

She says she's told them they have three more sleeps. This morning she says she heard them down the hall experimenting with the word Caloundra. It sounds like the name of a shampoo or something from the lizard family. She looks past me for the window. She says what a close thing it's been. For years they've watched the street empty out. They could have been stuck here. They could have died here. Of course it was up to her. Guy with his big blond shoulder tied up in sheet and sleep. Next to useless really, isn't he? She was the one who had to make the play and get Guy to apply for the paint technician's job with a marine company. Left to Guy they would be in the hold of a fast-sinking ship as everyone rowed away in lifeboats. She says they've been careful not to buy any more groceries. All week they've been eating the fridge back to its humming white panels.

'It's been a good fridge but now along with everything else I guess it'll go to you, Harry.'

She opens the window and yells at the kids to 'scoot'. The girl takes off. The boy stays nudging the grass with the end of his cricket bat.

'Go on, Michael. Daddy will be out soon.'

Closing the window she says, 'He's sad for some reason. Wonder why?' But she doesn't wonder; she doesn't spend another second wondering. She has leapt ahead to the matters at hand.

'Well,' she says, with an extravagant wave of her arm. 'All this we're leaving behind.' I start itemising as Kath calls them out—the bed, the vanity, the rug, the bedside lights. I tally them up and mention a figure. Immediately Kath looks away. She was thinking of a different figure of course. This is how it is. This is how we will progress around the house. I lift the duvet and test the mattress springs—this time when I mention the figure Kath looks frankly appalled.

'No. Really? Is that all? I really thought...'

I tell her I've got mattresses coming out of my ears. I can't give them away. People are funny when it comes to beds. They will scrimp and save on the other things. They will settle for a secondhand bed frame and splash out on a new mattress.

'Still,' she says.

I tell her, 'You could give Skinners a go.'

But I know she won't. Why would you drive fifty kilometres down the coast on the off-chance? I give her a moment to consider the option. The fluorescent patches on the roadside posts flash in her eyes.

'No. Take the damn thing,' she says.

This is an emotional business. People are often surprised to discover this. They just don't realise how wrenching the whole exercise can be.

Now Kath has sat down on a corner of the bed to take fresh stock. The tips of her hands dive between her thighs. She is looking up at a familiar print by an old Dutch master.

'You should take that with you, Kath. It'll be nice to have the memento in Caloundra. Something to remember us by.'

But I see she's not looking at the painting with any affection. In fact she's not really looking at it at all. In a dreamy voice she says, 'I've promised the kids surfboards. Guy says there's surf in Caloundra.' Her shoulders rise and fall with this information. She looks back at the painting. 'Nope. I don't think I want that thing coming with us. I don't actually want to think about this place. I want to make a clean break of it. I want everything to be new and without that old scene nagging away at me from a wall. I don't want to be looking out the window at Caloundra and then back at New Egypt on the wall. I don't want us constantly switching back and forth between the two. I don't want any second thoughts or maybes, or "Jesus, I wish we hadn't," kind of thoughts.'

Her head turns. We can both hear it now. Guy is instructing his boy on cricketing matters. Play with a straight bat. Eyes over your front foot…It's funny to listen to because I don't recall Guy knowing that much at school. What I do remember is his face tightening with concentration—he always wanted so much to succeed but his body just wouldn't deliver for him. He'd get himself tied up. He'd dream of hitting a six and end up falling back on his wicket. Guy was forever dusting off his dignity. I follow Kath over to the window in time to see the boy play and miss. Father and son look nonplussed, a hand on their respective hips as if to ask, how did that happen?

'I realise it won't be easy,' says Kath. 'But I'm not giving up without trying…'

As I turn away from the window I catch a glimpse of myself in the mirror. I look like a man who may have been thinking about Ophelia's pussy.

'The mirror, Kath?'

'Like I said, our bags and clothes are all we want to arrive with. It's just more junk, isn't it? And anyway, I told you Harry, I don't want our new life cluttered up with the past. I don't want it to be cursed. I want it to be bright and new.'

Two days later I had finally found a magazine with an African nude. Piles of lion and tiger skins for our Queen of Nubia to lie back against, the outside knee raised. Mahogany-coloured breasts. Large dark nipples. Ophelia undressed back to her African origins. I was completely buried in this stuff when a voice piped up, from the distance of the door, thank God.

'I can come back…'

It was Dean Eliot and he was nodding in the direction of the counter. He was too far away to see. And yet he seemed to know. The knowledge crossed his face.

But if Dean knew, he didn't care. He glanced around, his eye climbing the floor-to-ceiling pile of mattresses, and I slipped the magazine under the counter.

'I'm after a bed. A *new* bed,' he added, but not in time to erase the vision of old blankets and a hard floor.

'Well, what you see is what we've got. King-size or queen?'

'King,' answered Dean, but again he'd left the blocks early and was forced to quickly follow up with, 'they're the same price? A king and a queen?'

They're not as it happens, but at that moment due to the munificence of the owner I was prepared to offer him a special. 'Same price applies to all,' I said.

'In that case, I'll take this one,' he pointed at the Stuarts' bed. There must have been thirty mattresses piled there and he'd found the one I'd just bought from them. I felt an odd wish to deny him but couldn't think of a reason fast enough.

He'd come prepared. He had a length of rope in the boot of the orange Datsun. I helped him wrestle the base and mattress on to the roof and held it in place while he roped it through the open windows. It was unstable as anything. I mentioned the van—I didn't mind running it out to the beach. Usually it is part of the service. And in case he was thinking of an added expense I put his mind at rest. I should have insisted, but Dean was determined to do it his way.

There was a call from Guy on the Saturday night. He was ringing to say the Caloundra thing was off. The marine paints lab had gone into receivership. The manager had phoned him to explain. Apparently it was all a big shock. The manager hadn't known anything until the security people showed up at the gates. He was like everybody else at this point, pondering his future. 'I'm sorry. This isn't the news you were wanting to hear,' he told Guy.

There was a deep breath at the other end. 'So…everything is on hold, Harry.'

I said to Guy, 'I hardly know what to say.' Immediately Frances looked up from her jigsaw table. I mouthed the news to her and she rolled her eyes and whispered, 'Ask him how Kath is.'

'How's Kath handling it, Guy?'

'Not well,' he said in a very low whisper. 'She was so looking forward to this, Harry. It breaks my heart. But it could have been worse. She's not interested in hearing that, of course, but what if we'd got over there and been given the news? We'd be up the proverbial without a paddle. Anyway, listen, I'm afraid it means we need our stuff back.'

When he said that a fatigue of stunning proportions came over me. I'd just spent the best part of an afternoon finding places for their household stuff and now it was spread to all corners of the shop. There must be ten other frying pans that looked just like theirs.

'You can imagine how it's been. All day the same thing. Shall we go? Shall we stay? It's been terrible.'

'Well, everything is here…'

'Good. Good. That's something.'

'Except your bed.'

'You sold our bed? Already? Jesus, Harry.'

At first he sounded impressed, then injured like I'd just impounded their dog or switched off the power.

'I think we have a problem. Hang on a mo will you, Harry.'

There was some conferring in the background. Kath was snapping at the walls. At the Stuarts' end the phone fell against something. I placed my hand over the receiver and told Frances, 'Kath's gone apeshit because I sold their bed.'

'That's what you do,' she answered.

'Exactly.'

Then Guy came back on.

'You there, Harry? Sorry about that. I'm going to put you on to Kath. You two can sort this out. I just want to go outside and dig a hole and bury myself.'

'Harry! Is that you? Now, listen. I want that bed back. It's like we're camping in our own house as it is.'

'As I said to Guy, Kath, everything else is there but...'

'I don't care about anything else. I just want our bed back.'

'The bed is sold.'

'Then un-fucking-sell the bed! That's our marital bed. Michael and Abby were conceived on that bed.'

Now that she'd cracked my ear she began to sob. 'Please, Harry...Help us with the bed.'

There were some muffled noises and I had a sense of the phone swinging airily in the Stuarts' hall before Guy came back on.

'This is not a good time for us, Harry. In fact, this has just got to be the worst.'

The next day I drive out to the Eliots' with a new king-size bed that I aim to exchange for the Stuarts' bed. Hopefully that will make things right. It means of course that I've had to leave my mother in charge of the shop with the result that the magazine crowd won't come further than the door. It also means there will be some profit-taking. Word will get around that Alice is behind the counter, on her own, and every piece of worthless crockery will be winging its way to the shop even as I speak.

At the Eliots', Violet is hanging up the washing. I notice that the Datsun is gone.

I need to explain the situation with the Stuarts and come to the point as quickly as I can. I have promised Guy I will try and get their old bed back to them by noon.

I tell Violet, 'The bed I sold you and Dean, well it turns out that I shouldn't have.'

Her face seems to darken. I rush on with further explanation, the Stuarts off-and-on-again situation with Caloundra. The late-breaking news of the receivership. The importance of the bed to Kath Stuart in particular.

Violet drops her eyes. Oh God, there is a problem. I can feel it. Now she raises her face to look in the direction of the house. She says she just put the babies down. At first I'm not sure why I am hearing about the babies—I just want the mattress—then the penny drops. I wasn't expecting there to be a problem. I thought I could dash in here and out again. To make things worse, she says, 'Maybe you should speak with Dean. Dean is funny about things like this. I can make you a cup of tea if you like, but you're still going to have to speak with Dean.'

'Where's Dean?'

'At the cemetery. He's got some work there this week.'

Another ten minutes and I pull up behind the orange Datsun on Utopia Road. I climb over the broken gate for the path that winds up past the bones of adventurers from Dalmatia and Russia and Ireland, the same place I had mistakenly brought the cruise ship people to. Strategy. Strategy is everything.

Nothing concrete has formed in my mind when Dean pops up behind a headstone, looking crudely alive with a pair of hedge-clippers in his hand. The corners of his mouth are smudged with orange soft drink, the bottle I can see lying in the cut grass.

For the second time that day I start on the same story, although this time I up the ante and suggest that Kath has become unhinged with disappointment.

'These are very old friends of mine, Dean. I think we can work something out that is satisfactory to all parties.'

Dean is staring down at the grass. I can see the bit about old friends and working something out has skipped his attention. Now he raises his feral head.

'But technically the bed is ours, right?'

'Technically, I suppose that is right.'

Once more I feel an enormous tiredness descend on me. I don't think it can be jet lag. I've been back two weeks now, though I haven't quite felt myself since the day with the cruise ship people. And it isn't just that. The beaches have been hit with algal bloom. Kids run from the water complaining of scratchy eyes; they are vomiting in the night. Dead fish have washed up. Dead seals roll in the shore break. People, sane people I've known all my life, have been up to the strangest things. George Hands and Victoria are back in town to bury their son Dean (the irony of the name does not escape me). The funeral is in another week. George has asked me to say a few words. There are so many fronts to attend to.

Dean, though, sensing leverage, swings his attention out to the pine trees lining the other side of Utopia.

'So you're asking me for a favour?'

'Yes, Dean. I suppose that is what this is all about. I'm asking for your understanding...'

'But technically...'

'Technically the bed is yours and Violet's. But I'm asking that you reconsider. I've got another bed in the van that isn't just as good, it's better.'

The van is just visible over the top of the grey headstones. Dean sends his eyes there.

'How so?' he asks.

'The one I dug out for you has an extra layer of innerspring. Ventilation is better. This bed I got you and Violet breathes. When the Stuarts bought their bed no one was even thinking about breathing beds.'

Well, it sounds plausible to my ears. Dean though has tuned out. He's working the handles of the hedge-clippers, snipping at the air. At such a moment it's usually best to bite your tongue and sit back and let things work towards their final shape, but in this instance I feel the negotiations are going nowhere. I've also decided that I don't like the Eliots. How long have they had the bed? One night? So why are we are going to war over this thing?

'Okay, Dean. How about this? I will buy the Stuarts' bed back and give you the one in the van for free. How's that?'

I would have thought that sounded pretty good in anyone's language. But Dean looks put out; inconvenienced, you might say. This is amusing in an annoyingly ironic way. Dean is gainfully employed because of money I wangled out of the district beautification scheme. Maybe it would be wise to let him know who is responsible for the funds set aside for his employment? Maybe I should tell him to hand over the fucking bed and be done with it?

'I'd need to talk it over with Violet,' he says.

'I already did, and she said it was fine with her but to check with you which is why I'm here. I'm asking you.'

'Cash?' he asks then.

It is eleven fifteen by the time I reach the cottage on Beach Road. I pull back the sliding door and drag the new bed across the sandy lawn to the front porch. I have to yell out for Violet to give me a hand to get it in the house. She has to get the babies up. I stand in the hall while she puts the babies on the floor and strips the bed. It is embarrassing—but not too embarrassing.

I ask her to help me carry out the Stuarts' base to the van, then the mattress.

I speed out to the Stuarts' house. When I get there Guy is mowing the grass out front. Bare legs in gumboots. The front door is wide open, the hall looking desolate. As I get out of the van Guy bends down to switch off the mower. He drops his earmuffs to around his throat. The blond hair on his legs is covered with grass clippings. On his way across the mowed section of lawn he stops to pick up a dead blackbird. He picks it up by its orange feet and throws it into the nearby hedge.

'Where is everybody?' I ask.

'Kath and the kids are around at her mother's.'

I feel his pale blue eyes settle on me.

'To be honest, Harry, I was hoping you'd get here earlier. This morning would have made all the difference.'

13

This morning Frances looked at me across the breakfast table and said I seem so far away. Ever since I got back from seeing Adrian in London. I said, 'I'm all right,' and cracked the top off my egg.

'I haven't seen you like this before. Distracted. Elsewhere. I don't know what,' she tailed off and waited.

'I'm all right,' I said again.

She looked at me a while longer. She was in her dressing-gown. She would spend the rest of the day in that dressing-gown. Her lips moved to speak, but nothing came of it. She cleared her throat and looked away to her workbench. Her eyes came back with a puzzled look

'Who is this Ophelia?'

'Ophelia?'

'Yes. Ophelia.'

'How do you spell that?'

She ignored that as I tried to think back. I was sure—no, I was positive I'd never mentioned her name to Adrian. Unless, of course...it was possible he knew her, in which case it was possible…it could have come back through him, the little shit (that overpriced Soho eatery plus the theatre set me back a hundred and fifty quid), the name of the woman I spent no more than an hour with in that London nightspot.

I thought I'd bluff it out. I said, 'I don't know anyone with the name Ophelia.'

Frances gave me a peculiar look. Her lying bastard look, though it trailed off to a corner of self-doubt.

She said, 'I'm sure that was her name. Ophelia. I kept hearing her name. I kept asking you, "Harry, who is Ophelia?" but I couldn't reach you. You sleep so heavily these days.'

'Jet lag.'

'No. I'm certain. Actually, I do know. I've got it written down. Ophelia.'

'Well it could be anyone, Frances. If it was a name that came out of a dream how the hell am I supposed to know? I can't even remember such a dream.'

She sat up straight in her chair and turned her eyes away while she thought.

'I don't know, Harry. Dreams never come just out of nowhere. Dreams come from somewhere. They live somewhere firm and secure even though we may not know it. Some experience…craving. I don't know what, except they're connected. Everything is connected.'

Later, much later, after I cleared the dishes away, I stood watching her through the glass-panelled doors that separate her study from the dining area. And I thought, it isn't those doors separating us, or the sanctified air of her workspace. I could see too that she'd forgotten Ophelia now she was at her table, but I couldn't escape thinking about this woman who was my wife, arranging bits of mismatched landscape scissored out of magazines scavenged from the tip and in a rotting pile by her socked feet. What a strange place for a life to end up!

I could see her hands sifting through the layers of pictures. The stone walls of Scotland that had been lifted off the stony hillsides of Fife and dropped on to the fertile countryside outside Lisbon. She told me this morning what she was working on. The jigsaw manufacturers F W Horst of Frankfurt had asked for something rustic and heavenly to go with their Great Escape series sponsored by Holidays in the Sun. *Snip, snip, snip* went the scissors. My wife's hands moved. The head pondered. The hands reached for another magazine from the filthy pile on the floor.

She hadn't seen me through the glass; she was too engaged with finding a windmill. She flipped over the pages. A wind-mill would deliver a timeless element, restful to the eyes, soothing on the soul. Lovers or perhaps another lonely jigsaw enthusiast would piece together a future life in which they appeared hand in hand beneath the slow-moving blades of a windmill on the lake shore. A lake shore. Of course there had to be a lake shore. For the next five minutes as I watched, magazines were picked up and discarded. The expression on Frances's face was the same unyielding one that sat through my lies about Ophelia. Lakes. We were on to lakes. Lakes came in all shapes and sizes. She would persevere until she found the right one. It is a nice little earner for which she doesn't even need to leave the house, unlike Frank, and her own father, Dickie, who for decades punched a card into the time clock at NE Paints.

In the course of the morning the draft image for the jigsaw would be sent electronically. Some electronically delivered comment would come back. A problem to do with the windmill had been identified. It was standing next to a lake and yet its reflection was not obvious. Not to put too fine a point on it, there was no reflection. How could this be? Some further tinkering and by that afternoon Frances had sent a shadow digitally to Frankfurt. The email came back saying thank you. *Danke schön!*

I remember Ophelia catching a glimpse of my ring finger and saying with some satisfaction, 'So you're married, Mister Mayor, and what does Mrs Mayor do?' And knowing that she would never guess, that it would surprise her, I told her. 'She makes jigsaws of places that don't exist.'

14

The Eliots entered more fully into our lives over the coming month. The first lot of rent Dean paid Alma in such a flamboyant manner must have cleaned them out. I knew the job at the cemetery had come to an end. Now I heard Dean had been down at the wharves and paid one of the scallopers a visit. Unfortunately for Dean he had to zero in on Rob Sciasia who told him he could give him a job but first he'd have to sack himself.

We weren't used to having youth live in our midst. Usually they had cut and run by the time they reach Dean and Violet's age. For years we'd set our clocks to school holidays and in summer kids crowding the beaches like masses of sand plovers. It was simply the cycle of things, I guess. But a young couple like the Eliots were fresh air in other, unexpected ways.

Some of us hadn't seen a mother or babies in yonks. Beth Young who has the second-hand clothing shop saw a bit of Violet. Whenever she came into the shop Beth would emerge from behind the counter and take one or the other babies off Violet, sometimes both, in which case you'd see a weightlessness enter Violet; if she brought up her arms too quickly she might end up floating to the ceiling.

All the same, there was an uneven spread of feeling towards the Eliots. Whereas Violet inspired sympathy, Dean was a reason to lock your door at night.

The day the rent fell due I drove Alma out to the cottage. We knocked on the door, then pushed on it and tiptoed into the hall and out again. The girl was asleep. Alma didn't want to wake her. And Dean we saw rowing away like a pirate from the beach in a dinghy he must have borrowed or stolen from somewhere. Dean didn't row like others did, in unhurried bliss; he didn't stop to rest the oars. He rowed like he was trying to beat a storm. I was sure he must have seen me and Alma standing on the sand dune at the front of the cottage.

It was all an annoying waste of time. I'd gone up to the tip to collect Alma. We'd driven here and now we'd have to come back in the morning.

This time Violet was awake; in fact it was almost as if she was expecting us at precisely that moment. She stood juggling the twins on her hips; as we got out of the car she nodded in the direction of the beach and sure enough, as we came over the sandhill there was Dean. He was hauling up the dinghy and seagulls were flying in all directions.

He was barefoot and in jeans, those skinny white arms hanging out the loop of his T-shirt. Dean didn't look like someone with money. He approached us with his head down and passed a beggarly hand across his mouth. 'Sorry about yesterday,' he said. He'd gone out to set a cray pot.

Anyway, he said, he hadn't been able to get to the bank down in Clearwater. There was a problem with his car, a gasket or something. He pulled a battered-looking chequebook from his back pocket. He would have written a cheque if Alma hadn't stopped him. It would be more trouble than it was worth. Alma generously told him he'd wait, and while Dean should have been thankful he frowned and scratched his head. It wasn't as simple as that. He'd have to wait until his car was fixed before he could get to the bank in Clearwater.

It put Alma in a difficult situation. I knew he was dependent on me driving him down to Clearwater to bank the cheque. He looked at me for a nod. 'Go ahead,' I said. 'I can do some business there.' A lie, but anyway. So after all this mucking about Alma said he'd take a cheque after all.

Dean went over to the porch where he wrote with childlike concentration, his lips moving as he spelled out the amount; it was the same with his signature.

In the morning we drove down the coast. It was a nice still day. Blue sky. Blue ocean. Waves piling up on one another's shoulders for a glimpse of the land. Alma didn't notice any of this.

On the way back, after a particularly long and thoughtful silence, I said, 'You could throw them out and you would be entirely within your rights to do so.'

Alma raised an eye. 'Well, let's wait and see, Harry.'

Notice of an 'unpaid item' bears a stinginess you can feel right through the sides of the envelope. It arrived in the mail three days later.

Once more we drove out to the cottage. The Datsun wasn't there. This time we let ourselves in with Alma's spare key. The house stank of sand and urine. A few toys lay in the hall. A poster of a dreadlocked man with a head band was pinned to the wall over the bed. There was enough arrested activity in the place to suggest they hadn't done a runner, and it was hard to know whether that was reason for relief or regret. We were letting ourselves out again when we heard the Eliots drive up.

Violet looked relaxed. Crystal and Jackson waved iceblocks at the windows. Dean looked almost pleased to see us. He bounced out of the car and began counting from a wad of notes. Alma handed him the notice of unpaid item which Dean pocketed without a glance or even acknowledgment that he knew what it was or the trouble it represented for Alma first, and then for me. There was no apology, no explanation given. He paid the money and so that was that; the history leading up to the moment obviously held no further relevance. The Eliots had just bought themselves another hunk of time, in this case a fortnight, but without our knowing it then events were moving Alma to a whole new set of circumstances where a new generation of portrait subjects would avail themselves.

Living on borrowed time, the Eliots sometimes go out for a drive. It's a cheap thing to do. Dean drives carefully; he doesn't want to stress the car before he's sold it. At this time of the year the evenings are long and sometimes theirs is the only car out on the road. Violet loves to sit back and wrap her hair around her finger and have a sense of the countryside sliding by. Sometimes something will stick. Maybe Dean will point out something comical. Yesterday it was a whole lot of women's bras tied to a farm fence. Maybe a hawk hovering over road kill. A hare or a possum. They argue over that, and—*possum* or *opossum*.

At night when the babies wake he gets up and hands them to Violet in the dark, one by one, their little paws scratching at her shut-eye face. If he's sly about it he'll slip into bed and snuggle up against all that bodily warmth. If he's too awake he will go out to the lounge, stoke the fire and sit there until dawn listening to the tide draw in and out. Perhaps this was where the disintegration of things began, with Dean getting up in the night and keeping his own company? With all that time to himself, perhaps his mind went wandering.

They got drunk one night, just to treat themselves, just to go off the rails for once. They toppled into bed and made love and fell into a deep sleep. Violet slept through feeding time. She didn't so much as stir. So Dean had to get up and attend to the babies as best he could, walking them around the front room until they stopped bawling. He opened the door and the smell of the sea came searching. There was a rustling noise from the lawn. Probably a hedgehog. The babies, floating under each arm like tiny pink astronauts, looked around with wide-awake curiosity. In another four hours he'd be over at the cemetery trimming grass.

The new supervisor, Guy Stuart, picked him up outside Granger's abandoned garage. That was fine, convenient, but he drove so slowly along roads that were completely empty. Dean glanced past Guy's big immobile face to the mist rising off the backs of cows. They drove so slowly that each cow had time to lock eyes with him. When Guy spoke his lips hardly moved.

'I've got a new project that might interest a young fella like yourself. An opportunity's come up to purchase some shoe manufacturing machine. I think I can get it at a good price.'

Guy glanced across—he'd gone out on a limb. He hadn't even told Kath about this. He wasn't into making promises any more until he had them nailed down so they couldn't escape from his grasp. 'I was thinking I might move into footwear.'

And now silence—Dean waited and waited. 'Sure,' he said at last.

'I was thinking of calling it Gondwanaland Footwear. But I've looked into one or two things. If I use the Gondwanaland name I can't protect it. Someone else can come along and steal it. Whereas if I call the line Dodo Shoes then I'm on safe ground.'

Silence—this time even longer than before. But Dean couldn't for the life of him think what to say.

'Dodo kiddies shoes. I think we could move some,' Guy said.

Dean noted it was the first time that Guy had used the royal 'we'.

'Slippers, sandals, school shoes. What do you think, Deano?'

Deano. That was new too. Dean didn't have a strong opinion but as the supervisor's eyes were on him, and as by the sound of it he was more or less included in the scheme, he pretended to roll the question in his mind a few seconds more.

'Not Kiddie Gondwana?' he asked.

'Well now you're thinking laterally. I like that. But we'd run into the same problem. I don't want to get tied up with semantics. Dodo Shoes is definitely a contender.'

As the blackened cemetery stones, came into view Guy told him, 'Of course you must understand Dean that everything is strictly exploratory at this point. I've still got to get over the Main Divide and check out the machinery. There's a hundred and one things to inspect, but if everything goes to plan I'd like you on board, Dean. I like the way you work, you knuckle down, and best of all you go well unsupervised.'

This time they shook hands. They hadn't done that before. 'Oh, and Dean, keep it under your lid for now. Ideas are too hard to come by to give away for nothing. Thataboy. Catch you at four. Don't slam the door.'

To be included, to be in on something, how that raised the spirits! Dean couldn't stop smiling. He couldn't wait to tell Violet. All day he crawled over the ground containing dead people, clipping the grass and smiling at his change of fortune.

In the afternoon, on the way home, Guy picked up where he had left off.

'Your dodo, Dean, was seen by Portuguese sailors approximately around 1507. Imagine something bigger than a turkey. Blue, grey plumage, a big head.' Guy glanced across to see if Dean had got that, and Dean nodded. 'The bill measured nine inches, or twenty-three centimetres in your language, Dean. That's another thing. You'll have to look after the metrics. I'm too old to learn new tricks like that especially when they add up to the same thing.'

Later that night, the babies asleep, he and Violet sat around the fire talking. He told her about the dodo. All that remained of an entire species came down to a head and a foot at an English university, a foot at the British Museum, a head in Copenhagen.

'What about skeletons?' she asked.

'By the truckful,' he said, and Violet smiled. Dean was learning things. She was meeting new people as well. There were the women at the crafts shop. Women in their long green and black velvet dresses. One of these women had taken Violet down to the beach and shown her how to identify those bits of driftwood that contain the soul of a fish. Sun-bleached bits that arched—that's a dolphin. That's a seahorse. Slowly this place was opening up to them.

Towards the end of the month funding for the beautification scheme came to an end. Dean had a sense of foreboding when Guy dropped by the cemetery at an earlier hour than normal. He knew it for sure when Guy switched off the engine and actually got out of the car to wander up the knoll past the graves, hands in pockets, dragging his eyes over the broken bits of gravestone; evasive, but with eyes too that had glimpsed the bottom of the ocean. Dean knew a bad-news face when he saw one.

Guy gave him the news, told him straight, and afterwards Dean picked up his tools and walked down to Guy's car. They drove back to town without a word. Normally they would have talked at length about the dodo shoes, various designs. But there was nothing said. Guy didn't bring it up and Dean didn't ask. The feeling was one of flatness, signalling the end of something. The end of a plan, the end of dreaming out loud around those headstones. In the car he fell to copying Guy's manner. When they pulled up outside Granger's, Guy said, 'Here we are.' He nodded down at the clippers at Dean's feet. 'I better have those,' he said, and that was that.

They were back to the needle being on empty and free-wheeling God only knew where.

Dean got a day's work down at the fish plant watching filleted fish drop off a conveyor belt into a waiting bin. He wore a white cap, white coat, white gumboots. As soon as a bin was filled with hundreds of startled-looking fish heads he wheeled the bin across to the fish meal plant and returned to the conveyor belt with an empty bin. Someone came and told him it was lunchtime but as he didn't have anything to eat, and was embarrassed about that, he crossed the road and sat on the pier looking dreamily at the fishing boats at their moorings. A single duck cast its shadow across the glass estuary. It occurred to Dean that he hadn't made any new friends. He smiled down at the water. Here was one of those moments where you could feel sorry for yourself, bask and wash around in it a bit. It was a shame about the dodo shoes though. To have a dream like that snatched away. The sunshine, and these still shadows floating under the pier, put him in a mood.

At the end of the day with nowhere else to go but home, Dean passed under the bronze rifles and donkey of the Anzacs instead and entered the Garden of Memories where he sat on a bench by the rose garden. For a long time he was the only one in the gardens. So it felt like an intrusion when he looked up and saw a woman circling near the fountain. He wondered how long she had been there, and if she'd seen him bend to tie up his laces and come up with a profanity for the world.

She had taken some care with her appearance. Dean was not to know that this was a hallmark of Diane who is Dougie Munroe's wife. Diane wouldn't be seen dead in a dressing gown. Anyway, let's continue with the scene from Dean's perspective. The woman looked over his way and started towards him. She was pointing at her wrist and asking for the time. So he told her, 'Five forty-five.'

The woman looked down at her own wristwatch and she made a complaining noise. 'That's what I've got too.' She looked up and shook her brown bob of hair, shook loose some pleasing fragrance. She stared at the gates Dean had just come through. Now she turned and looked for the other entrance at the far end of the gardens. Then she wanted to know something else.

'Your watch is absolutely correct and not fast?'

'It's good,' he told her, and she said, 'Well, that's that, so why should I be surprised?' She looked fed up, and after thanking him she marched off under the gate entrance with the Anzacs.

The man she was supposed to meet turned up fifteen minutes later on the grass beneath a maple. Dean guessed he was the person the woman had been waiting for—the closeness in age, a matching preparedness, the man's shiny black shoes. He cupped his hands to light a cigarette but abandoned it when he saw Dean. He started over.

'You missed her,' Dean said.

'Woman with brown hair? Probably in a red top?'

'This one was wearing blue.'

'A blue top.' The man looked surprised.

Dean said, 'You were supposed to be here at five thirty.'

'No. I said six o'clock. I definitely said six o'clock…wait. She told you five thirty…?'

'She said you were supposed to be here.'

'Well that's bullshit for starters. Five thirty.' He threw away his unlit cigarette in disgust. Dean considered going after it but the man was sculpting a figure in the air. 'Brown hair… and kind of…you know…'

'Yeah. That's her,' said Dean. 'She said her watches always run fast.'

'Ah ha ha ha. Yes. We are talking about the same person. No doubt about that. That was Diane you just met. That's her without a doubt. Did she say if she was coming back?'

'She didn't say…'

'What else did she say?'

Dean thought for a moment.

'Nothing. That's about it.'

The man closed his eyes and gently shook his head. 'Oh Diane, Diane…' He took a deep breath and opened his eyes and pointed to the space beside Dean on the bench.

'May I?'

The man sat down and crossed his legs.

'So she didn't leave a message?'

'No.'

'Thank you, Diane. Why am I not surprised? After all, why would you do something so reasonable as leave a message?'

Dean stared at the ground. It seemed like this would be a better conversation if he wasn't there and the woman Diane was sitting here instead.

'A blue top. I find that interesting. Very interesting.' He sat up and crossed his arms and nodded back at the rose bed. Now he uncrossed his legs. 'So what else? Did she look happy or sad? For example, did she look disappointed at having missed me?'

None of the questions and their guesses quite hit the mark. 'Annoyed' might be the word but the man hadn't put that one forward.

'She was angry with her watch,' Dean said.

'Interesting. Interesting. That in itself tells a story. People always look to lay blame when they've lost something. Diane is my wife. Possibly former wife. I had better get used to that idea.'

He stopped himself and took a good look at Dean.

'I don't think I've seen your face. I'm Doug, by the way.'

'Dean,' said Dean.

He felt the man look him up and down.

'So Dean, what are you like with a paint brush?'

It was his next job. Not a big one. A few days' work at the Albion Hotel. Doug showed Dean upstairs and led him past suites named the Quagga Suite, the Giant Sloth Suite, the Jamaican Tree Suite. 'All this shit has to be painted over.' He pushed on one door which opened on to walls covered in forest and savanna. It wasn't one landscape or another. Patches of tropical jungle fought with Arctic waste for wall space. Snakes writhed around tree trunks, mammoths stood ornamentally in the background. A Tasmanian tiger peered back between branches. Birds with pink feathers turned on a sharp wing over ice floes. One large awkward bird caught his attention. Dean knew what it was. He pointed at it, waiting for the name to come to him. 'That's a dodo isn't it?' And he began to recite some of the stuff Guy Stuart had told him until Doug interrupted him.

'Anyway' he said. 'I'll be downstairs if you need anything.'

Dean had just stumbled on to one of my outstanding failures as mayor. After the wind-down of NE Paints the enterprise committee had come up with an idea to turn ourselves into a theme park called Gondwanaland. We worked ourselves into a fever over it. It seemed such a fine idea, so original. Our theme park would bring the extinct species of the world back to life. I managed to get a special local body business grant. We used the money to draw up plans. We called a public meeting and filled the old NE Paints community hall where I bounced up on stage and introduced the idea. A steering committee had prepared a number of charts. A large illustrated flap chart invited my willing audience inside to a reception centre, shops and cafeterias, and an auditorium. The artwork showed a lot of smiling faces, and in the uniformed park employees they saw their future selves on the Gondwanaland payroll, as car park attendants, guides, projectionists, restaurant hands, vendors, manufacturers of Gondwanaland maps and stuffed toys—the stuffed quagga, woolly mammoths made with the finest New Zealand wool, Eskimo curlews—and this was the moment when Frances had nudged my side with her idea for jigsaws. The park would need financing. We spurned big-moneyed partners; not after what NE Paints had done to us. In our small-town wisdom we decided on a private subscription. Five hundred dollars bought a unit share. That was quite a large amount and there had been some nervous shuffling in the hall. But could we afford not to be involved?

On the coast there are moments when a storm signals its end. The clouds part; the sky has never before looked so blue. The world appears radiant again. Gondwanaland was that shaft of sunlight. What a change it made to see people with some purpose in their stride! Suddenly everyone was an expert on theme parks. Discussion on the giant elk or Eskimo curlew flushed out the pedant. 'Your giant elk, Harry. It takes its name from the old Norse *elgr* and Old High German *elaho*.'

For all that, the buoyant mood made for a nice change. It was like we'd discovered oil.

There was much discussion on where to site the park and this led to some speculative buying of property. Merchandising ideas steamed ahead. Cupcakes in the shape of dodos, T-shirts with G logos, a map showing our town's approximate location back when these islands were part of a supercontinent. There was Frances's Gondwanaland jigsaw. The Gondwanaland burger which Heath pestered me to death over. We saw it would be crazy to hang on to the street names of the past— Green Way could become Moa Lane. Pacific Blue would turn into Curlew Square. We liked those new names. For one thing they finally shook off the yoke of NE Paints. They said something more about our place in the world.

It was a good idea, if a little wacky. This made it even more appealing. It made people smile. Everyone's enthusiasm was up. We bubbled along, encouraged one another. So when Doug took me aside to ask me if I thought it was a good idea, a sound idea, whether he should go ahead and launch himself at refurbishing the hotel and pick up the Gondwanaland themes embraced by the rest of the town, I said, 'Hell, Dougie, you'd be mad not to.'

We spent a lot of the money raised by public subscription on nailing down trademarks. Now we could see that we'd struggle to finance it on subscription alone. We would need institutional support, maybe government support, a benign loan, perhaps from one of the commercial banks. Our figures stacked up. We had growth charts. All in all, we had an impressive story to go to the bank with.

Yet it was rejection after rejection. It was hard to understand why, harder still to explain to the hopeful constituency. Face to face we'd get respectful and enthusiastic hearings, then the letter with its bad news would arrive some weeks later. I'd call up, sure there was a mistake, but I never got through to the person the steering committee had met with. I began to feel more and more desperate. The business kept me awake at night.

I didn't know which bank or funding agency to turn to next. I put all my hopes and those of the town in one last pitch to a rural bank.

I remember it was a fortnight later, getting the news and looking up from the letter with the bank's regrets and seeing a woman on a stepladder clipping a hedge; and I had this mad desire to rush out and stick my head between the blades of her hedge-clippers. The theme park was so stupid, so obviously stupid now that we'd been turned down. Worse, I'd led the flock down a blind alley and straight over the edge of a fucking cliff.

Tommy Reece hadn't done this bad. The Tommy of the sombre portrait—the last one by the way commissioned by council. Gondwanaland was the kind of disaster that should end a political career. But when the election came around eighteen months later no one could bear the embarrassment of remembering. I was voted in unopposed.

Long before then, however, the constituency found other ways to square things up. They filed in one after another with their worthless possessions and demanded ridiculous prices and I couldn't refuse any of them. Overnight Pre-Loved filled up with ships in bottles, plain wooden boxes talked up for their 'antique value', miniature cars that were really cigarette lighters, stuffed animals, stuffed toy animals, so many koalas I had to burn them, an embarrassing number of stag heads, wooden tennis rackets of a vintage more likely to turn up as an accessory in a clothing catalogue than on the tennis court. The slightest bit of hesitation on my part and they reached for their last card, but what a card. 'To be honest Harry, I did a bit of money on that Gondwanaland thing…'

A few days after Dean had finished up at the hotel they were on their way back from the supermarket when the Datsun blew up halfway along Beach Road. They had to abandon it. They had groceries plus the twins to carry, and a surfboard Dean had tried to sell me. I should probably have bought it but some mean-spirited bile kept rising up my throat. I took my time looking over Dean's surfboard, drew out the agony, pursed my lips and drifted into long silences while he twisted and burned before me.

That night he and Violet discussed what to do. They needed transport of some kind. They needed to get to the shops and what if the twins fell sick? Dean got up and walked away from the conversation. She followed out to the porch where he let her know he had seen a second-hand bike at the Pre-Loved place. 'If I can get him to come down on the price the bike will do for now.'

I made him work for the price he wanted. The hassle over the Stuarts' bed was still fresh in my mind, the way Dean stonewalled and sought to exploit the situation. I didn't want to be cruel about it. I let him have it in the end but not without a slow, sweated-out negotiation. I'll give credit where it's due, though. Cunningly he clinched it with, 'It's not really for me. It's for Violet.'

A steady spell of fine weather towards the end of January saw Dean disappear for days at a time on his bike. Often he was gone by the time Violet woke to find the two babies wedged up against her where Dean had put them in the night.

She assumed he was out looking for work so she was surprised when he told her he'd bought a small house truck which he planned to do up and sell. She didn't ask what he'd used for money or where he'd found it. She had a feeling Dean had cycled into some other life away from the one they shared, and she was afraid to ask. A bit of paint on his fingers and hands, a green fleck on his eyebrows—that was as much of his world Dean brought back to the cottage on Beach Road.

And since he was never there she asked him for the rent money just in case he wasn't back in time. Dean who was tying up his laces said he would be back.

'When?' she asked.

He went on tying his shoelaces. 'I'll know when I know.'

Later in the day when I turned up with Alma she insisted Dean was on his way home. Alma was more willing to be led along a merry trail than I was.

'Was that your car we saw up the road?'

There was no point denying it and its bad end. All the same, she turned the question over and considered it from every angle.

'So Dean is driving what exactly, honey bunch?'

'He's not driving anything. He's on a bike.'

'Your bike?'

This seemed to confuse her. What did I mean by 'her bike'?

Alma was impatient. He didn't care about the damn bike. He wanted to get to the end of the outstanding rent. He was tired of all the running around. He wished he'd never rented the place out in the first place.

'This is how many times I've run out here?' he asked.

'I know and I'm really sorry,' said the girl.

Now there were more promises made. She'd speak to Dean. She'd make sure he left the rent money with her if he couldn't be there himself.

We bumped our way back along Beach Road. Neither of us felt like speaking.

Well, Dean didn't come home that night or the next. There was no phone. If there was a phone he might have rung, and as far as Violet was concerned any excuse would have been welcome.

In the morning she left Dean a note and took the twins down to the beach. She walked for longer than she normally did because she was fed up with the waiting. She wanted Dean to find her gone. She wanted him to feel that stab of panic for a change.

But it was hot, and the twins were irritable. Today she didn't have the energy for it. Crystal kept dropping her rattle and she had to keep bending down to pick it up. The last time the little girl dropped the rattle Violet yelled at the pink face dribbling near her ear. They started pulling her hair until she shouted at the air behind to cut it out. A seagull hopped on to a log and looked at her. And suddenly she was sick of the beach. Tired of the idea to give Dean a dose of his own medicine. She would go back and if Dean was there she would say she had just gone out for a walk. If he wasn't there she would put the twins down and sit outside on the porch steps and wait for him.

Near the flax bushes by the cottage she heard someone moving about. She thought it must be Dean and rushed forward to find Mr Martin on the lawn. In that split second she knew he'd looked around and worked out Dean's absence. She could see his annoyance, and something else—hope was it, something preventing full-blown disappointment hogging his face. Some hope that Dean might have left the rent with her. She waited for the inevitable question. But instead she heard him ask, 'Was that Dean I saw out at the Riverside Community?'

She didn't know what to say. She didn't know the place. Dean hadn't said anything. Where did he say again?

'You know, Violet, where the house truckers park?'

She had no idea what he was on about. He gave her some directions but she didn't know of it. She shook her head and felt her eyes drop. She heard the landlord step closer. He must have reached out with his hand. She heard one of the babies coo.

'They're lovely babies, Violet. They're adorable. You get to my age and you just don't see babies any more.'

'Thank you,' she said.

'You know, I cycled out here. I hate asking Harry to come all this way on my behalf. He's a busy man. And it's such a lovely day I thought…what the hell…I'll cycle out there.'

He was being so nice to her. She felt bad that he'd come all this way on his bike. She wished she had something nice to say back. She wanted to hide.

She pulled a strand of hair across her face.

She said, 'I don't know what's holding up Dean.'

He didn't show any sign he had heard her.

'I noticed a bike leaning up against the house. Is that Dean's?'

She was so surprised by this she went around the side of the house to look. Black mudguards. The heavy pedals. The faintest ghost that was Dean. Her heart sank. He must have come home and left again while she was down at the beach.

Now she heard the man say, 'Violet, maybe you should let me know what is going on. What do you say? I won't bite your head off.'

Jackson and Crystal were wriggling in her arms. She pretended they were more of a distraction than they really were. She could have put them down to continue the conversation; instead, through the maze of little pink pawing hands, she asked Alma if she could have until Monday. Monday didn't promise anything better. It didn't promise anything at all, but it was the only stalling device she could think of.

'Monday,' he said. He didn't look happy to hear it. 'All right. Monday it is.'

After Alma left her she counted up her change. She found she had twenty-four dollars and fifty cents left. She needed things—bread, milk, tea—but she couldn't bear to spend the money because if she did there would be nothing left. So she stole milk from the letter boxes of farmhouses scattered up Utopia Road. The houses were a long way back from the road and the letter boxes. It was pretty much free picking. Though it turned out she was democratic about it. If she took a carton of milk from a letter box, the next night she would push the twins in their pushchair past that house for the next letter box. A carton here, a carton there. In other ways it wasn't so straightforward. A week ago and she'd have thought this was the kind of thing that happened to other people. But there she was stealing under the cover of night, taking what wasn't hers to take.

This was pretty much how Violet came to my official attention. A phone call from one of the houses. A sighting of a silhouetted figure with a pushchair running down the road in the moonlight. Any milk taken? Why yes, was the surprised answer at the other end.

In a moment of wide-awake hunger she lay in her bed thinking, I'm sick to death of milk. Tomorrow I will catch a fish.

She had caught spotties and some herring before but nothing that she would eat. This was a much more serious undertaking. She scooped a pen out of the shingle higher up the beach and laid Jackson and Crystal down. With the driftwood near to hand she fashioned a shelter. Seeing the pattern of shadow and sunlight fall over their pink faces she removed her purple blouse and hung it over the driftwood, before heading up the beach to the log where she placed the bucket with its tackle.

She'd woken up thinking about the fish she was about to catch. Before she got out of bed she'd cooked and eaten it half a dozen times already. Her stomach juices didn't remember any of it. Were those stomach cramps hunger? A wave drew up the beach seeking her bare feet. She said a prayer. Two prayers. One for Jackson and Crystal—'Don't yell out or I'll hit yis.' The second prayer was for the ocean. 'Let there be a bloody great blind eye of a fish headed this way, please?' She peeled some cat's-eyes off the rocks, smashed their cover and dug out the yucky green flesh which she threaded on to the hook. She did as she'd seen Dean do. She waded out into the tide up to her waist and threw the hook and sinker beyond the fringe of soft brown kelp; letting out the line as she backed her way to the warm shingle and the toothless complaints of the babies.

Shush Jackson. Shush Crystal honey or I'll whack you. Shush. You don't want the fish to hear. She made the sound of the sea. Two pairs of dark eyes shone up at her. *Shush baby. Were waiting for the fish…*After a few minutes a nibble travelled up the line. She closed her eyes, held her breath. *Concentrate. Concentrate. Please God. Concentrate. Shaddup Jackson. Shush baby.* She waited, waited…when she gave the line a rip she felt her hand come up against the fish's weight. She walked towards the water excitedly pulling the line in hand over hand. Already she could see its aspirin-white belly. The flash of blue, followed by a singular movement, a near thing as far as the fish was concerned. The line went slack in her hand and drooped over the stony part of the beach. *Fucking fish.* She began hauling in the line and almost immediately it snagged on the kelp. She walked along the beach trying to free it. She didn't have another hook or sinker. There was nothing else to do but strip off and swim out to the snag and free the line.

At this point Alma left the sandhills and walked back to his bike. He stood it up and balanced the bag of potatoes on the handlebars and cycled the short way to the Eliots' place.

That night she sat out on the porch. It was warm, one of those nights that light up the entire countryside. You could thread a needle in this light. You could play a hand of cards. You could ride a bike.

The last thought made her lift her head. She stood up. The bike was still where Dean had parked it. The front door was wide open. She turned her head to listen for wide-awake sounds at the end of the hall. She thought she'd better check just to be safe. She tiptoed up the hall and stood in the doorway for five minutes until she was sure they were asleep. She knew she shouldn't leave them. It was the worst thing you could do. It was irresponsible. Anything could happen. A fire, for example. The thought was so awful that she shook her head to get rid of it. It was almost as dangerous to think like that; to think the worst was to breathe life into the possibility of it happening. She stood the bike up and stared back at the peeling weatherboards. In the deep night she heard a morepork calling and the sleepier sound of the sea turning over. She knew she shouldn't leave. It was wrong. She should definitely not leave her babies but here she was lifting her leg over the saddle bar.

She hadn't ridden a bike for years. The front wheel wobbled to start with, and the handlebars shook loose in her hands as she rode over potholes. Along Utopia the way was smooth. She was able to stand on the pedals and cycle as fast as her legs would allow. Once as she passed under the deep shadow of a giant pine all the bad things that could happen suddenly returned and she stood higher and pushed harder to get away from the picture in her head.

She reached the T where she had to stop and think back to the landlord's directions. Only now did it occur to her that he had been telling her where to find Dean. He'd just been letting her know. How the hell had she been so slow? She turned the wheel left and was about to set off but paused to wait for a car from the direction of town to whoosh past. The night fell silent again. She pushed off. Soon the road began to climb. Her legs grew weary and the front wheel slowed. It became so difficult she thought about turning back. But she was past the midway point; she might as well keep going. She counted to twenty; she counted to fifty, to one hundred. There in the near distance was the wooden sign the landlord, Mr Martin, had spoken of. She turned down River Road. The air changed to a gorsy smell, and now there was the sound of a shallow river; there was a screen of thin trees but she could hear a narrow reach gurgle along a bank quite near her. Soon she saw lights, little pinpricks of yellow headlights. She cycled on. Now she could hear music. Someone was strumming a guitar. She heard a woman's laughter. Different shadows boxed up around her. House trucks. Caravans. Old buses. She got off her bike and wheeled it in off the road. She could see a circle of faces lit up by a small fire. That's where the guitar was. One person looked up, now another, and another. The person playing the guitar stopped.

She called out, 'Hi!' She hoped she sounded friendly; she wanted to. But no one answered. No one moved from the fire. It was a bit intimidating, really. She said she was looking for Dean. She'd come for Dean. Anyone here know of Dean Eliot? No one responded. She thought she might describe Dean, maybe that was the way to go about it, when a woman stood up from the circle around the fire and came towards her. She was barefoot. She wore a woollen shawl over the shoulder straps of a white cotton dress. One side of her face was fire-lit. Now that she was closer Violet could see her lip piercing.

'Who's asking?' she asked.

Violet began to say who she was but the woman looked away before she had finished. She seemed to know.

'Well,' she said. 'Dean isn't here.'

'What about the house truck?'

'It's here.'

That was something at least. Dean wouldn't leave without the house truck.

'Dean's gone?' It didn't sound right when she said it, it didn't sound remotely possible.

The woman pointed to a cutting on the edge of the dark. 'He left that way and followed the railway tracks down the coast.'

'To go where? Where was he going? Did he say?'

The woman shook her head. 'Nope, he didn't say.' She pulled the shawl around her shoulders. Her expression had hardened.

Now Violet tried to look past her. Maybe Dean was sitting with those people around the fire; sitting there and watching this, the joke on his face.

'Well,' said the woman. 'I think I told you what you need to hear.'

Then she thought to ask after the house truck. 'Dean wanted to show me,' she lied. 'That's why I'm here.' She could see the woman weighing up what she had said; she could see another lie was in order so she said, 'Dean wanted my opinion on a paint colour.'

The woman gave her a long and testing look. She just wished she'd go away. She wished she hadn't got up from the fire in the first place. She looked over at the fire. Her friends were getting up and walking away to different house trucks. She turned back and said, 'Five minutes. That's all you get because I didn't hear Dean say anything about you. What did you say your name was again?'

'Violet,' said Violet.

'All right, wait here and I'll get the torch. He doesn't have electricity in there yet.'

She started over to one of the house trucks and stopped and looked back.

'Well, come on,' she said.

Violet wheeled her bike after the woman. The light kept changing. One moment it was pitch black, then a square or rectangle of lead-lighted window, a candle flickering, now it was shadowed, and in the shadows she would see the outline of people sitting on the steps of the trucks talking and smoking. Underfoot the ground was bumpy. She hoped she didn't step in cow shit. She waited while the woman picked up a torch from the step of one of the trucks and they carried on to the dark oblong at the very end of the house truck community.

'Here,' said the woman. 'Mind your step.'

Violet took the torch. She found the door handle and pushed. The smell of paint hit her. She pushed the torch ahead, and the discovery took her breath away. Here were the places Dean had spoken of, places he'd described in detail back in the days when they both worked in the paint warehouse, when in the cafeteria he had first told of the travelling life he was saving up for. Here were the lakes, and forested hills, majestic mountains and long beaches with the curling waves he so admired, and she saw Dean had injected some poetic licence; he'd found space for a Turkish minaret, two unicorns and a vast bridge, a wonderful engineering accomplishment linking the forested mountain with the virgin beach.

Monday. We drove past the Datsun with its shattered windows. It had been stripped of its wheels as well. It was a desolate sight, and it was impossible to dodge the thought that the Eliots were in quicksand up to their necks.

Violet was sitting out on the step as we pulled up on the lawn. The quiet dignity we'd seen on the first day was still evident. She rose from the step, her face shifting with different impulses—gratitude, sincerity, a tiredness as well, I thought.

She said to Alma, 'I would have rung and thanked you for the potatoes—I guessed it was you. There's no phone though.'

Alma patted her shoulder. He looked at the house.

'So, I take it Dean's not here?'

Dean. Already. So quickly on to that subject. She shook her head and stared at her bare toes poking out the bottom of that faded purple dress she favoured.

Alma raised an eyebrow. I think he'd finally realised that he had reached the point where he could politely ask what was going on. Of course Violet didn't know what was going on. The truth is she didn't know much more than we did. She didn't know where Dean was, and she didn't know what to say. She'd run out of excuses.

'I hope this doesn't sound out of line, Violet, but I'm going to ask you anyway. Are you and Dean okay?'

She'd been expecting a question to do with the rent. When she looked up from her toes her expression was defiant.

'Why?' she asked.

Alma said he was just wondering. He hoped it didn't sound like he was prying.

I thought he should just get to the point and throw her out of there. At this rate there would trips galore between the tip and the beach cottage, all of it time-wasting.

'Nah. We're okay,' she said.

'Because if you're in any kind of trouble I need to know if I'm to help in any way.'

You could see how tempting that sounded. Alma gave her a moment to think about it.

'And if I wasn't okay?'

'Well, in a way, it would be to my advantage. I need to pay someone to model for me and I thought if that was to interest you, well we could come to an arrangement.'

Modelling. She hadn't been expecting that. Boy, was she not expecting that.

It was a surprise to me as well. On the way over there Alma hadn't mentioned it. Maybe he hadn't thought of it, except of course such an idea had a history.

Now he was warming to the notion.

'We could take it off the rent. It would be in lieu of...but that's only if you want to.'

She didn't say thank you. That was the thing about the Eliots; it was like they couldn't see or recognise a kindness shown to them. I didn't sense a trace of gratitude; it was simply a change of circumstance, something new to react to. In a blink she'd leapt Dean-style into that feral position of finding advantage; and now she was out to hammer it home as best she could.

'What kind of modelling?' she asked. And fair enough, modelling could mean a lot of things.

'Drawing, sketching,' Alma told her.

She was starting to nod now; starting to get the idea. Trying to picture it. She folded her arms to think:

'One thing though. I won't take my clothes off.'

'Good. That settles that. I won't ask you to then. I won't ask you to do anything that you're uncomfortable with.'

'And how much would you pay me?'

Alma thought for a moment. The speed and the direction the offer was moving in had caught him unprepared.

'Oh, I don't know,' he said. 'Three or four sessions a week to start with and that can cover your rent.'

There was the same deliberate slowness I'd had to put up with in Dean while negotiating the exchange of mattresses. Words weighed, pondered.

'So, would I get more if I took my clothes off?'

'After what you just said?'

'But if I did, let's say…'

'I hadn't thought about offering a different rate—but that's not to say I shouldn't.'

'And just modelling, right?'

'For purposes of sketching. Maybe even a painting. Portraits, that kind of thing. I'm sure you know what I mean. But you take your time and think about it.'

She looked up at the sky, then back at Alma—all of two seconds.

'I've thought about it,' she said. 'I'll do it.'

15

Late on Sunday night we were hit by a cold front. The rain was extremely heavy. I lay in bed listening to it flow over the guttering. The ground outside our bedroom window made that pudge sound. The rain didn't want to end. My thoughts ran to various disasters. Blocked drains, slippages, property damage. I waited for the phone to ring. And that's how I eventually dozed off, while waiting for news of the worst.

Most of the rain was let go of in the night. In the morning it was murky out. When I walked down to the store the air was still wet, soaked through like the washing. Alice rang to make sure I would run Alma out to the Eliots'. She didn't want him cycling in that weather. 'And you know he won't ask…' As she spoke I could see patches of sunshine hanging in a fine mist over Broadway. He could have biked. And anyway, the tip was closed (it would be a quagmire) and whenever that happens business gets down to a trickle. So I didn't mind, though just as I was about to lock up a very tall man bent over with hay fever came and bought the hydrography set that has sat around the shop hoping to catch someone's eye for nearly eight years. Then Guy turned up drenched in his raincoat. He didn't want anything in particular. He was just out and about and thought he'd drop by. Since the job with the beautification scheme ended I had no idea what he and Kath did for money. When Guy walked in I was about to slip the 'Back in an hour' notice on the door. Now it occurred to me that he could watch over the shop. I made it clear that he would be doing me the favour, and of course I would pay him.

'Absolutely,' I insisted. I couldn't have him do it for nothing.

Guy's face turned red when I mentioned money. His eyes shot up at the stag head. 'Well, I'm happy to do it for nothing, Harry. I wasn't meaning to hit you up for anything. There's plenty here to keep me occupied.' His eyes flitted across the shop and hesitated at the beaded curtain.

On our way out to the Eliots', Alma got me to stop at the supermarket. He came back with tea bags, milk, biscuits; things which he aimed to pass off as morning tea and leave with Violet. Alma often looked cross with the world. Alternately, he could just as easily seize up if you said thank you. That was the case when he put out the biscuits and tea at the Eliots'. As soon as Violet began to thank him he looked around for a distraction. He found me heading for the door.

'No point you leaving Harry. We'll be here an hour, that's all. You might as well join me.'

He was inviting me to draw. Was this what I was hearing? In all the years I'd known Alma, all the times he sat with a sketchpad perched on his knee drawing my mother in our house, I'd never known him to extend this invitation. It was an obvious one when you think about it, rain falling against the window, a boy restless in the house.

A funny awkwardness came between us, as though Alma had just logged on to my thoughts.

'The fact is, I can't draw.' But he heard that coming.

'Everyone says that, Harry.'

I said I hadn't drawn anything since primary school. 'People say that too.' While this conversation was going on Violet was looking from one to the other; now that it was decided—since Alma had decided for me, I was still standing like a limp rag with a big loopy grin—she said, 'Will that mean extra?'

Alma looked at me.

'How much?'

'Ten dollars is the usual going rate,' he said.

Violet seemed happy with that; there was a skip in her tail as she gathered up the goodies Alma had picked up from the supermarket.

It shouldn't be so threatening—pencil, paper. You can look at a sheet of paper and find yourself thinking ludicrous thoughts such as, 'I'm bigger than it is.' Or catalogues of past work drift out of the back rooms of memory. Pictures of brown boats sailing on blue seas, a perfect mountain cone in the background, a blob of snow on top. Round faces with yellow hair and hands like small thickets suitable for firewood. I had grown up with the neighbour drawing my mother so there were certain things I already knew about drawing. I knew the breathy silence, the scratchy sound of pencil on paper. I knew that strange practised stillness. I knew how to move around it. But I knew it as an audience knows a scene in a play, never as one who harbours a burning ambition to enter the scene himself.

Now as Alma took a free hand in moving furniture around, organising where we would sit, a chair for him, one for me, a place for Violet, I found myself trying to remember if there had been another time, just once, when Alma urged a pencil or piece of crayon on me. I began to feel strangely nervous, and as I do on such occasions I reminded myself that I am the mayor. We are the modern-day Hercules holding up the pillars of our little communities from ill winds of economic glut and ruin. We are the unseen, unsung glue, I often think…

'If you're thinking of making a mark on that sheet of paper you'll need to pick up a stick of charcoal, Harry,' Alma said then.

He was smiling to himself; enjoying himself, I think. Violet's mood was more like my own—apprehensive. Alma gave some instructions. First to Violet; he wanted her to adopt a number of poses. He demonstrated. He dropped his chin on to his chest and hung his arms so that everything about him had a downward flow. Next he placed a hand against the wall and leant his weight in that direction. He showed her two or three more poses and told her she could change whenever she got sick of one—apparently we were just after some quick gestural things. And then he told her, 'When you're sick of those, Violet, you can come up with your own.'

Then he directed his attention to me and explained what he meant by a gestural drawing. The body is hardly ever at rest. Weight hardly ever sits square as in a statue or a porcelain object. He showed me with a few quickly drawn lines what he was after and it came as a relief that I wouldn't have to get down to the detail of faces, eyelashes, mouths. He just wanted lines indicating the way Violet's body fell.

The hardest thing was to make that first mark. While I was dithering Alma picked up my wrist and crudely moved my handheld charcoal against the paper. 'There, now you're started.'

He worked quickly, dashing off one drawing after another. Ripping out sheets of paper that he'd obtained on the cheap from Persico's fish shop. *Quid pro quo.* Jimmy had asked for some fish drawings. Alma had said, 'How about drawings of your customers?' And now the portraits of Jimmy's regulars were pinned up to the wall next to a large chart of various fish species plus a very old NE Paints landscape calendar.

Violet finished Alma's repertoire of poses and began to explore a number of her own. She tried sitting on a chair, tapping her shoe. Alma told her that drawing a tapping foot was a bit beyond us, and after that she slid off the chair on to the floor and sat with her back up against the wall, her knees tucked against her chest, her face at a moon-gazing angle. Once more that glass dome of concentrated effort fell over us. Violet was away in her own little world, spinning to a distant corner of the galaxy. In her face I saw assembled various depths, layers, shadings, all kinds of cravings that I had no idea how to ever get down on paper. For the most part she appeared to be in a kind of reverie, then the circumstances would waken her and she'd look with that same mildly troubled look sometimes found on customers who come into the shop clutching something worthless that they nevertheless hope I will buy.

'You doing fine, Violet. Just fine,' Alma said at one point. Our eyes met and she glanced away and fell back into the former planetary arrangement of drawer and sitter. What a privilege it is to look at another's face, to explore it without causing offence. Of course you are free to stare at Robyn's blonde vulva out of the glossy glare of a magazine, and there are places in the world where it is possible to shuffle through a curtained-off area to sit and observe the same thing live as it were. But in the end that is just voyeurism without any useful outcome. My mother once asked a man in a picture theatre to stop staring at her. This was before the war, before George's drunken advances, back when my mother lived in a world of neutered desire. Drawing validates what that man in the picture theatre was ticked off for; it lets you get away with a lot more. In a street or inside a shop or in a train it is possible to look at the person at your side or in front of you or across the aisle but it tends to be a stolen opportunity. A quick glance which turns and runs. The bounty is all smash and grab—a neck view, the back of the head (grey hair, a neck wart, skin soft, puce-like, and you return to your newspaper). Eventually an impression forms and we race to fill in what we saw with words—happy, sad, forlorn, moody, anxious, idiotic. But these words are of no use whatsoever when you draw. Things are simply what they are. Neither the shadow beneath the chin nor the drawn one hold strong opinions about themselves.

After an hour the Eliot twins woke. I was pleased for the interruption because drawing all that time was tiring. Violet unscrambled herself and jumped up to get them. They emerged, pink, sleepy, black-eyed, over their mother's shoulder. For a while they were content to roll around on the carpet in piss-reeking napkins while Violet went off to make the tea and put out the biscuits Alma had bought her.

We were all feeling strangely skittish. Violet, I guess, because the exercise wasn't as daunting as she had worried it might be. I shared some of that self-congratulatory mood. Violet and I, together, had come through the first session. Touch wood.

Alma looked smug. Things appeared to be working out. When Violet returned with the tea tray Alma asked her how she was finding the experience. She gave a happy shrug. 'I don't know. It was kind of hard to get used to, you two staring at me...'

'Staring...?' Alma took issue with that. We weren't staring, he said. We were seeing. 'There's a difference. For example, hills stare. Hills are like faces in a crowd.'

Without a blink Violet asked him, 'How about the sea?'

'The sea glances.'

'Trees?'

'In high winds a tree will show an interest in its surroundings. Otherwise, in my experience, trees are reliably discreet. What they see is instantly forgotten.'

I don't know that Violet was hearing any of this, whether any of it sank in. She just wanted to keep Alma going.

'And the beach?' she asked.

'Ah, the beach.' He stopped to think for a moment. 'Pebbles on a beach are completely innocent. Pebbles as we know were blinded at birth which is why a female bather will happily undress in their presence.'

Violet gave a delighted laugh and for the first time in weeks, since we glanced up at the tip to observe her get out of that orange Datsun, we saw a happier, intelligent face.

Now she asked Alma where he'd learned to draw. Surprisingly this was a question I'd never really thought to ask, since what Alma did seemed eternal like the hills and sky and every other part of the world I'd come into; you'd no longer think to ask a question like that of Alma than you would of the sky as to how it had come to be there. Now I was glad Violet asked the question.

There were the drawing classes in hospital all those years ago. I knew about those. But now Alma dismissed those lessons. The man who really taught him was the patient in the next bed along from his own. A thin-lipped watercolourist in for a cataract operation.

This all happened years ago, after the train tragedy. For the next half hour he went back to that time and place, to a moment when his life as it had felt then was in the balance and he drifted about in a semi-conscious state while occasionally surfacing to voices around the next bed.

'You know I hate fruitcake.'

'No, Neil. It's sultanas you don't like. This fruitcake doesn't have any.'

'In that case, why bother? Why make fruit cake without sultanas?'

Silence.

'Edith? Hallo, Edith? Are you still there?'

Alma said the watercolourist was a crotchety old bastard with bandages over his eyes. By his own account he was also the man who had probably saved Alma's life.

In between times of wakefulness he would drift back to a staging post where the accident repeated itself over and over, with the night sky swimming in his vision, yellow trees flashing up at the windows, the sideways angle of the carriage, the surprise of the trees, he said, and their surprise at seeing him. The trees seemed to know. They seemed to know half a second before he did that the train had left the tracks. The trees were trying to point this out to him when he woke to another conversation.

'Is he awake, Edith?'

'No. He's out,' said the woman's voice.

'What does he look like?'

'Young. Thirty. He's got a wire running in and out of his jaw.'

'Well look at his clipboard at the foot of the bed. They'll have the whole story down there.'

'No, Neil. I am not going to look at another patient's notes. They are private and I am not going to…'

'All right, Jesus, Edith, keep your hair on. Let's not broadcast to the world…'

It was weeks before he was allowed up. The morning arrived they pulled the drip from his arm and to celebrate his new-won freedom he and the watercolourist had got up out of bed and taken a walk in the hospital grounds. Up till now the man in for the cataracts was reliant on his wife, Edith, escorting him over the grounds. Now it fell to Alma to direct the blindfolded watercolourist by his elbow across the lawns to the lily ponds where patients in hospital bandages perched between crutches or slumped in wheelchairs.

It was a few days after this that he heard about the drawing classes from Carmichael. Actually, it was one of his colleagues who came in to give them. Carmichael said he wasn't much good; that in fact Alma would be better off with himself as his teacher. They were out in the grounds sunning themselves when the watercolourist became suddenly excited. He'd just had a brilliant idea, he said. It was too good to tell there and then; he urged Alma to lead him back to the ward and got him to look under his bed for the carton of drawing materials and an easel and a stack of paper. The huge eye pads over a bald skull made the elderly watercolourist look like a bull ant. He trembled with excitement. He said, 'Now let's take a crack at that palm tree Edith tells me is outside our window.'

This, Alma said, was the first drawing he ever did, with the watercolourist holding on to his wrist and riding shotgun for the journey through the tree. The watercolourist wasn't an easy passenger. He became angry at one point and barked at Alma, 'I'm not interested in what you think a tree should look like. I'm only interested in the one outside the window.' And once at the start when Alma stalled, which came as a relief to me to hear, the watercolourist told him, 'You'll have a heart attack pondering the wherefores of getting down the detail. Concentrate on the spaces in the branches, draw them, and bingo—the rest of the tree will come into play.'

Soon, within days, hospital staff were crowding the door to watch a man who couldn't speak learn how to draw from a man who couldn't see.

Now Violet put her hand up to ask something.

'Where is he now?'

'The watercolourist? Dead.'

'So sad,' she said, and hurried forth with her next question. 'What then?'

'Well, he talked a lot. Here was a man who couldn't draw for the moment. He couldn't see for the bandages. So he would talk. He would talk all night about his favourite artists.'

It would begin with a soft croaking inquiry in the dark.

'Alma, are you awake? Just give me a sign if you are.'

And Alma said he would have to think for a moment. Was he awake? Could he be bothered with being awake? Then he'd decide, okay, he could be awake. He wasn't exactly doing anything such as sleeping, so he'd bring up his hand and lightly bang the bed head.

'Remember earlier, Alma, I was banging on about Rembrandt. Of course Rembrandt never painted flowers except in pictures of his wife Saskia. Interesting, don't you think? He painted her as Flora, the goddess of love and the goddess of whores. If you like I can get Edith to bring in a book with some nice plates. In a couple of them you can see Saskia looking sluttish. There's one, now let's see, think…Jesus, my memory's deserting me…that's right. *The Prodigal Son in the Tavern.* In this one Saskia is perched on his knee, the slut as tavern trophy. Before them is a peacock pie which according to all the commentaries was a contemporary symbol of pride and sensual pleasure. Twenty years on and all that mischief behind them, Saskia is more elegantly presented. She's in borrowed furs, feathers, lace and velvet. With these props he's levered his wife out of the gin palace and into the monarchal class.'

Silence.

'Well, they had fun together. At least you can say that. You know what Cézanne used to say of his wife? "She likes nothing but Switzerland and lemonade." In his portraits he pays her back with a cold blue palette, adding a fluey red to Mrs C's cheeks. She in turn pays him back with a drawn mouth; her left eye is flooded with an unkind thought. She's probably thinking, Your socks smell, your breath stinks. When you look at a portrait like that, you can hear the cross words whizzing about the studio, and yet, poor Hortense, well this is what you hear: she was said to sit for her husband for hours without moving or talking. Model and painter locked in a death silence like a slow-moving train…One of those marriages where the two combatants are handcuffed to suffer a long, slow suicide.'

Silence.

'Edith tells me I talk too much. Just wave a hand or raise a leg or whatever, Alma, and I'll put a sock in it.'

Silence.

'Tell you what, wouldn't some brandy be nice? A hit of something would put me away.'

Silence.

'I imagine you're a Jack Daniels man. I'll get Edith to smuggle some in. We can pipe it down a straw into you.'

Silence

'Funny though how they all put their wives in their pictures. Rembrandt squeezed two wives into his portfolio. He was twenty-six when he met Saskia, forty-three when he met Hendrickje. The Hendrickje version of Flora is more sober than its predecessor. He went outdoors with H—didn't with S. I'm thinking of that beautiful work *Hendrickje Bathing in a Stream.*'

Silence.

'One artist (I can't remember his name. I want to say Bonnard but Cézanne's keeps barging in), he points to a shadow beneath a tree and says, "See that shadow? Does it not look purple? Then paint it purple. And as for the tree, save your most beautiful green for it." I may be making this up, but the point remains. The invitation is not to transfigure but to heighten the emotional engagement. Alma?'

Alma flung his hand against the bed frame and the water-colourist continued.

'Constable described trees and meadows. Well, frankly, he might as well not have been there. The French painters by contrast put up signposts across the countryside saying, "I was here. I saw that. I saw that tree and its shadow!"'

Listening to all this, day in day out, Alma said, was like

travelling in a foreign country where at first you don't understand the language spoken all around you, then one day it
happens, understanding drops into place and suddenly you find
you can communicate. Drawing, he said, had been like that
for him.

The Carmichaels owned some coastal land, scrappy, unpro-
ductive, lovely for living though, fruit trees and vegetable beds.
Edith was the gardener. They insisted he convalesce in their
home and it was there that he learned to milk cows and lop
heads off chickens. The watercolourist and Edith had two
grown-up daughters and for the time he was there Alma slept
in one of the girls' rooms. Her dolls were still as she had left
them, arranged along the top of a bookcase. Her crayon drawings from childhood were still pinned to the wall. It was a
fitting environment—it served to remind him of his status in
this new world of drawing in which he was feeling his way. It
was like tearing out a sheet of paper and starting all over again.

When I got back to the shop to relieve Guy I had the strange
impression of a walrus blinking back at me. My head was
racing with various thoughts, stuff that Alma has shared with
me and Violet, and Guy was just too big and slow and ponder-
ous. It was the same when I got home and Frances looked up
from her jigsaws and waved through the glass doors; I thought,
things could be worse between us. At least it's not Switzerland
and lemonade. That made me smile, then I found myself laughing. *Switzerland and lemonade.* And now Frances got up from
her work table. I'd made her curious. She came through the
glass doors. She was smiling too. 'What?' she kept asking.

'What?' I shook my head. It was impossible to tell her. It would be impossible to repeat the phrase 'Switzerland and lemonade' and for her to get it; I'd have to explain where I'd heard it, at the Eliots' of all places, with Alma quoting from a watercolourist long dead.

In order to accommodate me the drawing sessions were scheduled for midday. That way I could get Guy in to cover for me. It was a good deal cheaper without my mother's charity days, and I was pleased to help Guy with a little pocket money, hardly enough though to keep a family ticking over, and when I mentioned that he gave me sad, slobbering look.

'Actually, Kath and the kids are still over at her mother's.'

It was just a temporary thing, he added, but given the speed at which he looked away I seriously wondered about that. I went out the back way, and as I closed the door I heard Guy's soft padding footsteps and the clatter of the beaded curtain.

I drove out to the tip to pick up Alma. With the reek of the tip all over him we continued on to Beach Road. Alma was grim; he sat tight-lipped. Something was bothering him. I looked across once or twice for him to spit it out and he just looked away.

I mentioned I'd seen George Hands the other day—but no Victoria.

'I had a drink with Victoria, and George, separately.'

'Sad about Dean.' Alma cast his eyes on the road ahead as if this went without saying.

Finally as we bumped along Beach Road, he said, 'This Ophelia woman, Harry. Tell me it's none of my business and I'll leave it alone. But you know how I feel about Frances. I think she's a wonderful woman and whatever difficulties...'

'Hold it there. Who told you about Ophelia?'

'Alice. She got it from Frances. I don't think she will mind me telling you that.'

'Fine. I don't know anyone called Ophelia.'

Alma turned his head to look at me hard for an uncomfortably long few seconds. Once that side of my face had turned red he looked away, satisfied.

'I've known you for too long, Harry,' he started to say. But I stopped him.

'I can't believe how out of hand this has got. Look, I don't know anyone by the name of Ophelia. I do not know of anyone called that in this community. Who the hell would call anyone Ophelia?'

'Frances has an idea it's that black woman you had that thing with in London.'

'There was no "thing" as you put it. There was nothing.'

'As you wish. As I started out saying, just tell me if it's none of my business and I'll shut up.'

'Fine,' I said.

For the next minute we listened to the stones flying up at the chassis. Alma stared out his side window and I stared out mine. Finally I couldn't stand it any longer.

'It's pure imagination. The whole thing is. It was a dream I had. I've already had this out with Frances. I can't believe she spoke to Alice about it. We talked and I explained and put her mind at ease and now she's happy.'

Alma still had his head in the side window.

'Alice is upset,' he said at last. 'She was the one who asked me to speak to you.'

'Now you have and now you know, and now it's over. A misunderstanding in about three different directions at last count.'

'As you wish.'

At the Eliots' I was in no mood to draw. I couldn't sit still and concentrate. Alma's instruction didn't sink in. I could hardly hear him for all the other stuff going on in my head. It upset me that Ophelia was everyone's business, it was essentially a private matter. For all the trouble it was giving me I might as well have accepted Ophelia's invitation. I should have played out the whole ritualistic dance to the end, and at least have the satisfaction of doing what apparently everyone back here at home had assumed to have happened. The facts were less spectacular. I remember I had put my beer down in the dark—her flashing white mouth and some delicious tropical smear of perfume—and Ophelia reaching for my hand and missing. Instead it brushed across the top of my trousers and as a kind of automatic reaction I found myself reaching for my beer again. What had been heating up suddenly turned down to cordial, and within minutes, as it now seemed, there was a puzzling withdrawal of interest before she upped and left with that glass held before her.

'You're not drawing,' Alma said at one point.

Violet broke out of her pose and stared at me.

'Is something wrong?'

'No,' said Alma. 'He's got other stuff on his mind.'

A few minutes later the twins woke—much earlier than Violet had planned. She had put them down only an hour before. Now she was nervously apologetic. I thought she must be worried that she wouldn't get her money. She tried putting them to sleep again. But when she tiptoed back to the front of the house and resumed her pose it wasn't the same— there was the tilt of concentration in her eyes, her head angled, cocked, for the small tinny voices floating up the hallway. Progressively they grew louder, whimpering, nagging, screeching, persistent, until at last Violet jumped up to attend them. She tiptoed back and within a minute they had started up again. We tried to ignore it; it was hard to think that it wasn't malice —they were just babies after all—but the bawling was intolerable and in the end Alma looked up and shook his head. Violet disappeared and this time the triumphant twins turned up with their black eyes glowing over their young mother's shoulders.

She put them down on the carpet and tried resuming her former pose. But the twins kept going; they kept rolling up against our feet. One of the twins, Jackson, I think it was, began pulling on Alma's trouser leg and in the end he put down his pencil with a sigh of exasperation and said, 'It's not working, sweetheart.'

Violet gave a hateful look to her babies who were sabotaging her potential earnings. She thought maybe they would go back down if they could stay up a while and tire themselves.

'Up to you, Harry', Alma said.

I glanced at my watch.

Poor Violet. The wheels in her mind must have been spinning for her to come up with an idea that would prevent the loss of chargeable time because before I could reply she got our attention with, 'This isn't the first time I've been asked to model.'

Alma closed his eyes. I gave the far wall a doubtful look.

'It's true,' she said.

It was in a town far from here. She didn't say where, exactly, but at the same time it was a town resonantly familiar once she spoke of its plans for a commemorative coin. This was an example of the kind of civic pride we had once gone in for. She said a search was launched to find the face that would be minted on the side of the coin. For a short time she had thought it would be her own.

Everything she said spoke of the ideal face radiating hope but not in a beggarly way. It would be in profile because a profile offers a certain decisiveness. That's the thing about the profile. It isn't just a face laid on its side like a lily pad. The line from the corner of the eye to the point of the nose indicates where the future lies. And this is what people would get in their hot little hands.

What happened was this. Violet happened to be standing on the porch to her house when a man in a van came to an abrupt halt—a squeal of rubber on tarseal, a forward jog of the chassis as the driver's face turned in the side window. It was like he had been looking for her all this while. Violet thought he must be a courier in search of an address. No one, she said, ever came to their house in such a deliberate fashion. He hadn't even parked his van properly—she could still hear the engine idling.

She assumed he was after directions. So she looked up at the clouds and counted to three; when she dared to look again she saw he had come no closer but had stopped at the edge of the dry lawn to look at her, as though he was checking that his initial impression was right. He shifted his head to the side, squinting, a squeeze of judgment in his face because he had been travelling at forty k's when he had seen her, this barefoot waif in the light and shadow of her parents' porch.

Violet's arms were stiff at her sides. The man's stare made her feel awkward. She pulled down the hem of her skirt and experienced that annoying rise of butterflies in her tummy, which was what she felt like when she entered rooms in which people were already seated and acquainted.

The annoying thing was, she said, the thing that would get her offside with her father in the first place, was this idea that she had deliberately sought the man's attention, as if by raising an eyelid she could bring traffic to a halt. As if in spite of herself and whatever else her intentions might be, she could detach a man from his van, and even—or especially in a neighbourhood as scruffy as hers—have him leave his senses behind him where he'd left the engine of his van running. Even the neighbour's dog sat up. The clouds seemed to drift down for a closer look. She told her father all she'd done was come out for air. He seemed to think her face was a lure and that her cast had been perfect to catch that wily trout in a passing van. But in fact—as she told her father—she had been thinking she would cross the road and see if the neighbour's dog was dead. She had stood on the porch a full five minutes and it hadn't moved a whisker of hair. She didn't want to touch it though in case it was; she didn't want to touch death. Three weeks earlier there had been a death in the street and she had stood at a distance watching the ambulance people pass the body up through the back doors of the ambulance parked next to the green recycling bins and bulging black rubbish bags. These were her random thoughts when her father asked her what the hell she had in mind standing out on the porch if she wasn't looking to lure a man—if she wasn't some suburban siren operating from her porch.

And who the devil was this passing ship, so called? As it happened, breathing calmly and outwardly at the thought now, she wasn't sure what she would do. The day wasn't as inviting as she had hoped it would be. The sky was too blue; it made the windows appear dull and witless. They made her wonder at what moment, precisely, did the man along the road decide to drive his car into the garage and close and bolt the doors and engineer the exhaust pipe up through the floorboards of a car she had seen pass up and down this same street with groceries, sometimes the man's wife aboard, observant always of the speed limit. Days like this made you ache to be elsewhere.

She was still to discover that elsewhere. She was no longer at school, but not yet at work. There was a home, but a home with so little space, so little air of her own. She had come outside to the porch to escape the whine of her baby siblings. Some days their sounds drilled into her brain. Some days her mother lay like a sow, the faces of her tiny brothers panting and suckling and sometimes turning their faces to their older sister standing in the door. They could look so knowing, so alert to the circumstances they had arrived to; almost as though they knew that if they didn't get this attention now they would get nothing later. Some days were so unbearably alike that she wished she could just draw her curtains and default on them.

She didn't say any of this to her father. He would say she was spoilt. Maybe slap her and call her ugly names as he was prone to do when he worked himself up. Maybe she was disporting herself like a common slut? Why else would a total stranger bowl up with his visiting card and leave a van running?

It was about now that she noticed his camera. About now she brightened. And this despite what her father would later scoff at—any old jackrabbit with a camera. Some seducer! Her father would walk to the window and point out to the street. 'Out there, you say? Out there our friend pulled up and offered you the rainbow?'

She recalled his keen oval face; an honest face, she remembered thinking at the time. A clever face spinning out words, entreaties. *Coin. Visage. Profile. Opportunity. Fame.* The words linking to form a rope with which he could, the man said, with her blessing haul her out of this world of burnt lawns and finger-smudged windows. If she would take hold of this rope he was offering she would find herself catapulted—that's what he'd said, catapulted! And that's when she began to laugh, which was okay because the man laughed with her and said, 'Hell I know what I must sound like.'

She remembered the clipboard with the ballpoint attached by string. He needed her signature, which she gladly gave. And when she handed back the clipboard he nodded back in the direction of the house to ask if Mum was home. In that direction came the noise of toilets flushing, doors closing. She said her mother wouldn't mind which was true up to a point as far as raffles or lotteries were concerned. The man's offer seemed to sit squarely in the lottery basket.

Now that he had her signature he fell back to examining the house. His face was not quite as friendly as before. He said, 'We'll take that picture, shall we?'

She stared back at the lens and on the edge of hearing babies were calling and crying. The man told her to stop looking so cross, then she heard a click and then another. 'Hold it there,' he said. 'Just like that. Good…Good.' *Click. Click. Click.* He raised his head, smiled, lofted his eyes past her to the house and hurriedly rolled on more film. This was definitely one of the strangest things to happen to her. She'd left the house to get some air and now look what was happening. She was having her photo taken.

'We're almost there,' he told her. 'Almost. Hold it. Hold it… Yup. That is gorgeous.' *Click. Click. Click.* Still with his eye attached to the camera the man had asked, 'What's your favourite side? Sunny side or the other?' She didn't know what he meant by the other until he explained, 'Your deep secretive side, honey bunch. The side that no one gets to see. That piece of you that lies out of bounds. That part which each of us takes to the grave more or less intact.' He swung the camera up to his face and once more asked if Mum was around. He took his face away from the lens and poked at the dials. She realised she was being given the chance to lie if she wished. Presented with that option something pushed her to say that her mother was in there but she was tied up. He received the news thoughtfully and appeared to make a snap decision there and then. He reached inside his pocket and handed her his business card. He told her he really thought she was a good shot. He said, 'I hope you realise it's not every day that you get your face minted on to the side of a coin. It could change your life, Violet. Think of all the places you'd end up! In people's deep pockets. In their hands. Set on velvet cushions. Life is short, gorgeous. It's over in a blink. If you're not going to climb Everest this isn't a bad option…' She was thinking as he spoke, thinking that what he said made sense, thinking that she would like to…'

'Costs twenty-five bucks to enter and I need the signature of your parents, one or the other,' and as he glanced back towards the house he thought to add, 'or a guardian.'

Later she watched her father's mumbling lips move down the clauses and sub-clauses on the form. To hurry him up she pointed to where his signature was required and he snatched the form away.

'Damn it, Violet, you don't just sign any old thing. I have to read it first.'

He went back to reading—but in a little while she saw him sneak a look at her and she knew he wasn't reading. He was putting her in her place. All the sharp angles in his face and his narrow eye-slot spoke of denying her, because to deny her would mean she was back in the same sinking ship. She had to learn she wasn't anything special. She might as well get used to reining in false hopes, otherwise it would lead nowhere but to disappointment.

Later, she sat on the edge of her mother's bed. Her mother was nursing and in that musky half-light she sat fondling a fifty-cent coin. On one side was a young-looking queen with a tiara, on the other the raised edges of the wind-filled sails of the *Endeavour*. It was a funny way to bring up the subject with her mother. She only wanted to know if she had signed the form that would allow her portrait to go forward into the competition.

The Queen caught her mother's eye and she began to reminisce: there were two occasions she had seen the Queen; once riding in the back of an open car looking floral and waving a gloved hand, and more recently when she had opened parliament and the disgrace of our prime minister choosing a smart trouser suit over a dress. Her mother had opinions on such matters. As Violet's youngest brothers suckled on her teats she talked about the Queen's problems with her own children, their marital difficulties, which just went to show no matter who you were, even the Queen, trouble could sneak up and touch you on the shoulder, though more often than not, sighed her mother, it was trouble in the shape and form of offspring.

'Now about that coin nonsense, Violet, if you fall for a clunker of a line like that, the first man who pretends to speak just half the truth will have your pants off in a flash.' A half-stifled laugh rose in her chest, creating a rolling wave that made the two babies bob their heads. One became detached and its little red face looked up angrily. It opened its mouth to cry but had no time to. Her mother, unsighted, shoved her large nipple back in to the complaining mouth and the tiny package grunted obscenely and went on sucking. Here was rude life unminted, breathing, preoccupied. Her mother hadn't brushed her hair that day. A stale odour of old bed sweat stuck in Violet's throat when her mother shifted the duvet. She continued in her tired dreamy voice, 'I don't know why Charles doesn't marry that horsy-looking woman. Why do people make things so difficult for themselves?' She drew in the silence and thought deeply. 'I don't want you going to that photographer by yourself. I'll speak to your father.'

Her mother was suddenly aware that she had slid too far down in the bed because now there were two suction noises as she detached herself without ceremony and dragged herself back up the sheets, a movement like a heavy seal dragging itself up the beach. The angles of the room changed and now that she could see the window a softer, more considerate voice came from her.

'At least you have your good looks, Violet. That's no secret. You have a head on you. And just by the way, between me and you, whole cities make room for a pretty girl. It's not supposed to be so, it's not the way you probably hear it at school, but it's the bloody truth, Violet. There's other things a mother should say so I'll say them now. I have always found it better to allow other people to tie themselves up with their foolish tongues. You might also want to think about using Optrex to make your eyes nice and bright, and one last thing. A thin smile will serve you better than a generous smile. Don't ask me why. And don't laugh too loud otherwise men in snakeskin shoes will take you for all tits and teeth and an easy lay.'

Violet listened politely and when her mother had finished saying her piece she was able to counter with an interesting opinion of her own. She asked her mother, 'Which side of your face do you prefer to show? Sunny side or the other?'

The question that had seemed to just blow in from nowhere lodged in her mother's face and pulled her away from the dark boozy countryside of memory. Gobsmacked, she asked, 'What do you mean, sunny side?' And Violet was able to repeat the photographer's sentiments, pretty much word for word what he had said, and watch with delight the effect these had on her mother. Something like a shift of light from the window to a distant corner of the room; a shift in worldly know-how, the unthinkable possibility that Violet might know something about the world out there that had escaped her mum and passed her by.

Two nights later her mother intercepted her in the hall, took her by the hand, led her into her bedroom and said, 'Just come and talk with me.'

Violet could smell the booze on her mother and after she shook free she went out to the kitchen where she found her father sitting at the kitchen table next to his drink. His face was covered in mischief. Delight showed even in his molars. In one hand he held the form from the photographer and in the other a lighter.

After she had been paid, after she heard the car go, she sat by the window looking at the listless sea and the grey sky and wondered where Dean was. 'Where are you Dean? Have you gone out to the world or have you disappeared inside of that painted one? Where are you, Dean?' she said back to the day. 'Where are you?' And she turned her thoughts back to where she had first found him.

She had left home and was on a bus on her way to one of those cities where her mother promised buildings would jump out of the way to make space for a pretty young woman. Her face was lost in its own window reflection. Bits of countryside tangled in her hair gave way to motorway, housing development, traffic, street lights and finally the city itself. When she got off the bus not knowing where to go she followed the national flags of two foreign girl backpackers. She didn't want to lose them. She didn't want to turn up someplace as a lost dog.

The buildings, she noticed, were stubbornly anchored in place. They seemed not to know what her mother had said about them, their windswept foyers unwelcoming with that shooing noise. Two more turns and the backpackers led her into a busy street with cafés and lights and people entering and leaving a supermarket.

She followed the girls into a backpackers' hostel where she paid for a first-floor room overlooking the busy street and that night she sat on the edge of her bed looking down at the street, at the people going in and out of the laundromat, the carousel lights of the picture theatre. She was there several days when she noticed the foreign girls had left. There were new faces. And around this time the manager, Dale, a large man who sat in a low leather armchair so that his head and shoulders never rose higher than the desk top, asked her if she'd like a job setting up the buffet, filling the dishwasher, mopping down the halls. It meant she got her room for nothing, and that was a saving while she looked for a job. She had to find something because there would be no going back. If she went back her world would close up like a clam.

She got a job as a trainee stock controller at a paint warehouse. The hardest part was boredom. The next-hardest part was walking on the concrete aisles. For hours she and two Chinese girls who didn't have much English between them, but who nonetheless were quick to pick up the various codes of paint pots, walked up and down aisles under a vast roof of white plastic light.

The movies were her treat. She went there as often as she could afford to, deliberately seating herself next to someone else, but no one ever spoke to her. Sometimes there was brief eye contact before both parties retreated into the bashful dark.

The traveller who made her pregnant arrived in her life at 2 a.m. She woke to hammering downstairs, pulled on a coat over her undies and tiptoed down the stairs to open the door to a backpacker like any other, the practised heave of the pack through the door, the accented English, the apology for the lateness of the hour. As he straightened up from lowering his pack he said, 'You were asleep. I am sorry.'

It didn't matter. There was a room left, one room, and he breathed a sigh of relief to hear that, but then came the catch; the key was in Dale's office and he wouldn't be in until 8 a.m. However, if he liked he could sleep on her floor.

He answered by picking up his pack. And as they climbed the stairs she was amazed by her offer—it had just flowed out of her without any pause between thought and speech.

She lay awake the rest of the night listening to the heavy sleep of the traveller. When she got up to go downstairs to set out the buffet he raised his forearm and laid it discreetly across his eyes. Then as she was letting herself out she heard him say, 'Thank you. My name is Hans.'

As it was a Sunday she accepted his offer to accompany her around town. They visited the museum. Walked in the park. Talked with increasing ease and intimacy, especially after he told her a joke about a crow that she didn't really get but recognised when to laugh, which she did a bit generously, she worried about this, but needn't have because he slipped his arm around her after that. They hired paddleboats and afterwards sat in a courtyard café. They laughed. This time he touched her hair. He said what nice hair she had, and she closed her eyes and drifted on praise. When they reached the steps of the hostel she glanced up at her window and felt a surge of joy. For once she was where she wanted to be, on the threshold of something exciting and new. And as they arrived on the landing, their sides touching, he held up her room key and asked, 'Yes? No?'

'Yes,' she said.

He was gone a few days later. He left while she was at work. He had South America to do, then North America. Within a week she was back sitting next to strangers in picture theatres.

Three weeks later, feeling queasy, she bought a pregnancy test kit from a pharmacy and spent the best part of a Saturday sitting on the edge of her bed daring herself to find out. She thought it might be worth a day of not knowing. How would she spend that day of not knowing? The pictures? A walk? Whatever she did it would be with the knowledge it might never be the same after that. In the end she didn't do any of these things. It was enough to experience the thought. It was enough to hold the options in her hand and see the world gently tilt this way and that. In the end she lay down on the bed and fell asleep. When she woke it was dark and instantly she knew what to do. It took less than ten minutes and she sat on the bed dazzled with the sequence of events. This was one of those times her mother meant her to ring home. She couldn't bring herself to do that.

But she had to tell someone so she decided to tell the skinny boy who kept coming in from the loading bay to sneak looks at her. She found Dean in the canteen and sat herself next to him. He was hopelessly shy. He would turn his head away to take a bite of his ham roll. She introduced herself and because she actually had to ask for Dean's name she thought he probably wasn't the right person, then two days later he'd seen her rubbing her stomach and asked if she was all right.

One afternoon a large number of paint samples fell out the end of a loose carton. The cans wheeled and sprawled. She stood disabled by the task before her. She didn't even hear Dean sneak up behind her. He gathered up the cans in half the time it would have taken her.

He was more talkative these days. Warming to her, she supposed. In the canteen she heard about his travel plans. As soon as he had saved for a van he would roam in whichever direction the road took him. He'd just drive anywhere and everywhere until he found a place he liked and he would pull over and see what that part of the world had to offer. As he talked she felt an envy, envied him his plans and his going places. Her mother had got stuck, and now she would be like her.

The gentlest questions seemed to come out of his white chattering frame. Sometimes he would look away at the moment of asking, as if to distance himself from a question such as what names she liked best. Which one did she think would be right for her baby? It was baby. Not babies. The shock that she was carrying twins would come much later.

Dean had made up his mind it was a boy. She had liked that, liked it that Dean involved himself in this way; it made it feel like a joint project.

Away from Dean though she worried about supporting herself and her baby. She would have to give up work. She would have to find somewhere else to live. At night she sat on the edge of her bed staring down into the glistening road streaked with neon and reflections; it reminded her of a school trip to the rock pools, they were searching out different niches. She would have to find one of her own; knowing this and at the same time not being able to do anything about it drove her to doing something she never thought she'd do. Because she had to do something, make preparations of some sort and feel that she was progressing towards the new life arrangement, she began to take paint from the warehouse. She had never stolen anything in her life. But now she filled her coat pockets with paint samples, taking some home every day. At night she got them out from under her bed and out of her wardrobe and spread the small sample cans over the floor, arranging them in pyramids, proof that she was building for her future. And because it was the only thing available she couldn't stop stealing.

One day she felt another person's hand in her pocket. She nearly jumped out of her skin. But it was only Dean, straight as a bowling pin at her side. He nodded down at the paint sample in his hand. 'It was sticking out,' he said. So he knew. Possibly he'd known for a while, the way he watched her; he watched her like a hawk.

A week later the thin boy in the all-weather T-shirt saved her from herself again. The siren went for what she thought was one of those tiresome fire drills. It was near the end of the day when they filed out into the yard where the warehouse manager, a rarely seen man, came out, removed his glasses and rubbed at his eyes, then addressed them on an entirely different matter. In his twelve years, he said, this was the first time he had had to deal with the matter of employee theft. Paint was disappearing out of the warehouse. He said some other things. Out there in the frigid yard the word 'amnesty' had a jailhouse sound to it. She tuned out and filed back with the others, the line moving past the manager and the supervisor; and it was as she was asked to step aside that Dean rushed up and rudely asked her for his coat back. Dean must have seen and understood what was about to happen. A storm gathered in his face as he demanded back his coat. It wasn't his and yet he was so fierce about it she didn't want to deny him. As she shrugged out of it and passed it to him she could feel the sagging weight of the pockets, and in that little transaction all interest shifted from her to Dean.

She didn't see him in the cartage dock after that. She didn't see him until she left for the day and across the road she spied him in that orange Datsun she'd seen him in before. He was waiting for her, because as she appeared he climbed out and grinned over the rooftop at her.

He said he didn't like the job anyway.

They went to the movies that night. And the next day when she finished work he was waiting for her again. In the car over the smell of oil rags and the noise of the fan heater that smelt of melted plastic they talked and talked. She had an idea he liked talking in the car. That way he didn't have to wholly commit to whatever he said because he had to concentrate on the road. His eyes darted left and right, and sometimes they seemed to go right up into his forehead if he had to think about something or pull on the handbrake. One night when they were driving nowhere in particular she asked him if he wanted to kiss her and Dean was able to nod and at the time accelerate as the lights turned green.

Later, in the hostel, after sneaking Dean upstairs and giggling under the duvet, he picked at her. Finding his way around. So this was a breast? And this was the part between the legs? She felt like a stocktaking. It was not quite dark in her room. The curtains she'd left open, and the streetlights played over Dean's bare white body. She looked up at the green and white arrangement in his face. Dean was like a gecko to touch—his skin was cold, everything was drawn tight over his forehead and bony ribs; his fingers were bone and skin like someone severely dehydrated. When he arrived at his moment he released his breath in a series of shortlived hisses.

16

Violet had gone a long way into herself to retrieve the story about the photographer. Alma scoffed at the word 'photography'. He said all photography proves is that the camera worked. He possibly felt a bit more short-changed than I did. Stories were fine but he was there to draw. There was an awkward moment when it came time to leave and the unspoken subject of payment jarred the air. Violet was hopeful and at the same time tense, her arms stiff at her sides. When I plunged my hand into my pocket her eyes automatically followed. Alma had no choice but to follow suit.

'Less than ideal,' he said as we got into the van.

After I dropped him home I drove back to the shop to relieve Guy. Around five I rang Frances to say I would be late. I locked up and went to the back room to find the special edition on assorted African nudes. There was one woman, clothed as it happens, with a gorgeous pear-shaped mouth. She walked along a path through shoulder-high corn with a basket balanced on her head, a machete swinging from her hand. This image was more like that of someone from the Caribbean, not that I have been there, but it looked like it could be Ophelia's home and that I was entering the blue and green landscape that she had played in as a young girl. As least that was my version.

I kept switching between the clothed woman walking through the corn and the open-legged shots, but in the end—well, eventually—I found myself not so much bored as unsatisfied. I wanted more. I wanted to know more. Actually what I wanted was to hear her voice. And I wanted her to hear me sober and sound of mind.

I knew she worked for a bank. Where? What bank? Then I heard myself say out loud, 'What the hell is that?' Staring back at me was a stuffed polar bear. It was hard to believe that it had taken me this long to spot it. Guy hadn't said a word when I came in the back door. Its glassy eyes stared at me. It stood on its hind legs, its forearms extended like a wrestler's, a head higher than me. There was a tag hanging from its right paw. 'On appro' it said, with name and contact details of the person it could go straight back to in the morning.

I looked up at the bear's sad eyes. It must have been there the whole time I was thumbing through the African spreads. Somehow the whole unsettling experience of the polar bear helped to flush out the name of Ophelia's bank. I remembered then that she had said South London. Definitely she said South London. I rang up international directory and within minutes I was speaking to the bank in London asking for Ophelia. Ophelia who? Oh God, wait. Think. In the end I had to describe her. The person at the other end said they had three Ophelias. One in accounts, a cashier and a personnel manager.

'That's her. And can I have her surname, please?'

Ophelia Williams. A second later Ophelia Williams was speaking to me.

'Hallo, how can I help?'

It was her. That voice. Accentless, educated, interested. Helpful. And now puzzled—she had no idea who I was. Then she was puzzled in a laugh-out-loud kind of way.

'Who did you say you were? Mayor who?'

Then she was alarmed as if she may have to ring the cops at any moment. 'Wait. Where are you calling from?'

I was too embarrassed to carry on. The creepy night-time menagerie effect of the shop—shadowed stag heads, golf bags, piled mattresses—made me seem even more ridiculous.

'But you are the Ophelia who sometimes goes to the Fridge in Brixton?'

There was a slight hesitation then she answered in an out-side-of-work kind of way, 'Yes, I'm that Ophelia...' It was an admission, sad, regretful. I had torn it out of her but she didn't want to go back there right at this moment during office hours. Especially with a nut she apparently didn't know, and more joltingly of whom she had no memory. A shooting star in a night of shooting stars, interesting and diverting for the moment but that was all.

I could hear her tapping a pencil from half a world away. I said, 'Thank you. I'm sorry. I made a mistake,' and hung up.

For a while I sat in the dark, drum-rolling my fingers. I wish I could report on some clear path of thought but there wasn't one. I sat there with my loss, thinking what to do with it. I don't recall any conscious decision but after a while I stood up from my desk and went into the back room to get the magazine with the African spreads. There is a dumpster bin out the back. I tossed it in there. I felt like I was removing something in order to improve something else. Feelings, strategies—none was especially clear at this point. Except on my way home I had an inkling of what to do when I looked up at the clean painted side of the Lyric Theatre and remembered the lurid and mocking scene that used to sit there of two huge moa walking through reeds at a lakeside. It had been awful to have that glowering back at us after the collapse of the Gondwanaland theme park idea. Its cheap house paint seemed to sneer back at the civic vanity and greed that had put it there. I had to look at it every day to and from work until one day, sick and tired of hearing me complain about it, Alma had said, 'Why not paint over it?'

This was the night I picked up a pencil and began to draw Frances on the back of a power bill envelope. She looked up from her jigsaw and asked what I was doing. She sounded puzzled—she still didn't know about my involvement in the drawing lessons at the Eliots'.

'What does it look like I'm doing?'

The chair leg scratched on the floor as she got up.

'Now you've moved,' I said.

She didn't know whether to grin or call for help. She moved her hands to her hips.

'Harry, what exactly are you drawing?'

'I'm drawing you, Frances.' I pretended to be drawing, head down, though in fact I wasn't because that is not how you draw; at least it isn't the way Alma had expounded. You look at what you are hoping to draw—not down at the sheet of paper. But Frances didn't know that. She sat down again and turned to her scissored pieces of landscape.

'You're being silly,' she said.

That was all right. I could carry on drawing. She was in her dressing-gown, a characteristic pose: right elbow on table, hand supporting the side of her head, head turned slightly away and down at the scraps of paper covering her bench space. She was back to considering different scenes, this lake with that mountain; I'd seen a covered bridge from Vermont and a horse-drawn carriage outside Prague. Now the pencil squeaked on the envelope and she looked up.

'Harry, stop it.'

I waited for her to turn back to the jigsaw and resumed. This time she spoke down at her desktop.

'You're being silly and I wish you'd stop. I don't see what you're trying to prove.'

I told her I wasn't trying to prove anything.

'I'm just drawing you. Be still, please, Fran.'

That's all I said, nothing more. She brought a shy hand up to her cheek, her delighted cheek as it appeared from where I sat.

'Really, Harry? Is that what you're doing? Drawing me?'

'Rembrandt used to paint his wife,' I said, and I saw my wife think things were getting queerer by the second. Rembrandt. Harry's never mentioned him before.

I didn't say anything more since it seemed self-evident what I was doing now. I wished she would be still, however. She really needed to be in better light. At the Eliots', Alma always took care to arrange the light. Light and shadow, he liked to say, are in constant negotiation as to which parts of the world the other can have.

The spare chair at the nearer end of her workbench would be better. I stood up and pointed with my pencil.

'I'm sorry Fran, can you change places? The reflection from the window is getting in the way.'

She looked amused to hear this. She repeated what I had said. 'The reflection in the window...' Her tone was gently mocking, but that was all right. After all, what did I know about light and shadow? I heard myself regurgitate some of the stuff Alma had to say on the subject and Frances began to laugh in a quiet, pleasant, head-shaking way. She couldn't believe this strange chick that had hatched before her eyes. Could it actually walk? And because I guess she wanted to see what would happen next, she happily complied.

I helped her shift the chair and table into a better arrangement. I played around with the desk lamp and ended up with a nicely shadowed effect. Then I walked back to the chair, picked up the pencil and envelope and waited for Frances to compose herself.

Of course what happened next was entirely predictable. She sat as she would like to be seen, her hands flat on her knees. She raised her face with a smile that aimed to please. But that wasn't Frances at all. It was simply the face that she was willing to show, entirely different from the one I saw devouring the landscapes scattered over her work bench. So I didn't draw. I did what I did out at the Eliots' and instead I just looked and from time to time she asked me, 'Is this all right?' or, 'Are you finished yet?'

After a while she didn't say anything. Her face began to relax and settle and I was reminded of the very last ripple moving to the edges of a pond, the final reminder of the stone thrown into its calm middle just a few minutes earlier.

For a long time I waited. Frances was so still I could have walked up and pinched her skin. She looked like she did the first time I saw her at high school. She was walking with a group of girls but at the same time she was apart. She looked now as she did then, as if waiting for the world to come and touch her.

Frances was always tall for her age. She deliberately walked half a step more slowly than the other girls to prevent her loping ahead like a giraffe. Of all the girls in our final year Frances was everyone's favourite bet to be first on the train out of here. You never really felt you had her full attention. You could see her long legs walking past the hills and the ranges to that distant and as yet unnamed place that waited to claim her. Maybe it was the result of her putting so much effort into appearing graceful, but the first time she gave up the far horizon for what lay nearer and more conveniently to hand she discovered me.

I don't know how long I stared at Frances—ten, twenty minutes. But suddenly she drew a long breath and snapped out of wherever she had been.

'Finished?' she asked.

'For now I am.'

Immediately she sprang up. I knew what she was after and turned the envelope over.

'Come on, Harry. Don't be a tease.'

'I'll show you when I'm finished.'

'You said it's a sketch. A sketch by definition is finished when you are finished.' She demonstrated with some rapid brushstrokes in the air. 'There. Done,' she said.

'This is more work in progress,' I explained.

'A work in progress,' she said after me, so we were back to that. She looked at me carefully, trying to see behind the corners of my very being. 'You have been acting so strange lately. Ever since you got back from London.'

She gave me one last searching look and dropped her eyes to the envelope in my hand.

'Let me see. A peek. Just a little peek. Come on, Harry. The world won't end. What are you trying to hide? You've seen something, haven't you? You've seen something and now you're out to hide it. One little peek, come on Harry.'

I told her, 'There's really nothing to see.'

That's when she made a half-hearted grab for the envelope. I whipped it away and she said, All right, fuck you, Mayor. You can't just draw me and not let me see. That's the new rule from now on.'

'I will. I will show you, I promise, okay, but not until I finish it.'

In fact I'd just had this wonderful idea. With Alma's help I would do a portrait of Frances and unveil it for her birthday. The idea was beaming out of me.

'One teensy look won't cause the world to end. Jesus, Harry.'

She'd worn me down and so this time I decided, what the hell, and handed over the envelope for all the good that would do. I watched her turn it over. She turned it over again. Confusion and hurt hung from her face.

'There's nothing here, you teasing Mayorfuck.' She threw the envelope back at me. 'I thought you were drawing. You said you were and I actually believed you.'

'I was looking. Looking is a preliminary step in the process.'

'Process,' she said. 'There you go again.'

By now I must admit that I was enjoying the baffling curiosity I'd become in my wife's eyes.

'What do you mean "just looking"? Not thinking?'

'Once, maybe twice, but most of the time I was just looking.'

'You must have thought something. You can't have just looked and not thought something.'

What she said was true. I knew what she was thinking—I must have thought something because to look is to take physical stock. To look is to weigh up and judge, at least that is what she was thinking. Had Alma Martin been in on this conversation he would have butted in then and said, 'Well, actually no, that's not quite right. When you are drawing you are actually learning how to see. You do this through looking. Looking is untarnished glass. No green bits of judgment hang from its lens. In order to draw you must learn to see how things are— not how you wish they were, or once were.'

This piece of insight from Alma did a quick dash through my mind; I didn't really feel I could bring it off were I to say it out loud. So what I told Fran was this.

'Well actually, yes, I was thinking. I was thinking about your mouth.'

Predictably she placed her hand there. There must be something wrong with it. There must be some defect.

Now she looked worried.

'My lips are too thin. Is that it? Well thank you, Harry. I really can do without you highlighting that to the world.'

'I love your mouth. There is nothing wrong with your mouth. I was just looking. I should have been drawing. Frances, I'm still getting the hang of this.'

For a moment we stared at each other as if we were two entirely different species who somehow, by way of the zookeeper's oversight, had slipped into the same cage. We'd never had a conversation like this one. Now we were both feeling and fumbling our way as it coursed between what had been said and something more intimate. She looked at me as if she was trying to figure something out. She experimented between looking doubtful and looking aggrieved.

'Okay,' she said finally 'It's been interesting but now I have to go back and finish this thing.' She nodded through the glass doors to her workbench where a piece of Pacific sky waited to be fastened on to an Adriatic town.

Later, in the dark of the bedroom, my wife said in a piping voice aimed at the ceiling, 'That was nice before. For a while I found myself enjoying it.'

'Enjoying what?'

'Being looked at,' she answered, and it brought to mind a story about a rat catcher that I could have told but would have taken too long at that precise moment. Instead, I found myself thinking how this drifting apart had come about; at what point had I stopped looking? After the birth of Adrian and Jess? I don't think so. We had wonderful times together. Family times. I think it was around the time they left for university and overseas and we bought this house believing we wanted something new of our own as well; and around that time, before we'd even tied up to new moorings, the Gondwanaland thing had come up and suddenly I was preoccupied, preoccupied in an excited kind of way, and after it turned out to be one more golden calf (as doomed and vainglorious as George's hill), Frances had her jigsaw thing, at least that was one good thing to come out of it, and I was left looking off in half a dozen directions at once, filled with shame, embarrassment, apology, determined not to lock eyes with anyone. Avoidance. Evasion.

I banged down those twin doors of escape as fast as I could, burying myself in the shop as I tried to acquit myself of blame and shame by buying up whatever cast-offs people had stowed in their wardrobes or in their garage. When I got the letter from the bank and gazed up at that woman with the hedge-clippers I remember turning the car around and driving slowly home in what I can only call a jacket of cold sweat. In my mind's eye I saw Tommy Reece, his little rooster body and outlandish arms crucified against that Dutch landscape, the one on the fading calendar on the greasy wall down at Persico's, and I thought, I can't do this any more. I can't carry this place. I've failed them.

At home I walked in circles saying over and over, 'I don't know what to do. I don't know what the fuck more I can do.' Frances was magnificent. She kept saying it wasn't my fault. I had tried. Done my best. She bundled me into the car and we drove up Paradise Valley. There is a ghost town up there with lofty views out to sea. Here and there a gate swings on a broken latch. It swings until the long grass catches it, holds it briefly, then lets go. Once upon a time five thousand people lived up here. Main Street marched from A to B, gathering and collecting lives. My God, elections were held up here. Here, in the long wavering grass of Main Street, people in Paradise Valley voted for a smartly turned out fellow. His promises were made in a particular register. There were no visible signs of distress in his face when he said, 'All this here in Paradise Valley, this here is our children's future.' Brave words, and yet on the other hand the future is always gilded with promise. It is the trophy on the mantelpiece with our name on it. The future is waiting for us to step up. All of us will be there when the roll-call takes place. Who would not vote for a man who spoke so ably about the future? And now, now that the future has been reined in, what do we find? Another experiment in living. Traces here and there. Scattered evidence. The Historical Society has been active. You can tramp around in the long fairy grass and stumble over the foundations where once there stood a Bank of Australasia, a drapery, a colliery, a school, a church; forget-me-nots still come up each spring faithfully tracing the plots of the dead. Once upon a time people had been happy to be buried there. Here and there photo displays are posted across the paddocks—put up by the Historical Society—of dolls, toys, clothes of an abandoned wardrobe. Traces of life lived. Offcuts of material and shadow.

When Frances and I got out of the car and wandered around, me in my benumbed state, we stopped by a photo of a woman dressed top to toe in black on the steps of a store and in her eyes I saw the look that had plagued us from Day One—*life is elsewhere.* Life is always elsewhere. I could see it in the woman's eyes, there, scored against the dead walls of her eyes the thought that in the morning she will break the news to the man who is taking her photograph that she is leaving this place. You can see by the backs of her eyes that she has already left. She is planning her way out of Paradise. She has seen the future. Tomorrow morning, when she wakes up she will break the news to her husband.

I found myself unusually affected by this woman's face and its pessimism. So much so that when Frances sat me down on the grass and stroked my knee and proposed, 'You know, Harry, we could always leave,' I heard myself say, 'Nope. I'm staying.'

Frances, bless her, kissed me on the cheek.

Late the next morning I caught up with Guy on the matter of the polar bear. As soon as he shambled in the door I knew he'd driven here with the bear on his mind and how he would explain it to Harry. Now he circled defensively, saying, 'It seemed like a good buy,' and although my intention was to be patient, since I had woken up in that kind of mood, I found myself asking the obvious question, 'And what do you suppose is a good price for a stuffed polar bear?'

Guy shrugged and looked hurt. He said he thought I would be pleased. And why would that be? Because, he said, as far as he knew and I should correct him if this wasn't the case, there had never been a stuffed polar bear in Pre-Loved Furnishings & Other Curios.

He was correct. There hadn't been a polar bear and soon, I hoped, there would be none. I told him he'd have to phone up the owner of the bear and get them to come in and pick it up. I saw him inwardly wince at the thought of having to disappoint someone. I had no idea what he could have been thinking. A polar bear for Christsakes. But then I wouldn't be the first to notice he hadn't been the same since Caloundra fell through, and I'd heard it from Kath that for a while after their setback he started daydreaming again and rekindling the old idea to manufacture children's footwear.

Despite the business with the bear and Guy, I was in a good mood as I drove out to pick up Alma. This morning he was waiting at the bottom of his drive for me. As soon as he got in the car he handed me a photocopy of a sketch. He said, 'I saw this and immediately thought of you.' It was Schiele's *The Artist and His Model.*

In the sketch there are three elements—a mirror, the model and the artist, Schiele, himself, looking on with vampiric interest at the naked upright figure of his model. Schiele has the rear view. The mirror has the front view. In the mirror we see the perky tuft of pubic hair, a look of high disdain on the model's face, and further back the artist sitting on an apple box, a sketchpad on his knee. 'The artist,' explained Alma now, 'sometimes finds himself divided between the woman on his left and the one on his right, the one who is sitting for him, and the other one that is emerging on paper. There is a third woman which is really of no use to anyone. It is the one in the artist's mind. The idealised woman. She neither breathes nor speaks. She does not live except in his mind. So it is useful when you draw to keep your eyes and full attention on the subject before you.'

I had to smile and yet at the same time I didn't feel like explaining Ophelia, how we met, or confessing to the thinly grounded experience from which her substance had grown to preoccupy me. I did tell him about trying to draw Frances the previous night, and he asked me if she'd demanded to see it. Looking straight at the road, and older than Methuselah, Alma said, 'They always do that.'

There are times when all the years he's lived congregate in his face and his eyes blink impatiently at what is before him. Out at the Eliots' there was another moment like that when we found Violet tiptoeing around the cottage with a raised broom ready to strike. She explained she'd seen a rat. Alma's shoulders appeared to stoop and his head advance on this ancient information, and again there was that concentration of years in his face, a complexion like white dust, red-eyed, crumbled skin.

For the second time in a row the modelling session was far from satisfactory. In anticipation of our arrival Violet had put down the twins. The cottage was quieter too, quieter for our nervous whispering. And we spent a few minutes rearranging where she would sit and playing with the light. But we couldn't get Violet to sink fully into herself and properly relax. Her head was cocked ready for distraction and even when asked to look directly ahead, her eyes appeared to turn corners.

Her expectations were duly met. The cries of Jackson and Crystal travelled up the hall. Their mother groaned and slapped the floor. She started to get up but Alma rather curtly told her to stay put. The look was still there, although it was in danger of drawing attention to itself. Child and adult swilled back and forth in Violet's face.

She made a move to get up and again Alma told her to be still. There was just the dashing sound of pencil and paper and the enraged cries of Violet's babies from the hall. Poor Violet looked more and more distressed. And when Alma flipped a page over and held up a hand to show he wasn't finished she looked to me for help.

I got up and walked down the hall to the bedroom. When they saw me the bundled red faces stopped their bawling and gaped up at the stranger's face. I had two to three seconds in which to do something. I picked up a music box and wound on the 'Sugar Plum Fairy'. They listened to that, their black eyes glistening up at me. 'Sugar Plum Fairy' finished and I wound it up again. This was easy enough. The Eliot twins listened. The third time I began winding they started to twist inside their bundled nappies and cry. In a few seconds I heard running feet. Violet came in and scooped them up.

In the sitting room Alma was packing his gear. He put his money under a saucer and I put mine there as well. I poked my head into the hall and called out, 'We're off!' Alma was already out the door. As we went down the side of the house Violet came to the window with her babies, one pressed against each shoulder. She looked scared so I gave her a reassuring wink.

Alma was already in the car, strapped in, sullen. When I got in he said, 'This isn't working. You're going to have to find that Dean kid. Get him to babysit. Otherwise we're wasting our time.'

17

Dean had got into the habit of sitting in the Garden of Memories. He liked it there, surrounded by flowerbeds, and it was amazing how often someone would turn up and come and sit next to him. If you sat there still enough, the world would wash up and share itself in unexpected ways. And he had to admit it beat lying inside that wheel-less house truck; for all the painted landscape it didn't really do much for him. It didn't talk back. He didn't come away from it better for the experience.

Yesterday he'd been sitting there in the same seat as he sat now, when a man of indeterminate age had wandered through the gates. A hawklike face had poked into different corners of the gardens and then, on seeing him, had set off in his direction, an old-fashioned leather bag swinging at his side. At a distance the man's clothes had been deceptive. They had made Dean think the man was younger than he turned out to be. He wore a white cheesecloth shirt with loose coloured threads of the kind that hang from sails of yachts to measure wind speed, a black jerkin, glossy bits of it catching and shining in the sun, black jeans and black boots. His hair was jet black. Too black to be real, he saw as the man came nearer, and then, a deeply wrinkled neck, a turtle's neck, heavily tanned, a face the same colour, sun-split and crossed a hundred different ways.

He pointed to the space next to Dean just as that other fellow Dougie had, and because that meeting had led to a job Dean thought, hell, this could be another opportunity. So he moved over for the man to sit down.

It was only as he lowered himself that Dean was able to see that the man was a whole lot older than he first had thought, and that probably he didn't have loose coinage in those tight frayed pockets anyway, but again what the hell, he had committed to this end of the bench.

The man felt the slats under him and only then did he risk the rest of his skinny body and lean back to allow the park bench to collect him fully. His beaky face made another investigation and glancing around, said how much everything had changed; it was deader than he remembered. It was smaller too; he had been expecting that since he'd been living in Queensland all these years and he'd still be there but for a death in the family.

Dean said he was sorry and asked who. The man's gums trembled a bit when he said it was his stepson, Dean, strictly speaking. And Dean had thought, no, this was like hearing he was dead. This was like getting late news of one's own death. And he'd blurted out halfway through the man explaining who this Dean was, blurted out that his own name was Dean. At which point the man turned and stared at him a full minute, at the end of which he said, 'No kidding.' And, 'How many Deans do you reckon there are in the world, Dean?' He dropped his eyes to his thighs. He said his Dean had no legs, and more sarcastically, 'So you must be all right. You must be alive, Dean.'

Eventually after that unpromising start they had warmed to each other. He asked how come this Dean, the man's Dean, this half-son of his, this stepson, had no legs, and the man told him it had happened in the war, though he didn't say much about that. He said, 'He was lucky to have lived as long as he did given the amount he drank and smoked.' At this point the man had extended his hand and said, 'My name's George, by the way.' And Dean had seen no point in repeating what was already known but did so to be friendly.

'I'm Dean,' he said, and the man said, 'Still?' And they had a laugh over that.

That's when he'd pointed down at George's bag and asked him what he had in there and George said, 'Oh, I'm collecting stories of human daring and folly. The whole shooting works in there.' And he tapped the top of his bag.

'Like what?'

'Like what?' the man repeated as if it was an obvious question but one he'd put up with in the interests of friendship. 'Well, let's see, like whatever you want to hear. Whatever you'd like to capture.'

That seemed a strange thing to say. *Whatever you'd like to capture.*

Not everything had fur and feathers or scales on it. Dean had to think about it, but after a while he'd gone with it and asked, 'Capture anything?'

'Anything. Sure.'

'Absolutely anything?'

'Try me.'

Warming to his task, Dean had glanced up at the landscape and said the first thing that came to mind.

'A hill.'

'A hill. That's a good one. Well, in total I have in this bag about fifty descriptions of how to capture a hill.' The man closed his eyes while he thought for a moment. 'Okay, here we go. The first thing is and this is important…'

'Yeah,' said Dean.

'…first, turn your back. Don't let it know that you are interested.'

'Well, that makes sense,' Dean said, playing along.

'Next,' said the man. 'In due course follow the track to the summit and keep climbing to where the mountain narrows to a point no larger but small enough to enclose your arms around it. Make sure your fingers touch—you don't want the damn thing slipping out and making a fool of you.'

'Hell no,' said Dean. He could have laughed at that point but something in the man's manner prevented him.

'And be sure to use your legs when standing up. No point putting your back out.'

'Right again,' he said.

'Mountain safety is everything. For example, you're at the top, scratching your head, it's getting late in the day and you're liable to think, bugger me. What I want to say is this. Stay calm. Do not panic. Remember you are the one with the brain. You are the adult in this situation. The hill will still be there in the morning.'

Now Dean had to laugh and the man he was relieved to see didn't take it personally. Not at all. He had a way of laughing and nodding himself.

'What else?'

'Well, there is a mountain in a northern country that stands on the edge of a plain. Think of a man lying on his back, his head raised high enough to see his big toe. The mountain can see you coming when you're still a day's walk away. Its gaze is said to be unendurable. Of all the hill stories I have collected I have to say this is the one I like least. My favourite hill stories tend towards the heroic end of things, or ease the pain.'

'Like?'

'Like,' he said, closing his eyes to think. 'Perhaps this will do. When Dean, our Dean, was hit by leukemia he lay in bed dreaming to see a hill again. He'd decided in his final days that he wanted to look upon a hill. It was a special request. He wanted me to bring a hill to his bedside window. Not an ordinary request, granted, but there is a history to do with this that I won't go into. Anyway, within a day I had it worked out. In the morning I came into his room and told him I'd done what he'd asked. I told him, "I only got it as far as the drive. But this afternoon, by four or five, you will see its shadow cast in your window." So later that day I got my wife Victoria to switch on the Holden headlights to high beam and train them on a big triangular-shaped piece of ply. With some juggling and manoeuvring of ply and headlight eventually we got the distance right and the shadow of the hill settled into the bedroom window of my crippled war veteran stepson.'

Dean replied, 'That's a sad one,' and the man thought for a moment.

'There's sad and then there is sad. I've got one, a true story, as it happens, where the capture of a hill was passed off as a grand gesture of love. But I don't have time to tell that one.'

With that he glanced at his watch and stood up in that way of the elderly, as if they have forgotten how. And after the man had gone Dean sat there a while thinking that this was one way of experiencing new things, one way of feeling the world in all its changing texture and behaviour, to have it come up and rub against you in all its many guises. And best of all you could do that just by sitting still and silly as a tulip.

It would have been nice to have someone, Violet, say, to pass on that story to. His own near-death, which is what it had sounded like he was hearing—he'd have to stress that, and he'd even felt a shiver of proximity crawl over his skin, like it could be him, that he was on his way out, or could have well been him, only this Dean didn't have any legs and his last wish had been to see a hill in the window which, as far as last requests go, hardly tips the scales to the extravagant end of things. It wasn't much to ask for as you anticipated your last breath. Now that he related it back to himself it didn't sound so convincing, and yet at the time of hearing it had sounded the most reasonable request in the world. Of course you would want to see a hill in your bedside window. What else could you possibly want? He thought a bit longer on it, and decided maybe it needed that old man's way of telling, his walnut-coloured face and shiny fairground vest.

He must have been sitting there in the sun a whole hour at least and was thinking he might give up because no one else had come into the gardens under the Anzac gate apart from two skateboarders and an elderly woman with a bag of bread-crumbs who walked the length of the gardens with a flock of sparrows behind her and a funny little smile on her pinched face. As far as Dean could see she didn't throw a single crumb.

He stood up to leave—he might as well accept the truth of good and bad fishing days. But as he did so he couldn't think what else to do that was any better and that it was silly in that case to wind in your line when you had nothing better to do; you might as well hold on and sit tight. A sparrow hopped down off a branch onto the grass and looked up at him. Something about it gave him the uncanny sense that he was being watched. And sure enough when he turned and looked behind, who should he see but the mayor.

The idea was to approach Dean, talk to him, and persuade him to come and see Violet and her babies. I had left them sitting in the van over at the car park. Violet thought Dean was probably embarrassed by his absences, but once they overcame that initial concern things would quickly improve and she would explain the babysitting proposal that would free her up to make some much needed money.

Unfortunately Dean saw me and some old game known to the pursuer and the pursued came between us. He stood up from the bench and moved away in a sideways fashion, one eye to his escape route, one eye on me which to tell the truth I found unnecessary and embarrassing. I was there to help, not stick him in irons.

So I thought I wouldn't take another step. I stopped still and called out, 'Dean, all I want is to talk to you.' But it was like a starter's pistol shot had gone off in his ear. He ran out through the gates. Stupid of course. Peculiarly mindless and irritating. A conversation would be much to his and Violet's advantage, not to mention two babies who were entirely blameless in the situation they found themselves. All I wanted to do was help. So when he ran it was an invitation for me to chase him.

I jogged to the gates. I knew he didn't have a car. A bike would make it difficult. But looking right and left I saw him turn on foot at the Public Trust building on to Broadway. Actually I hardly saw him at all—it was just a glimpse of his shirt-tail lifting off his black T-shirt. By the time I reached the same corner Dean was another hundred metres up Broadway. Soon he would pass the shop. If I'd had my mobile with me I could have rung Guy. Dean wasn't running any more but walking—bouncing on his heels like he might be feeling quite good about himself, having given the mayor the slip like that. I called out to him and as he turned around I raised a friendly hand in a gesture of, Wait a moment, Dean, you don't understand; he replied with a stupid shake of his head and broke into a jog as far as Endeavour where he turned. At this point he might have stopped to think for a moment, Wait a second, this isn't such a large town that I won't ever see Harry Bryant ever again. You'd have thought that would cross his mind and some rational acceptance drop into place. But no, Dean had made up his mind. He was the hare and I was the dog. And a hare and a dog know only one thing.

A cutting runs between the Lyric Theatre up the back of the shops, behind Pre-Loved, and comes out three-quarters of the way up Endeavour, almost opposite the school. I jogged up there with a big happy grin on my face. I was going to surprise Dean with a bit of local knowledge. I couldn't wait to see the look on his face when I squirted out of a blind spot to nail him.

I had turned into the dog Dean thought he'd seen.

He was still climbing Endeavour when he saw me. He stopped, puzzled. Once more I raised the hand of reason. Once more Dean thought differently. This time I ran at him. He went up on his toes. His eyes shifted to all points of the compass. The school, he decided. He ran across the road, reaching the gates ahead of me, banging his knee in the process which must have hurt because he swore out loud which I'm ashamed to say was reason for joy; then near the playground equipment he tripped on something and fell headlong onto the grass; two seconds later I arrived on top of him, forty-four years of living as I prefer to think of my weight upon his thin scrawny frame. He tried wriggling out from under me. I could feel the steam of his face near mine. All of this was so unnecessary. I said, 'I just want to talk to you, Dean. Now will you cut this shit out.'

He made one last effort to buck me—he failed of course and it seemed to take everything out of him; his hips fell back and the air expired from him. His shoulders went weak. He closed his eyes and panted for a bit. I thought he could be playing possum you could never be sure with a sneaky individual like Dean. I moved my legs up his chest and pinned his arms with my knees. Away across the fields in the classroom windows I could see rows of tiny faces looking back in our direction—at their mayor; and strange to say, at that moment Ophelia snuck back in to my thoughts with, 'What kind of mayor did you say you were?' It was a valid question. What kind of mayor pinned down a runaway like Dean in the playing fields of his own youth where for hours, as it seemed back then, Dougie and I held opponents in fierce headlocks for the duration of the lunch hour, their sweating faces against our own, their pounding chests. I remember the day that news of the death of Felix Sampson, founder of NE Paints, spread across the school playground; everywhere you looked you saw kids unravel themselves from headlocks and stand up and brush the grass off themselves, and as one gaze up at the Sampson villa on the hill. I remember that night, Frank acting all weirdly serious at home, and my mother shooing me out of the kitchen while Frank sat down to compose a letter of commiseration to Felix's sons, Brian and Aubrey, both shits as it turned out, who eventually wasted no time in selling us to the highest bidder.

Over at the classroom block a teacher emerged and moved gingerly in our direction. A female teacher. She stopped and went back inside. A few minutes later a teacher with male swagger started over. It was the headmaster, a man I had once shared the mat with at this very same school. Dean turned his head and saw him too and a misguided flush of hope entered his face.

I called out to him. 'Hi Phil.'

'Harry! I wondered if that was you.' He looked briefly behind him and came forward. 'The children,' he said rather awkwardly.

'Right,' I said. 'I understand. But it's okay Phil, despite how it must appear. It's nothing at all. It's just a little difference to sort out. Dean's not such a bad bloke, are you, Dean?'

Dean stared up at me tight-lipped with eyes of hate.

'We're almost done here, aren't we, Dean?'

'In that case,' Phil said.

I gave him a nod of encouragement.

'Really, it's nothing.'

He looked absently down at Dean. He said to me, 'Okay, Harry. Regards to Fran.'

'Thanks,' I said. 'Same to Meg.'

Under me Dean stared up with a bewildered face. Phil started on his way and stopped. He turned around.

'I almost forgot.' He stood there as if inviting me and Dean to guess. His delighted face was beaming. 'Our Olivia is pregnant.'

'Little Olivia? Holy mackerel, Phil, that makes you a grandparent.'

'I know,' he said. 'I feel too young.'

'Well don't you get old on me too fast.'

'I won't. See you, Harry.'

After he moved off again I slapped Dean's face. It sounded louder and actually much worse than it really was. Phil stopped and looked back. Behind his black bifocals his eyes narrowed.

'It's all right, Phil. It was nothing.'

Phil nodded, a bit more disapprovingly this time, and went on his way.

Dean twisted his face this way and that. He spluttered up at me, 'What did you do that for?'

'I don't know. It just felt right,' I said. 'Didn't it feel right for you?'

'You're not the fucking mayor. A fucking mayor doesn't do that sort of shit.'

'I am the fucking mayor. You're looking up at the fucking mayor. Get used to it. Now are you ready to talk like a civilised human being or do I have to slap sense into you? What's it to be, Dean? Give me an indication. Civilised or barbarian? I can do both.'

'The first one,' he said.

'Good choice.'

There are days when Frances asks me, 'How was your day?' and I hardly know how to begin to answer. This was shaping up as one of those. Later that night I told her—'You know Phil Anderson from the school, remember his daughter, Olivia? Well she's pregnant.' Her answer was much the same as mine, 'No, she can't be,' and just like that in dressing-gown and socked feet she took herself off to thoughts of the future, old age, shortened horizons, and I was spared the need to explain the rest. She would have been appalled to hear that I had spreadeagled myself over Dean Eliot on the local school playing field. She would have clasped a hand over her chest and thanked God or someone lurking in the ceiling that she wasn't downtown when I had chased after that poor boy Dean. Being mayor is a thankless job, and I would be reminded of that the next morning when I picked up Alma from beside his letter box for him to say offhandedly, 'I trust you've organised the baby-sitter...' So much of what a mayor does is off limits. There isn't a grandstand of home support cheering our every move. I know that and accept it. But from time to time it grates just a touch when the same beneficiaries upon seeing you wipe the sweat from your brow fail to ask, 'Is there anything I can do?'

At the schoolground I was conscious of the need to provide a morality play for those small faces gaping out their classroom windows. They had seen the mayor astride the youth—a confusing and troubling spectacle. Now they would see him gallantly offer the same youth a hand up to his feet. They would be treated to a quieter view of world peace as the two figures left the schoolgrounds by the gate, and perhaps they noted the way the mayor stepped aside for the other to go through ahead of him.

On our way along Broadway I stopped at Angie's Koffee Kafe and bought Dean a soft drink. I was feeling remorseful. I shouldn't have slapped him. There was no need for it. I didn't know I was going to until I had done it, enormously satisfying though it was. But Dean hadn't actually done anything wrong. He hadn't actually done anything to me—stolen, flung abuse. His only crime had been to run from me. *Flight.* And that is what had enraged me.

At Angie's while he slurped on a straw I explained my vision for the town. Before they shovelled me into the ground in a plot next to Tommy Reece I hoped we could look in the mirror and not run from ourselves for the next boat or plane, or take to the road. I gave the word *run* a bit more play than it warranted but I wanted Dean to think maybe he was actually to blame for some wrongdoing just in case he was thinking of getting litigious over being slapped. So on I went. People run when they've got no reason to run. It becomes a lifelong habit, and then when they reach the end what is there to look back on? A life of running over the surface of the globe and a colossal failure to dig down deeper. Always the next thing and never the ground under your feet. Dean slurped his drink, his eyes tilted up at me, watchful, suspicious.

'Anyway, Dean, I need to ask a favour of you...' As soon as I said that he straightened up on his side of the table and suddenly he smelt of the feral opportunism I'd experienced out at the cemetery that day I turned up hoping to exchange the beds. By the time I got to the end of the proposal his face had grown in confidence.

'You *want* me to babysit,' he said.

'Correct,' I said. 'For Violet so she can earn some money.

Yes, that's the idea.'

'Want me?' he said again, getting weird about it now, looking around as if this was an amusing idea.

'And when you say *want* you're talking about something free, right?'

'Correct.'

Now he was very amused. I hadn't seen him look this amused before. He shook his head down at the table like I just didn't get it, did I.

He said, 'You want me but you don't want to pay me. Is that the wonderful proposal?'

His moral blindness really was staggering. Did Dean really think he should be paid to take care of his own children. By now I couldn't even bear to look at him. That's when he said, 'They're not my kids.' Just like that. The element of surprise had swapped places at the table.

Later, after we had parted with a promise that he would turn up the next day, I felt differently about Dean. I heard about the paint warehouse, and everything that he'd done for Violet, and what he had hoped to achieve by buying the house truck before running out of funds and as a result feeling washed-out and derelict and of no hope or use to Violet whatsoever. He had taken himself off so he wouldn't be a burden on her. He'd planned to come back as soon as he found a job. Now he had one.

There was something else. Something he seemed itching to ask.

'You are the mayor, right?'

'That again,' I said. This time what I thought I'd do was take him back to Pre-Loved and show him my mayoral authority stamp. I keep it at the shop rather than down at Chambers. It's easier that way since I do my own correspondence.

In the end I aborted that show-and-tell because the man with the polar bear, moustache, glasses, was there. I could see Guy was talking, explaining with his hands. The other man was shaking his head down at the floor. Between them was the head of the polar bear with its silent roar and raised paws. I was getting used to the idea of Guy being there. I was discovering that I quite liked it.

'Another time, Dean,' I said. Dean nodded like he thought so.

About now I remembered poor Violet and her babies. I'd left them in the van back at the car park outside the gardens.

The same tree with its bronze leaves was in the side window. The same wedge of sky in the windscreen in front. The world seemed stuck. They seemed stuck. The Eliot babies began to squirm and agitate on their mother's lap. They began to agitate for something different. She offered them a breast each but they weren't interested and she knew what they wanted was what she could use too, some change of air, so she laid them on the driver's seat while she got the pushchair out. The man from Pre-Loved had been gone for much longer than he'd told her to expect. Either Dean was there or he wasn't. If he wasn't he should be back by now.

She was so sure she would see them and so surprised when she pushed the babies under the arch that nothing more than rose heads nodded in the gentle breeze from the direction of the port. The air smelt of fish meal. Even the rose plants seemed to know this. That is how alone in the moment she felt. She smiled, pleased. It would have been an observation to share with Dean but he was nowhere to be seen. She pushed on. There was a bench not far away with a pocket of lawn. The twins could crawl around there.

Soon a woman by herself wandered beneath the arch. The points of her shoes crossed when she walked and she held her hands behind her back which made her hips appear wider in a womanly sort of way. She looked to be lost in thought. But when she glanced up and saw she had company she smiled and started over.

She didn't sit down though. She stood with her arms folded and she smiled down at Jackson and Crystal rolling on their backs over the grass. As the woman shifted her interest she swung her hands down at her side.

'Let me guess,' she said. 'High school sweethearts?'

Violet guessed she meant the twins were thereby the product of this. Any other explanation was too long-winded, so as a matter of convenience she nodded.

The woman looked delighted. She said, 'Oh, they are the best, the absolute best. Fierce and uncontrollable.' She shuddered when she said that and shook her shoulders, and Violet laughed. She was pleased to have the approval; well it was more than that.

'You can sit down if you like,' Violet said.

'May I? Thank you.'

She made it sound like it was Violet's bench, hers alone. That it was her own personal space and that she had just opened the door to welcome the woman inside. On second thoughts she approved of that idea. And she was glad for the company.

Emboldened, she asked the woman if she was married and

if she had kids of her own, and then if she herself had married her high school sweetheart. With a great display of arms and teeth, like a giant bird hovering, she laughed. 'Oh no. No. No. Guy came later. I found Guy lost in the toiletries section of the supermarket. That should have told me everything I needed to know right there and then.'

The woman's mood changed. The tide went out in her face. She swung her foot under the bench while she gazed off into the distance. Still, Violet wondered if there was someone who'd come earlier.

'High school. Let's see,' she said. She became thoughtful, as if looking back inside herself. 'There was someone. But he didn't look at me. I wasn't much to look at it. A skinny kid with crooked teeth. I used to follow him around at a distance. He was so popular. All the girls adored him. Douglas. Dougie. I would watch him at parties. And years later too I would close my eyes and dream, and then, guess what?' Violet sensed the woman's itch to tell and at the same time felt her examining eyes upon her.

The woman sat up. She folded her arms, and leant forward. 'Okay. This is strictly between ourselves. Girls' stuff. Top secret, understood?'

Violet nodded eagerly.

'About four days ago, we met. It was at a funeral for a man who lost his legs in the war. Poor Dean. He was such a nice man. At lunchtime at school we used to go into his shop and he'd show us his knives from Borneo and bits of World War Two shrapnel. It's funny a bomb couldn't get him but something like leukemia could which at his age, sixty-something, apparently is more unusual.' She stopped and Violet felt the woman's eyes on her. 'Sixty is no longer old. It used to be, but believe me, from where I stand sixty is no longer old. You find yourself taking stock around my age. What have I done? What have I failed to do? The failings sadly leave everything else in their shadow. Anyway, Miss Maudlin me, I was telling you about Dougie. So, anyway, as expected I run into Dougie at the funeral. We're old friends of course and after the others have filed into the church we find that we're the last ones left outside under the trees, just talking. Anyway, we have a cigarette. Over the way is the hearse and from where we stood you could see the hydraulics of the hearse. Ghastly. Yuck. Anyway, just then music comes pumping out the church doors. Not just any old music. Not anything you might expect, say a church organ, but Edith Piaf. Can you believe? The pallbearers grin back at the church. One of them stamps out his cigarette and goes in. The others follow. Then it's just me and Douglas Monroe who I adored at high school out there, beneath the trees. We're the last ones left.

'The next part I'm not so proud of. I hear this song in my head and I start to sing. I stop, because suddenly I'm weeping. These tears. I mean, my God, Kath, get a life, please. Dougie gives me his hanky. I tell him, Carole King. That's who I want at my funeral. Well, by now Edith Piaf is winding down, and that's when another Carole King melody comes to me. I stop there because I need another cigarette. I dig around in my handbag without much success. Then I lay the bag on a gravestone. Eloise. Eloise Sim. That's whose grave it is. I just remembered that. "Excuse me, Eloise," I say, "while I have a cig." Dougie has one too and we sit on the gravestone, smoking, then he leans forward with a song of his own. And he starts singing Louis Armstrong's "Stormy Weather". Not my choice for a funeral. Definitely not, I tell him. I want people to cry at mine. Louis Armstrong would just have them dancing in the aisles. No one's crying. None of the shits care because they're singing "Stormy Weather". Well, screw that. Then I see all the faces at my own funeral. I see them sitting there. I can see my coffin up the front. And it's so, so awful, so awful that I start crying, and Doug puts an arm around my shoulder. He puts his face against mine. Then he kisses my cheek.

'Well, we both have a list of songs we want played at our funerals. We start sharing those. He wants Bob Dylan singing "Ballad of a Thin Man". But then he changes that for Al Green's "Take Me to the River", which in my view I don't really think is appropriate. Too much on the driving side. He agrees and says, "Maybe something soft and gospelly then?" And just like that, without a signal, we both start to sing, "I Bid You Goodnight". So that is what we're singing, not loudly or obnoxiously, just quietly on Eloise's gravestone, Eloise Sim born eighteen hundred and seventy-eight, when we see the pallbearers coming out of the church. They glance across the churchyard and we both bounce up as if we've been caught out, which we have in a way. I pick up my bag, dust the leaves off my black funeral dress. Now, listen to this. Dougie threads his arm through mine and draws me across the yard away from the entrance. Nothing's been said. Not a word. It's as if we are being guided. We cross the lawn beside the church. We can hear the shuffling of feet, the sharper noise of a pew moving, someone's cough. We have forgotten poor crippled Dean. I know where we're headed before I actually see where we're headed, if you follow me. Across from the church is a KFC.

Beside it, a SKY TV-winking vacancy. Vacancy. "Hello? This way." That's what it might as well be saying. So Doug, he gives my hand a little press, and at the first gap in the traffic we're pulling each other across the road, then we're hurrying across the flagstone parking area.

'Our room is on the street side, and there's that nice downy light of curtains closed in the afternoon. While Dougie undresses I pull the curtains back a whisker. It has started to rain and the funeral people milling around the hearse have put up umbrellas. Poor Dean must be in the hearse because I see this white-gloved hand reach up and close the rear. There are faces in that crowd I've known from high school, one or two I have kept in touch with. But the one I desired back then, twenty-five years ago, is raising my funeral dress over my shoulders. I don't look pretty. I mean, the youth has gone. My boobs sag. There's a bulge of white flesh tumbling over the waistband of my panties. Oh God, it's not pretty. There's a long scar from a caesarean. Another scar on my thigh is from an op to wind up my veins. My body is a battleground, let me tell you. So I let go of the curtain and I say to Dougie, "Tell me I'm not ridiculous." That's the word I use. Ridiculous. And he says, "You're not ridiculous, Kath. You're lovely."

'Lovely,' she repeated. She smiled, mysterious, enmeshed in all kinds of complexities of belief, make-believe, faith. She may not have believed Dougie but she's glad to have heard those words, and especially that word, *lovely*.

'So, we make our way over to the bed and you'll never guess but by some weirdly strange coincidence we both start humming Carole King. See, the melody was just to get us across the carpet and under the bedcovers. The rest you don't need to know about. Except this. Later, much later, I'm talking about after we've left the motel unit now, in sunglasses and with an unspoken vow never to see each other again, at least until one or the other's funeral, we all die, after all, I'm picking up pasta in the supermarket, bumbling along with my cart, thinking, What the hell were we doing? Just what were we doing running from that funeral? I'm sure we must have looked like we knew. To those people in their cars going by, all that traffic, I'm sure they thought we knew.'

She looked up sharply into the corners of the sky, a funny look lightly sketched on her face, now a quick exploratory look at Violet.

'What do you think? What do you think was going on there?' She spoke slowly, almost with exaggerated slowness, and watched carefully the impact of each word on Violet's face. She said, 'You know something? It's like watching a jug fill, to hear me and watch you.'

18

The world is off-balance most of the time. You can never see it in its entirety. All you really ever manage to obtain is a glimpse, an angled view, three-quarter, quarter view.

This is what you get to hear if Alma Martin is your teacher and you are into your second or third drawing lesson.

Here's another. When sketching your wife there are always three people in the room with you at the time. There's yourself, the artist, your wife who is the subject, and there is the figure emerging on the canvas.

The first time I heard that was in the car on our way to the Eliots'. The second time was at my mother's place. Doug and Guy and their wives were in attendance, Guy with a look of apprehension, Doug with his raised smile, like he's along for the ride to see what will happen.

Diane was sitting rather testily doing her best not to look Doug's way. Kath, as it appeared, was also trying not to look Doug's way, and at the same time finding it hard to look back at Guy. Frances was smiling back at me as if to say, Isn't this a hoot? Only my mother was in professional mode, silent, moving quiet as a shadow into position while the old master held court.

Alma gave me a searching look and held it on me as he explained the next part. 'The trick is to make sure that the woman sitting for you and the woman emerging on canvas are the same person.'

Doug gave me a nudge. Alma saw that and switched his attention to Doug.

'Douglas, how well do you know your wife?'

'Pretty well.'

A scoff from Diane.

Now Alma found Guy.

'And you, sir?' He'd forgotten Guy's name.

'We've been married seventeen years.'

Alma's eyes twinkled while he considered that answer, unexpected you would have to say, possibly misunderstood by Guy, but Alma decided to let it pass. He still didn't know Guy that well.

'And Harry, of course,' he said. But that wasn't a question. It wasn't anything in particular but it had the effect of making me feel guilty all the same, especially when Frances raised her eye my way.

Nowadays this is a sample question from Alma's introductory classes on portraiture. 'How well do you know your wife?' It's designed to disarm.

You're not supposed to actually answer. The question is the preliminary step to finding out.

At my mother's house that night Alma invited Doug and me and Guy to take a final look at our wives (the 'end-of-the-pier view' Alma calls it). Then he asked us to go into the next room and draw what we think we saw.

He said, 'Take your time but don't take too long about it—the National Gallery isn't holding its breath.'

We pushed into the dining room with our pencils and sketch pads. By dint of the sessions out at the Eliots' place, I knew the drill. I said, 'Don't procrastinate and fart about. Just get it down.'

Doug started to say something—I cut him off: '...and don't talk.' We scribbled in silence. Once Guy cleared his throat and half stuck up his hand for my attention. He asked if he could start again. 'There are no rules,' I told him. 'Just get Kath down on that sheet of paper.'

'How much time is left?' he asked.

I told him, 'There's no time. A sketch doesn't know time.' Though less than a minute later Alma opened the door and invited us back in for step three, which is: *Take your sketch back to the other room and compare it with the woman sitting/reading/eating an apple in the model's chair.*

Alma waited until Guy was through the door. Guy would rather have stayed in the dining room and closed the curtains and hid behind the couch.

'Now ask yourself. Are there two different women in your life? No? Really?' (Smirking now.) 'Okay, let's put it this way. Is the woman who sleeps in your bed and who bore your children the same woman you carry around in your head? Let's find out. Harry, let's start with you. Let's see your drawing.'

It's a cheap fairground trick designed to rattle and alarm, but effective, because it sets the student up for the first lesson. Memory is unreliable. Secondly, seeing is not the same as looking. And in learning how to draw what you really learn is how to see. Once you learn how to see, good or bad or better

276

doesn't come into it. Yearning just flies out the window. The only thing of consequence is what sits before you.

In recent weeks there are things I have wondered about the old rat-catching days of Alma's 'in lieu of' arrangement. I can't understand why it didn't catch on. Why, in those first uneasy truce-making months of soldiers returning to their women after an interval in some cases of years, why drawing classes weren't introduced. Imagine if drawing had become an activity with a community focus? Imagine if Alma had wandered up to George in the early days of his quixotic hill removal exercise and tapped him on the shoulder and led him back to the house, sat my mother down and put a pencil in George's hand. The one and only explanation is that he was in love with my mother and he couldn't give her up as he almost certainly would have had he shown George in which direction both to look and focus his efforts. Far better to watch George labour day after day on that hill and have his wife to himself. Of course Frank Bryant was a surprise; he never anticipated that event happening. Yet I can't help think that if Alma had put my mother to one side he might have killed that yearning for better things that spawned in the years following World War Two.

Still, it is never too late to make amends.

The day I changed my mind about Dean Eliot was the day I led him back to the Garden of Memories where Violet was waiting and somewhat unexpectedly talking to Kath Stuart. They were sitting on the same bench, the Eliot twins playing on the grass by their feet. Violet was first to see us. Then Kath looked up. She rose to her feet, smoothing out her skirts. She kissed Violet on the cheek, gave me a little wave and started to move to the far gate. She was out to avoid me and I wasn't going to let that happen.

'Kath,' I called out. 'Why don't you come down to the shop? Guy's there.'

She stopped to think. There's surely a dozen reasons why I can't do that. She must have had a total mind block because at the moment when she so desperately wanted an excuse she couldn't think of one.

I made another discovery ten minutes later back at the shop. No matter how much you may want to, you can't force people into doing what they don't want to do.

In retrospect I blame my heady success with Dean. Flush with that, I thought I could now wave a magic wand over Kath and Guy and make things better between them. Moreover I was convinced that I knew how.

As we came into Pre-Loved, Guy was touchingly shining up some bronze doorstops and that immediately enamoured me of him, especially after Kath's attempt to slide away from me at the gardens. I had heard whispering. I gathered something had gone down between her and Doug. I didn't know the details and didn't want to, and I hoped I was wrong. Still, if I had the feeling that something had happened then I'm sure Guy was also well aware of it.

He looked up from the brass doorstops, pleased to see me. Then he saw who I had with me and suddenly he looked unhappy. His eyes started blinking. For an awful few seconds I thought he might cry. Kath looked away. She'd just discovered the child's zebra rocking-horse. In retrospect I was a bit too loud, forceful, eager to make things happen after my success with the Eliots, still bathing in the warm feeling of seeing them drive away to the beach—in my van, I should add, reflecting the new cooperative spirit between me and Dean. He said he would bring it back and walk back out to the beach. I told him, no, he could return it in the morning and even Violet looked surprised. I was still feeling bad for slapping him. All the same, it was a good result. Well, anyway, for all that I felt like I was on a roll; that of all days this was one where I might be invincible. I should have just bought a raffle ticket and been content. That's what I should have done.

Instead I said to Kath, 'Why don't you draw Guy?'

She gave me a crazy look. Guy stopped blinking. I said, 'Sure. It's fun.'

A stubbornness took hold of Kath; she folded her arms.

Guy said, 'What's this about, Harry?'

'Not about anything. Just thought it would be interesting if Kath drew you. That is, it would be interesting for you both. It's something I'm getting to understand and enjoy. Something I want to share with my friends.' Kath and Guy eyed each other wearily.

'Perhaps another time, Harry. I don't think Kath...'

But I'd made up my mind and nothing was going to stop me. Kath was going to draw Guy and that was that. I pulled out a stool and made Guy sit on it. I went out the back for my sketchpad and pencil; and when I returned Guy was standing again and Kath was whispering furiously at him.

'Sit!' I told Guy.

He gave a helpless look, his hands moving out to his sides, and sat down.

Kath said she wasn't drawing anyone. This was stupid. Who the hell did I think I was anyway? She was sick of me ordering people around.

The other week a man from another town had brought in a World War One rifle. The rifle happened to be standing behind the counter where I'd left it before driving out to the beach to pick up the Eliots. Now it was within handy reach, and to my shame, to my ghastly gut-wrenching eternal shame I picked it up and trained it on Kath and said, 'Now fucking draw Guy.'

Guy started to say it really wasn't necessary.

'The sitter does not speak, Guy. The sitter sits and shuts the fuck up and the drawer draws. That's you Kath, so start drawing.'

She started to cry. I don't think she really thought she would come to any harm. It's just the way things had got out of hand.

Guy grumbled from the stool, 'You're upset and emotional, Harry. Honestly, I don't need to be drawn.'

Kath was sobbing into her hands. I lowered the rifle. It was only for a few brief seconds I'd held the rifle on her. But of course it wasn't the best persuasive route. Drawing requires absolute concentration and a still heart. These conditions were entirely wrong and all I'd ended up doing was frightening good friends.

I felt terrible. I tried to apologise. I tried to buy them Chinese. Guy said he didn't think this was the right occasion. I said, 'Persico's? They'll be still open.'

Guy said. 'No, Harry. Give me the rifle.'

I handed him the rifle.

'Thank you, Harry. Now I think it's about closing time. If you like I can close up.'

He put the rifle away. Kath was still sobbing but every now and then she peered out her fingers at Guy. She didn't want to be left alone in there with me.

That's all in the past. I don't try to promote drawing in that way any more. There's no need to.

After that incident with Kath and Guy I got on with my ideas and activities more quietly. I let word of mouth do the rest. Word got out that the mayor was spending all his waking hours drawing, sketching. 'Harry's doing what?' 'Why would Harry do that?' And so people came in to look for themselves. They crowded the door. The only things missing were the cage bars and bags of breadcrumbs. I didn't mind it, though. For one thing this was a quieter way to proceed. I didn't need to call a public meeting. I just went about my thing and allowed it to rub off on the population.

Doug and Guy joined me early on. How long ago that already feels! How long ago it is that we had our first tentative start at my mother's house where the walls were used to the activity and it had felt right. Soon the same space had become too crowded to accommodate everyone's easel.

Over the winter months we opened up the old paint factory. Guy and I went through with a lantern, skirting puddles, gazing up at leaking ceilings. We got a grant from the Lotteries Board to buy this old relic, and over summer we formed teams to do up the space. With Dean I drove the van over the Main Divide and picked up two cheap potbelly stoves. We visited second-hand bookshops and came out with armloads of books on various artists. I had a shopping list. Everyone had their favourite.

Alma's advice on mentors—pick yourself a dead artist and save yourself the humiliation of presenting yourself at a live one's door. There's the example of Schiele who picked Klimt (still alive, and herein lies the moral). Schiele turns up at

Klimt's door after godly anointment. Klimt was in his blue working smock. He could have quite reasonably sent the younger man away. Instead he looked over Schiele's portfolio and to the question, 'Do I have talent?' he kindly replied, 'Talent? Yes! Much too much.'

Think what he could have said—or for a clue, listen to what our wives said about our first fumbling portraits. That's not me. You've made me look like a tart. My hair's not right. My God, look what you did to my neck! Do you not believe in necks? All in good humour—mostly.

Goya's example gave Dean a roaming commission. These days we saw him on his bike with drawing materials, his rat's arse hoisted off the seat. Alma and I had finished our Violet series. And besides, the relief emergency was over. Dean was back at the fish-processing plant, bored silly, until Alma asked him what he did with 'all that time' it took for a bin to fill with fish heads and skeletal remains. The light returned to Dean's eyes.

'Remember,' Alma told him, 'you can draw any time, anywhere.'

In his lunch hour Dean sometimes caught the final hour of the morning court session. He'd sit back in the public gallery in silent rapture at the details of Saturday night's misdemeanours. He divided the accounts into a six-panel narrative. *Girl jilts boy. Boy gets drunk. Passes her house, sees girl with another boy. Original boy knocks on door. Heated words. Later returns to throw brick through window.*

Okay. So it is a cartoon. But look at Goya's narratives of the Spanish War of Independence. And the gory stuff that features there.

282

The first time Dean latched on to Goya he took down the heavy volume from the shelves at the local library and its pages fell open at a gruesome castration scene. The victim's legs point up in the air as the sword is viciously lowered into the area of the victim's crotch. On the page opposite is a hanging; a general sunnily reclines before the swinging corpse. The general's face records amused interest in the detail of the other's death.

Dean was instantly smitten. Up to this point he had no idea that drawing could be so out there in the world. He'd never heard of this dude Goya. Now he made up his mind to look into the man's life. Alma chose not to steer him elsewhere. Dean needed to follow his own instincts, act under his own steam.

Soon Dean had rattled through everything the local library had on Goya. Gloria said she could order in more books from city libraries, and then swallowing hard said there might be some she would need to buy. She was apologetic about that.

Granger used to say something similar whenever we brought our cars down to his garage. He'd lift the bonnet and poke around for a while, then he'd straighten up with a dazed look and pull at his earlobes. He could fashion a part out of most things. He climbed over abandoned cars with a spanner. We used to see him up at the tip at the rusted scrap end. It was almost a point of embarrassment with him if he had to order in a new part. Embarrassing for him, expensive for the rest of us. We clawed blood from our breast while we awaited the news.

At the library I said to Gloria, 'Why don't you order those books in?'

She whispered the filthy word 'money' and I waved it away and said I'd see what I could do. Gloria knows my weakness for the extravagant gesture. She smiled down at the floor. She wasn't holding out hope.

I spent an hour digging through council accounts and found two thousand dollars sitting in an escrow account, paid to us by the National Roads Authority for an easement. It wasn't doing anything, just sitting there. Within the month the shelves at the library were filled with new titles.

So we draw and we draw. If you come down to the paint factory on a Tuesday or Thursday night you will be struck by the silence. Newcomers invariably are. They report the same sensation of 'hearing' silence. What they mean is the sharp intake of breath, the scratchy sounds of crayon and lead on paper, maybe a muttered oath of personal condemnation at a line taking another deceitful turn.

We tolerate mistakes; in some ways we encourage them. What voyage of discovery would not? We are also mindful of Bellinghausen's error—his failure to trust what his eyes were seeing. We can always tear out the page and start again. Or else we can cover our mistakes, bury them so that the past mistake becomes texture.

Otherwise the silence you might hear is simply that of women concentrating on being themselves and of men paying attention. Sometimes it feels like we have come into a new and quieter arrangement with the world. The incessant rain that beats down on our roofs is not the problem it used to be. It's there registering above our bowed heads its right to exist. The salty wind that blackens our vegetables and the ferocious sun are just one or two of the many things we've learned to grin and bear. Things are just fine the way they are. Things are because they can't be any other way.

19

Rembrandt began sketching Saskia in their first year of marriage. Two years on and Saskia shows up in a series of portraits—there she is gazing directly back at her husband; here, away from him, and through him. She appears almost to be paying attention to the fact that her husband is paying attention to her. She is aware of her role, so much so that it's easy to think of her as contributing.

When Frances first began to sit for me she would do so with her eyes closed. These days she forgets I'm there. She sits in the bath staring at unflattering magazine pictures of film stars lifting their heavy thighs out of the breakers in the Caribbean. She sits on the phone twirling her hair around a pencil discussing with Diane what to do about Doug. She dozes off, half her face closed to a smile.

You discover early on that portraiture is a collaborative act. The subject cannot sit for long periods like a landscape can. A sitter never quite achieves the inner contentment of, say, a vase or a bowl of fruit. Gainsborough never had to rest those English meadows or put aside his brushes while the sheep got up to make a cup of coffee.

Portraiture can also be a dangerous business. Some tough decisions have to be made. Risks taken. Saying what *is* can be a lot harder than running from it. You can get yourself into hot water. You have to feel sorry for poor Sutherland after Churchill tore up his portrait. Sutherland had argued that to put feet on the great man would be to reduce him, make him merely mortal...I tried sketching Frances without legs and the results just looked like forgetfulness on my part. Then, for fun, I added back the legs but lopped off the feet and that effort looked more callous than forgetful.

'My awful bum,' a sitter is sometimes likely to complain. That's another thing about our classes—the subject is given to talking back. We don't encourage this, but vanity has its own persuasiveness.

'What are you talking about? Your bum is wonderful.'

'No. Marthe's is wonderful. Mine is awful,' comes the reply.

Bonnard's wife is also dead. It's hardly worth mentioning except to say that this is the broader community we move in these days. And also to make this point: in our drawing classes there is no such thing as an awful bum, or for that matter a superior bum. Again, things simply are what they are.

On that point there are no flatterers amongst us and this is something we are proud of. It's also why we steer away from the example of Rubens who is guilty of having made one or two of his women more lively and intelligent than they reportedly were in life. He had a habit of enlarging their eyes and exaggerating the darkness of their irises. For the record, let me say here, unequivocally, 'We don't tart up our women.'

287

I also know that other drawing classes like to make their models comfortable and surround them with electric bar heaters. But all you end up with is a drawing of a fat contented cat sprawled on the rug before the hearth. We are after a larger, more varied truth, so we let the weather in, and if one of the sitters complains of the cold and draws up her arms we're just as likely to call over to her to 'hold it there' and let the breeze go unchecked, let our sitters feel the chill.

Certain women, no names, try to hold in their stomachs. We let them fight it out on their own. We play around with little sketches in the top corner of our sheets of paper. An hour is a long time to sit and wage civil war with one's own body. Occasionally the struggle will tip the balance in our sitter's face (anxiety, fright, guilt —all trying to cram into the same square inch of space) and usually I will have to speak up; or Alma, who is not averse to demanding what he thinks he needs or wants, will say quietly but firmly, 'Just as you are, please...' And you think, what a simple phrase and why did we have to wait until our lives were half over and the town was on the brink of collapse to hear this said?

Things are just fine the way they are. You can't move the hills back—I have heard that said and often paused to consider whether I should say something to correct that viewpoint.

By the way, in case you are wondering, it's not an easy or comfortable thing to look upon another man's wife without her clothes on for the first time. You find your eyes making all the usual stops and this is in spite of the counselling you gave yourself on the way over to the paint factory that night. The stern words you may have addressed to yourself have a way of burning up to nothing when faced by the nakedness of a neighbour for the first time. It's not the same as looking in a magazine. This is real, terrifyingly real. This isn't Robyn and her horsey hobbies and most fervent desire for world peace. *This is it.* But if you stop thinking and start looking then what you see, that is, what you slowly begin to see, are lines and areas of light and shadow—or valleys and plains. This is what was meant when the question was put by an out-of-town reporter to one of the artists: 'It's about as sexy as a geography lesson.'

The night Frances was rostered on for the first time I didn't know what to do with myself. I sat down with the telly and turned on the news. The pictures showed rescue workers with surgical masks moving around the edges of a stagnant lagoon filled with bloated bodies. Victims of a tidal wave that had swept a whole village of Papuans out of their beds and into oblivion. Briefly I put aside my anxiety to listen to a survivor describe the middle-of-the-night noise of a jet plane half a minute or so before a wave as high as a five-storey building swept through the village. Sleeping bodies ended up a kilometre away. Small children and fish were discovered in the branches of trees. The pictures shifted to the newsreader and as quickly I had left the scene of disaster and was back to fretting over the scene down at the paint factory. Three times I got up to open the fridge and stare at food prepared and half-eaten a month ago. Leftovers wrapped in silver foil at Fran's insistence. I don't like cooked food lying around the place. Once I've nibbled from it I'm no longer interested. It's just me and Fran these days and yet we stock the fridge with food we never get round to eating. When Adrian and Jess were here it was different. It was like living with food hoovers. The final time I opened the fridge I decided I wasn't hungry. An altogether different appetite gripped me. I was curious.

At 8.30 I opened the door and stood on the front porch in the evening air. Our house is at the very end of Brunner Avenue, named after the explorer and surveyor, one of the few streets to have survived regime and name change over the years. I looked out into the New Egypt night, darkness piled upon darkness, and decided, no, I didn't need a coat.

The paint factory is eight minutes' walk away. I didn't hurry. I didn't tell myself I was headed for the paint factory. I told myself I was out for a walk and if our paths happened to cross, then so be it.

Of course very soon I found myself approaching the small outside light at the entrance. In another minute I was feeling my way in the dark to the side window, broken glass and rubble underfoot.

I saw a tidy arc of heads, all with their backs to me. It was like sneaking up on a religious order. And there on the small stage we had built sat my wife—bare-breasted. My attention alternated between the milky white of my wife's breasts and the equally attentive arc of heads. I must confess to feeling initially uncomfortable. But as I stayed at the window it began to pass. What had presented itself as a stunning, even shocking view really was now familiar and I went back to studying the look on Fran's face, her white toothy smile of triumph, the years exerting downward pressure on her pendulous breasts, and yet she did not look like a woman with two grown-up children—not at that moment she didn't. While my eye was pressed to the window she looked like some other possibility of the woman more familiar to me in dressing-gown and socked feet hunched over a work table bringing together bits of a dissociated world.

I felt I could leave that scene now. I could continue on my walk. I was back in the shadows of Furness Lane when I remembered with striking clarity what a model, a nurse, once said of sitting for the American painter Andrew Wyeth: 'I feel the colour going right through my face. That's the intensity. My nipples were erect three-quarters of the time.'

Colour, face, intensity—all that I was comfortable with. Nipples, though. I thought perhaps I had missed something and went back to the window for another look, just to check.

Of course it was ridiculous, and I felt ridiculous. You could argue, rightly, I think, what business is it of mine if Frances's nipples choose to react? You could argue I shouldn't feel so bloody proprietorial about it. You can run all these things through the chamber of cool reason in your brain and still you march forward to press your nose against the windowpane. You simply have to see. You need to find out.

For several generations the factory produced only paint, a fact we find embarrassing today. It brings other anomalies to mind, factory workers arriving on bicycles to car assembly plants, vegetarian butchers moving past swaying carcasses on the chain at the abattoir. It does seem crazy now to think that when we swam in paint we didn't know what to do with it. We used it for all the wrong things. We used it to cover up our lives. We were quite open and forward on this. We spoke about the need for a coat of paint. Paint was something to pull around our shoulders, take refuge in, use to cover up. But no one could say, truly say as our advertisements boasted, that our paint knew local conditions. In truth, it only knew itself as a fast-bonding chemical adhesive that came in a number of colours, though pleasing to the eye. This isn't paint as our early forebears knew and understood it. In the caves of Lascaux a colour chart is not as important as the rendered figures of bison and mammoth. Closer to home, the pre-European rock art on the limestone escarpments worn away by grazing cattle still make sense of the moa and their prehistoric hunter. Along the shore where NE Paints used to host their picnics, thin men in hair knots and rain capes used to stalk these huge flightless birds. It was an unfair contest—wit and prior knowledge versus the witless—but one which has given us our most enduring art. The giant birds with their small heads look very much like women on all fours under hair dryers. One year while digging a hangi the men uncovered a pit into which the stick men had driven the giant bird. All of us kids were hauled over to stand at the edge of the pit and gape down at the white markings of the moa, its flight plan ensnared in clay sediment built up over centuries of windblown deposit and floodwaters. How sad it looked in its spina bifida arrangement. The mayor and other dignitaries were due soon, so the men shovelled in another layer of dirt, dropped in the oven stones, and lit the fire. Hours later when they hauled up the sacks of steamed chicken and pork and kumaras, the thought of the giant extinct bird heating up another foot down wasn't as remote as some of us would have liked. We picked at our kumara and left the chicken wings on paper plates to rot in the hot January sun.

Sometimes I like to think, what if the paint management was to come back? What if that row of generals in shiny off-the-rack suits and fleshy faces were to stand in the doorway scratching at their freckled scalps to see these old walls once covered in calendars and pinups now covered with the portraits of various wives, ours and others, Rembrandt's Saskia with pearls in her hair, Madame Bonnard in her shallow bath, half her body washed away. In one corner the hissing and roaring potbelly that sees us through the dark winter nights. Along one wall we are growing a handsome library. And among our choice of mentors we all have our favourites. Bonnard is one. Chagall another. Matisse's *Interior at Nice* lends a more cautionary note to our aspirations. Is it his wife? I'm not even sure it is. I imagine it could be. Let's assume it is Matisse's wife, this woman who sits in the doorway on the far side of the kitchen. It is as if Matisse has said to himself, I cannot understand this woman. I cannot know her. However, I can understand the kitchen in all its surface simplicity so I will place this woman on the edge of what is understood.

One night Alma produced Hilary to sit for us. She looked a bit like Queen Victoria, but that isn't something to share out loud. When you draw, comparisons are unhelpful. All the same it was hard to shut out thoughts of Queen Victoria as we concentrated on that red rumpled face and folds of heavy curtain material.

The curtains had come from the Boyers. A year ago, after the Gondwanaland fiasco, the Boyers sold up and announced they were moving to Ireland. Ireland! 'Ireland!' we gasped. We tried to think where in Australia there was an Ireland. But they meant *Ireland* Ireland. It gets wilder. The Boyers hadn't actually been to Ireland but they'd seen Ireland in the movies. In other words, the passing-ship view. A glimpse. A taste. The Boyers didn't care. Ireland's was a go-ahead economy. It was booming, in major forward-thrust mode.

So off they went leaving us with their cast-off furniture, some oddities in amongst it all.

A cannon ball from Waterloo. I said to Jamie Boyer, 'How do we know it's from Waterloo?'

Jamie looked suitably put out. He said he knew because his dad said it was from Waterloo, and his dad before him. Family history is always the last thing I rely on when matters to do with provenance come up. On the other hand it doesn't pay to fool around with family history. To mock it or doubt it is to play with fire.

After thinking about it, I decided, well, the cannon ball *could* have come off the fields of Waterloo. Then we came to that difficult point in any negotiation. I laughed out loud when Jamie mentioned the price.

'Well it *is* from Waterloo,' he said. He had me there, and suddenly we were back to discussing origins and matters to do with authenticity. I pointed out that while I was happy to accept that the cannon ball came off the fields of Waterloo it didn't mean the next customer would see it in the same way.

'You see my point, Jamie.' In my game value depends on proof.

Things became heated. Julia Boyer said it was this very small-mindedness that was driving them away. In the end I talked them around to a price reflecting the value of a cannon ball that might have come from Waterloo. No sooner had I done that and I began to have second thoughts.

Who would buy a cannon ball? For what purpose? A cannon ball is a bit kitsch these days. I could feel myself getting cold feet. The Boyers also sensed my waning interest, and panicked. They were so determined to see me buy that cannon ball. They glanced around their living room for another chattel to throw in with the cannon ball.

The curtains! Of course.

'Tell you what, Harry, why don't you take the curtains and the cannon ball.'

I could see the determination in their eyes. It scared me to tell the truth. If I declined, what then? A brick through my window?

As it happened, Doug picked up the cannon ball a week later for a bit more than what I paid for it—reflecting the fact this was a cannon ball that may have rolled off the very fields of Waterloo. The curtains were a bit more of a problem. Long heavily braided drops that no one wanted or came near for months on end. Occasionally someone would rub the material between thumb and forefinger while I stood behind the counter, holding my breath.

The morning of our session with Hilary, Alma came in and sniffed around. He said he didn't know what he was after until his eye fell upon the Boyers' curtains. For tax purposes I put the curtains down as a community donation.

At the paint factory Hilary sat compliantly as Alma wrapped her in curtain. He could have wrapped her in seaweed and she wouldn't have minded. He spent some time with the lamp until Hilary was side lit. Some instruction followed.

'I don't want anyone to draw for ten minutes.'

We were just to sit and look at the crumpled face of our old schoolteacher, a woman who, as the expression goes, was once pretty as a daisy, and who had once lied to Alma that she had a rat in her kitchen just so he would draw her, and she would get to feel the sunshine on her body while her Jimmy was away at the war.

We saw the cheap foliage of the curtains, their second-hand wretchedness. We didn't see a movement from Hilary, not a breath. Only her eyes moved. At first her gaze went over the top of us. Then she seemed to reel it back to her frontal lobe interior. For five minutes we stared. I remember several years ago, plans for a historical route. There was talk at council and the subject of Hilary came up when we paused to consider what our visitors, hungry for local experience and history, might see, and it went without saying that such a historic route would have to get around the public ruin of Hilary. One suggestion was to relocate her as you might a public building, or walk her to a bench inside the Garden of Memories. The idea was abandoned, and some blamed Hilary. She was an embarrassment to us all.

I looked at the Boyer curtains. I saw how comfortable she felt in them, as if they were years she could feel against her. If you looked carefully you could see her mouth move. Hilary was shaping to speak and when she did it came unexpectedly and ghostlike, as though a mummified corpse had suddenly found its voice through all those bandages.

'I thought I saw Harry Bryant out there?'

I stuck up my hand.

'I'm here, Hilary.'

'And little Dougie Monroe? Is that you?'

'It's me, Mrs Phillips.'

Guy had his hand up though she hadn't mentioned his name. But then he stood and introduced himself. He said, 'I remember your lessons on the Russian...' He couldn't remember his name.

'Bellinghausen,' I said, and Hilary moved her head my way.

'And what do you remember, Harry?'

Her voice was firm and gentle as it had been all those years ago.

'I remember a man who was looking for the Great White Continent and who mistook the ice shelf for fog.' And I did what Doug had done and called her Mrs Phillips.

A tear ran down her cheek. She sniffed, then looked down, possibly for something to wipe her eyes with. We all waited for Alma to do something. He seemed unsure of his role and chose the easel for refuge. In the end it was Guy who got up and lumbered onto the stage with a handkerchief.

'Thank you,' she said to Guy. 'You were always such a nice boy.'

Guy beamed—he turned around to see we had heard that.

In the coffee break I said to Alma, 'Hilary's changed. She seems transformed.'

His eyes went still.

'Hilary has, has she?'

Okay. Point taken. The world never disappoints a jaundiced eye. Alma still tells newcomers that it helps to actually like your wife if you're planning to draw her. Otherwise, how you feel will show. There's no way to keep that out.

The jaundiced eyes sees the poor wager slumming it for extra cash in the Christmas parade. The kids see Father Christmas.

Just supposing one day I had sat down with her on that bench outside the video store, leant forward with my head hanging between my legs, grinning back at the pavement cracks, would I have heard a sane voice? There's no way of being sure, but I doubt it. The paint factory made it possible. The light. The circumstance. Even the Boyers' curtain fabric. The moment, shall we say. Our collective gaze stripping away the crust we'd all had a hand in building down through the years, and at last the long-suffering inmate inside of Hilary feeling it was okay to venture back out into the open.

20

There have been other successes. Another story is on its way, I'm afraid.

I don't think I will mention names except to say of this young couple (which will almost certainly give the game away, but discretion in this instance is outweighed by the lesson learnt so public good wins again), one was always coming and going. He had come and gone. Now it was her turn. This was mere prelude to a future tearful reunion where they would cling to each other and wonder how they could have ever been so stupid to wander off when they did. Briefly, a kind of domestic balance was achieved. You'd see them out and about, hand in hand or cuddling each other in the Garden of Memories, laughing and having a good time. She with her tee-hee Maori laugh. Him with his Pakeha snigger. They couldn't have kids of their own. *They.* Well, it was her. She couldn't have kids. Something to do with her Fallopian tubes, some past injury she was vague about. It was a shame, a great shame after everything they had been through, because like everyone says, what else are we here on earth for?

The unfortunate thing is, of all the places to shove blame they chose to blame each other. For a while it was his sperm count that came under fire. It was low, and some who'd worked with him at the fish plant thought that was likely as he was a lazy bugger, always drawing and scampering off in his lunch hour to 'some other place'. It was devastating for her to discover the real problem; though a let-off for him, you might imagine. She threw herself into work with glue-sniffing street kids. She was always palming off her own kids while she took herself off to a distant hui. It was amazing where she rang back from—the Far North, and once, memorably, Hong Kong. It was a spur-of-the-moment madness that saw her board the plane. Now she had phoned to say she was working in a nightclub which, he said later, explained the jukebox in the background. Eventually when she came back from Hong Kong she looked very smart, her hair was done up differently, there was a wardrobe of black skirts. She was home for a fortnight and then he ran off up the coast.

It is this couple that comes to mind whenever the grounding effect of drawing classes comes up for discussion.

When she sits for us she smiles. She holds her knees together, one foot on the floor, the other foot dangling in a way that puts us in mind of a Hong Kong bar stool. Still, we are left with the feeling that she is finally where she wants to be, with all of us looking at her. Her smile beams only in one direction, however. Craftily, he pretends not to notice.

On the subject of Dean...There have been some more changes down at the paint factory. A community arts board gave us another grant and with Guy's help we've built a proper studio space. Dean runs the downstairs art supplies area. Aisle upon aisle is filled with tubes of paint, sketch pads, crayons, pencils, charcoal. Customers creep up and down the aisles on their private shopping missions.

Newcomers are prone to feeling overwhelmed and unsure where to start. They tend to thrust a sheet of paper with its list of items across the counter, then Dean might say, 'I see Alma has you working with charcoal. I see he neglected to put down the HB 6 pencil. Shall I add one of those? I have a set on special.' And so it goes. Dean enjoys his expertise. He's developed a range of frowns and purse-lipped deliberations to go with his newly acquired know-how. 'About the pencils,' he'll explain. 'You will want the darker and heavier lead for hatching. I know Alma favours the HB 6 but that's not to say you can't go darker.'

21

We're up at the tip one afternoon when the rain comes. It is sudden and violent. And across the tip face the rats scramble for shelter. Alma and I make a beeline for the Eliots' old banged-up orange Datsun. When we sit in it, shuttered into that confined upholstered place, it is almost possible to hear the spluttering of the Eliot kids in the back. You can feel Dean's white-hot silence, and the gentle corrective glances of Violet from her side of the car. It is just a passing sense, a sniff as we close the doors and silence walls up around us, quickly followed by the aromas of the tip.

'This woman Ophelia. That's all over now, is it?'

There are any number of ways to answer this. The easiest thing in the end is to say, 'Yep. It's all over.'

Alma is pleased to hear that. His fingers tap on the steering wheel. His face livens up.

'I'll tell Alice. She'll be relieved to hear it.' He turns his face to look at me. 'That is, if you don't mind, Harry.'

'If you need to,' I say.

'I don't like your mother feeling burdened…'

We watch the rain fall.

In a while Alma says, 'That Douglas is a strange fish, isn't he?' And so it goes.

Guy has increased his hours with me. Alma won't be able to grub around up here in the tip forever.

'Well, it's that time-of-life change thing, isn't it Harry?' Guy said the last time we spoke about it.

Another time all three of us are up here. There are some guiding principles to pass on to Guy. Once more heavy rain sweeping in from the hills in the west has everyone running for the Eliots' car—me, Alma, Guy and this time Raymond as well. Though when the talk shifts to art Raymond falls quiet. As soon as the rain stops he's out of there.

For a while longer we stay in the car chatting; at least Alma is chatting. Guy and I are listening. Alma is recalling the day he heard on his wireless that Bonnard was dead. He went out to his porch. He said he felt numb. He looked down the far end of the paddock where George was shovelling away the hill. It was the one time he felt like grabbing George by the shoulders and shaking some higher purpose or goal into him.

'What hill?' asks Guy, leaning between us from the back.

Alma gives me a quick glance.

'You can tell him.'

Guy has his mouth hanging open.

'Back at the shop, Guy.'

'Right,' he nods.

Then Alma says, 'Cézanne used to complain about his wife. She liked only two things. Switzerland and lemonade.'

Guy rocks back and claps his hands. 'I like that,' he says. 'Switzerland and lemonade.'

And Alma winks across the divide at me.

22

The other day at the tip I picked up a book on the French Romantics. In it I found a poem by Blaise Cendrars. Blaise is one of ours now, one of New Egypt's chosen sons. In the poem 'Portraits', this is what he had to say about his friend Chagall, which speaks to all of us who meet down at the paint factory on weekday nights.

He sleeps
He is wide awake
All of a sudden; he paints
He takes a church and paints a church
He takes a cow and paints with a cow
With a sardine
With heads, hands, knives…
He paints with his thighs
He has eyes in his ass
And all of a sudden it's your portrait
It's you, reader
It's me

It's him
It's his fiancée
It's the corner grocer
The women herding the cows
The midwife

I have shortened Blaise's poem. This is a trick for which we have Alma to thank. We've learnt in that old magpie way of ours to take what we have a use for and leave the rest out.

I think I will end here, on one fine crisp Saturday morning in June. There are sunny skies. All the women are running and every man is smiling with his wife's towel draped over his shoulder. The women are running in a benefit to raise funds to purchase easels and brushes and canvases in order to on-sell them down at the paint factory.

The circuit takes them past the school down Endeavour Road and on to Broadway; there they cut across the railway line to run along Port Road and back up Stitchbury Hill through the reserve and back to the school. Three kilometres in all.

A pleasing number of women have their sponsor's name on their T-shirt or it is crudely written over their legs in black marker pen. All are red in the face. Their legs are covered in the same rash of exertion. For some it has got to be too much already. They look like they are drowning, especially up Stitchbury Hill where the motion of their legs becomes scrambled, the points of their knees are whacked out of alignment, their thighs are on the point of caving in. The whole shambling works looks ready to implode and would but for the determination shining in their eyes.

They have all stopped hearing our cries of encouragement. Blindly they snatch at the paper cups of water. They have seen their face on a canvas, and this is what they are running, gasping, sweatily towards.